HE NEVER FORGOT

HE NEVER FORGOT

ZACHARY GOLDMAN MYSTERIES #9

P.D. WORKMAN

Copyright © 2020 by P.D. Workman

All rights reserved.

No part of this book may be reproduced in any form or by any electronic or mechanical means, including information storage and retrieval systems, without written permission from the author, except for the use of brief quotations in a book review.

ISBN: 9781774680100 (IS Hardcover)

ISBN: 9781774680094 (IS Paperback)

ISBN: 9781774680117 (IS Large Print)

ISBN: 9781774680063 (KDP Paperback)

ISBN: 9781774680070 (Kindle)

ISBN: 9781774680087 (ePub)

ALSO BY P.D. WORKMAN

Zachary Goldman Mysteries
She Wore Mourning
His Hands Were Quiet
She Was Dying Anyway
He Was Walking Alone
They Thought He was Safe
He Was Not There
Her Work Was Everything
She Told a Lie
He Never Forgot
She Was At Risk (Coming soon)

Kenzie Kirsch Medical Thrillers
Unlawful Harvest

Reg Rawlins, Psychic Detective
What the Cat Knew
A Psychic with Catitude
A Catastrophic Theft
Night of Nine Tails
Telepathy of Gardens
Delusions of the Past
Fairy Blade Unmade
Web of Nightmares
A Whisker's Breadth

Auntie Clem's Bakery

Gluten-Free Murder

Dairy-Free Death

Allergen-Free Assignation

Witch-Free Halloween (Halloween Short)

Dog-Free Dinner (Christmas Short)

Stirring Up Murder

Brewing Death

Coup de Glace

Sour Cherry Turnover

Apple-achian Treasure

Vegan Baked Alaska

Muffins Masks Murder

Tai Chi and Chai Tea

Santa Shortbread

Cold as Ice Cream (Coming soon)

Changing Fortune Cookies (Coming soon)

Hot on the Trail Mix (Coming soon)

Recipes from Auntie Clem's Bakery

Parks Pat Mysteries

Out with the Sunset (Coming Soon)

Long Climb to the Top (Coming Soon)

Dark Water Under the Bridge (Coming Soon)

High-Tech Crime Solvers Series

Virtually Harmless

AND MORE AT PDWORKMAN.COM

For those who remember
Even when it hurts

1

Zachary was on the highway driving home from Jocelyn's house, thinking over his visit with Joss and the young man she was helping out, now known as Luke. It was going to be a long recovery period for Luke, after being trapped in human trafficking—both servicing his own clients and forced to recruit and train new teens—for a number of years. Successfully separating himself from that life was going to be more challenging for him than rehabbing from years of drug abuse. But if there were anyone who could help him through the process, it was Jocelyn.

Joss had only recently come back into Zachary's life. Separated from his family when he was ten, he was gradually reuniting with his siblings. Joss was the oldest, and the hardest so far to reconcile with. He sensed that she blamed him for the hard life she'd led, and rightly so, since he *was* the one who had accidentally lit the fire, the straw that broke the camel's back. His parents had relinquished the children, severing all ties, and they had all been placed in foster care. So far, none of them had led particularly happy lives. Tyrrell seemed to have led the most normal life. Zachary hoped that the youngest children in the family would turn out to have had an easier time. They had been almost two and four when they had been put into foster care, and under-fives had the best chances of recovering from trauma and leading a happy life.

But despite their differences and Jocelyn's generally bitter attitude, when Zachary had freed Luke from the trafficking ring, she had agreed to take him in and help him out. Zachary had a feeling that they would be good for each other. Joss already seemed to be gentler and happier around him. She didn't have any children of her own—as far as Zachary knew—and she seemed to have taken Luke under her wing. He was legally an adult, but still needed her protection and direction, and it seemed to be working out so far.

He was enjoying the smooth highway drive, one of the only times that his restless brain would settle down and enter a more relaxed, meditative state, when his phone rang over the car's Bluetooth system.

Zachary hit the answer button without looking at the number, assuming it would be Kenzie. But the voice that answered his greeting was not Kenzie's.

"Mr. Goldman? Is this the right number?" an uncertain male voice inquired.

"Yeah, this is Zachary." Zachary looked at the number on the radio screen but didn't recognize it. "How can I help you?"

"Of Goldman Investigations?"

"Yes, sir." Zachary waited for an explanation, hoping it was a client and not the IRS or a reporter.

"Uh… my name is Ben Burton. I'm interested in retaining your services. That's how they say it, isn't it?"

"You don't have to use any special jargon. What is it you need to hire a private investigator for?"

"Well…" Burton still hesitated, unsure of himself. It wasn't an unusual reaction from a client hiring a private investigator for the first time, thinking of TV show PI's they had seen. Hard-drinking, gun-toting, brilliant investigators. Wondering if they could really hire someone for their own problem, or if it were just ridiculous. Knowing that TV was not reality, and not sure what to expect. "I'd like to discuss it face-to-face, if we could do that. It's really…" Burton groped for a word, drawing it out painfully long.

"Private?" Zachary suggested.

"No. Um. Unusual, I guess. I don't want you to just laugh it off as a prank call."

Zachary raised his brows as he navigated around a few slower-moving cars, intrigued. "I wouldn't laugh it off if you're serious."

"I'd rather not take that chance."

"Okay. Are you in town? Where do you want to meet?"

"I'm just visiting. I'm at the Best Western. I don't know the city; maybe you could suggest a place to meet."

"I could come to you there. If you don't want to meet in your room, they have meeting rooms and a restaurant and lounge."

"The lounge sounds good," Burton said, sounding relieved. "So, you will meet with me? You'll really come?"

"Yes, of course. I'm out of town right now, but I'm on my way back. When do you want to meet? How long are you in town?"

"However long it takes, I suppose. Hopefully… not too long."

"All right. I've got a supper date, but maybe after that? Seven or eight?"

"Yeah. I'll be around. Why don't you just call me when you're done and on your way over?"

"At this number?"

"Yes. Ben Burton," he offered nervously, and rattled off the phone number.

"I've got it. I'll give you a call tonight, then."

"Thanks. I really appreciate it. That's great."

Because Zachary had thought it was Kenzie calling him, he felt the need to connect with her. He told his Bluetooth system to call her, and the call started to ring through. She would still be at work, but she would answer if she could. He was getting more used to the idea that they were a couple and he was important enough for her to interrupt her routine work to answer the phone when he called. For a long time, he'd been worried about calling her during her work hours, unless it was about something to do with the medical examiner's office. He'd worried that she would chastise him, haul him over the coals like Bridget would have.

But that was Bridget. And as he was learning, he couldn't judge all other women by the way his ex-wife behaved. He had thought that she was just honest, that other women all thought the same way as she did but were just too polite to say so. But Kenzie wasn't like that.

"Zachary." She sounded relaxed and cheerful. A good day at the medical examiner's office. "How did things go with Joss?"

"I think it's better every time I go there. She's... less defensive. More relaxed."

"That's good. It seemed like there were... a lot of walls there. A lot to get through before anyone could see the real Jocelyn."

"Especially me."

"Maybe," she conceded. "She has her issues. I'm glad that you've stuck it out and didn't let her scare you off."

Zachary considered that. Joss was prickly. And he remembered how she had treated him when they were both young and she was in charge of him. He was always getting into trouble, and that would get her in trouble, so she was sometimes too harsh in her reactions to him when he was doing his best. But he still loved her. He'd loved her then, and it hadn't even occurred to him to walk away.

"Zachary?"

"Yeah, I guess," Zachary agreed. "I just... I've missed my family for so long. I'd never consider not having a relationship with her."

Kenzie laughed. "Well, you are unique, because most people wouldn't persist with someone who was so cold and put up so many barriers. But you've worn her down."

Zachary shrugged to himself. It was hard for him to take a compliment, even from Kenzie.

"I was calling to let you know that I have an appointment tonight. After dinner, though. It's not bumping our date."

"Oh, okay." She was probably disappointed that they wouldn't have the full evening together. Zachary was working hard on that relationship too, but he couldn't always meet her expectations. "That's fine. Is it a client?"

"Yes. A prospect, anyway."

"What kind of case?"

"He didn't want to tell me over the phone. Said I would think he was crazy. So... I don't know whether it is someone I will end up working for or not."

"Yeah. That's a little suspicious. Let me know what happens; it sounds intriguing. If he is crazy, I want to know all about it."

Zachary laughed. "Okay. We'll see how it goes."

2

Supper with Kenzie left him feeling pretty mellow, which was unusual for Zachary. He was happy to go with it. If he could step out of his stress and anxiety for a while, it would make his life a lot easier. After supper, he headed over to the Best Western lounge, giving Burton a call to let him know he was on his way. It was only a few minutes away.

"The bar is pretty empty," Burton informed him. "Why don't you just meet me there."

Zachary agreed. When he got there, he scanned the bar briefly. There were only a couple of men sitting on stools along the counter, and only one of them was watching the door anxiously. Zachary nodded at the man and approached.

Ben Burton was maybe a bit younger than Zachary, in his mid-thirties. He was pale, with black eyes and hair. What Zachary guessed was Italian or Greek heritage. Burton had a slightly receding hairline, ears that had probably earned him nicknames as a child, and thick arm hair that went all the way down the backs of his hands to his first knuckles. He held his hand out toward Zachary, looking as though he was going to pull it back again any second. Zachary took it and gave it a squeeze, trying to reassure Burton. Whatever he wanted investigated, it was stressing him out. A wandering wife? Child custody problem with an ex? Someone stalking and harassing him?

"Don't get up," Zachary said, as Burton shifted to slide off of his bar stool. Burton stayed perched there in an awkward position. Zachary sat down on the stool next to him. "Nice to meet you, Mr. Burton."

The bartender approached, eyebrows raised.

"Coke," Zachary requested.

The bartender nodded and filled a glass from the fountain. He placed it on a napkin in front of Zachary.

"Coke?" Burton demanded. "Don't you drink?"

Zachary glanced at the shot glass and half-full beer in front of Burton. A hard drinker, if Zachary didn't miss his guess.

"I generally avoid alcohol," he explained. "It interferes with my meds."

Burton rolled his eyes as if he'd heard this excuse a hundred times before, which wasn't how most people reacted to Zachary's explanation for not drinking alcohol. Usually, if people knew it was a medical thing, they would accept it and not harass him further to join them in their spirits.

"They're just covering their butts," Burton told him. "Most of the time, it doesn't have any negative effect at all."

He appeared to speak with the voice of experience. Zachary made a mental note of the fact but didn't pull out his notebook. He sipped his cola and waited for Burton to make the next move.

"So, I guess you want to know why I wanted to meet with you," Burton said finally.

"Whenever you're ready."

"Let's get a booth." Burton cast a suspicious look toward the bartender.

Zachary agreed, and let Burton pick one out. He did not, Zachary noted, pick a seat with a view of the doors. Not someone who was watching his back. So probably not worried about a stalker.

Zachary sat opposite Burton in the booth. He took his notepad out and laid it on the table beside his hand. "You don't mind if I need to make notes?"

Burton shifted back and forth, thinking about it, then nodded. Zachary started on a fresh page and put Burton's name at the top. He wrote the date carefully. Too many of his notes had dates that he had to guess at. A six or an eight? A one or a seven? He wanted to improve. Digitizing his notes meant that they would be in his cloud storage indefinitely. He wanted something he could read later on down the line.

Zachary looked at Burton, waiting.

"I don't know how to start this," Burton said.

"Just let me know why you want a private investigator. And don't worry about it, I've heard all kinds of stories."

Burton cleared his throat. He looked up into the corner of the ceiling of the lounge, fingering his glass. "I don't know. It's not like it's anything embarrassing. I just want to find the house I used to live in as a kid."

Zachary nodded. "Okay."

He waited to see if Burton would explain further. Burton remained silent and brooding.

"So you lived here in town when you were younger," Zachary suggested.

"I think so."

Zachary raised his brows.

"From what I can remember, I mean. I didn't grow up here, but I think *before*, I lived here."

"Your parents can't tell you?"

"I was adopted. I don't know anything about who my bio parents are. Or were. I don't know very much at all about my own history."

"Ah." Zachary nodded. "I grew up in foster homes and institutions, so I know a bit about what that's like."

"I'm not saying it was bad. It wasn't. I have great parents; they gave me everything I needed. I just… I need something else. I need to know where I came from. *Something* about my past."

"Sure."

Burton drank, not looking at Zachary.

There were physical similarities between the two of them. Zachary was also pale-skinned with dark hair. His was buzz-cut short so that he didn't need to do much to take care of it. He had enough to handle without having to worry about styling his hair too. He was shorter than Burton, shorter than most of the adults he knew. The result of poor nutrition before he was put into foster care and growth-stunting meds after.

Burton was clean-shaven. He kind of looked like an actor from a noir movie. That pale face and his dark eyes and eyebrows. Very dramatic and brooding.

"Maybe you could outline what you do know about your childhood. You came here, so you have reasons to believe this is where you came from."

"I don't know. Maybe it's something I just made up as a kid. Because I had to be from *somewhere*, you know? A lot of the things that I used to tell people about myself... I don't know how many of them are true and how many are just things I made up because I didn't have anything else to tell."

"And you told people you were from here. What else did you tell them?" Zachary wrote a couple of words on his notepad to help him remember everything later.

Burton studied him, his dark brows drawing down in a scowl. "What makes you believe me when no one else does?"

"Believe you? You said that you might be from here. I don't see anything particularly unbelievable in that statement."

"When I think about living here, when I try to picture the house that I came from... my heart speeds up, and I start to sweat, and I get this feeling in my chest. This... pressure."

Zachary nodded. "Because you can't remember, or because of something that happened in the past?"

"I don't know. I think that something happened, but I can't remember what it was."

"How did you end up with your adoptive parents? They didn't know your bio parents? You went to your adoptive family from..."

"I was in DCF custody. In a foster home, I guess. They didn't know much about the circumstances I had come from. Or they didn't tell my adoptive parents. Or Mom and Dad just couldn't remember the details anymore."

"Or didn't want to tell you about it."

Burton scowled again. "They wouldn't keep it from me."

"Social services would have to know something about what kind of home you came from. And they would need to fill your adoptive parents in with enough details to handle any problems."

"Why would there be problems?"

"Were you apprehended from your bio family? How old were you?"

"What difference does it make?"

"Because the older you were, the more likely it was you would have behavioral issues. And if you were coming from a home where you were abused or neglected, it would be that much worse."

Burton gulped down what remained of his beer and motioned to a waiter, pointing to his glass. "I was... five years old. And I didn't have any behavioral problems."

"So maybe you came from a stable home. And your bio parents were killed suddenly. Nowhere else to go, so DCF comes into the picture."

"Maybe," Burton agreed, giving a brief nod.

"Do you remember anything about your bio parents? Not necessarily anything concrete like their names or what they looked like, but... impressions. Two parents or one?"

"Two," Burton answered immediately, then looked thoughtful.

"What did you tell people you remembered about your home and family?"

"I lived here... in a house... My parents..." Burton frowned, trying to remember. "Two parents, I'm sure. A mom and dad."

Zachary nodded. "Any siblings?"

Burton rubbed his forehead. He looked around for the waiter with his beer. It was a few minutes before he got his beer, and then he looked at Zachary as if he'd just remembered he was there.

"Mom and Dad said I was very quiet, very well-behaved. I got good report cards at school when I started. I have copies of those. I wasn't a troublemaker."

"You can have a lot of different issues without being labeled a troublemaker." Although Zachary had always been labeled a troublemaker himself. Unfairly so. He hadn't been trouble. He'd just had problems. Problems dealing with his traumatic past, his abusive upbringing, his impulsivity. He'd been unable to control himself and never stayed in a home for very long.

So maybe he *had* been a troublemaker.

He'd always been singled out as one.

"Do you have any adoptive siblings?"

"No." This didn't seem to be as difficult a question for him. "Just me."

"Did you have imaginary friends?"

Burton puffed out his cheeks, his forehead creasing. "I don't know. Maybe. I don't remember much from when I was that young."

"Most people have a few memories from when they were five or six. Or maybe your parents had cute stories about you. What else have they told you about when you first joined the family?"

"Not a lot... they were really happy to get me. They wanted a kid and couldn't have their own, so they picked me out." Burton shook his head. "Is that right? Would they have been able to pick me? It's not like I was in an orphanage where you can go from bed to bed and pick out the kid you want."

"No, but most agencies have books of pictures you can look at. A little blurb about each child or family group. So they might have seen your picture in a 'waiting children' book."

Burton nodded. "Yeah, that must be it. I don't know. My mom just says how quiet and well-behaved I was. I didn't really… get my own voice until I was older. You know how teenagers are." A shrug.

Going from five to thirteen without having a voice of his own was a long time. Most kids would have explored their boundaries long before that.

"Were you in therapy?"

"For what?"

"When you first came to your parents. Were you in any kind of personal or family therapy to help you with the transition? Or to overcome any emotional issues."

"No. I didn't need any."

Zachary nodded and scratched a few words into his notepad. "What do you remember about the house you are looking for? Anything?"

"You'll take the case?"

Zachary nodded. "Sure, it sounds like an intriguing case. I think we'll be able to find something." Zachary reached into the satchel he had brought with him and pulled out an envelope. He handed Burton a one-page retainer agreement that set out his rates and usual terms. They discussed the various aspects for a few minutes, and Burton signed his name on the appropriate line.

"Do you take credit cards?"

"Yeah." Zachary turned his phone on and entered his payment app. He put the initial retainer amount in the field and handed it to Burton. "Go ahead and enter your credit card information."

Burton tapped in a long string of numbers without taking out his wallet. An impressive feat. He entered the expiry date and handed it back to Zachary. Zachary waited for the transaction to go through, then turned his phone back off.

"Great, that's all covered. So we're ready to get started."

Burton was gazing at Zachary's phone, his eyes glazing. How much had he already had to drink? It couldn't have been so much, or he wouldn't have been able to remember his credit card number.

"Mr. Burton. Are you ready to begin tonight? Or do you want to set up a time tomorrow?"

It was a minute before Burton blinked and looked at Zachary. "You can call me Ben. What did you say?"

"Let's set up a time to meet tomorrow. You look like you've had a long day. You should get some rest, and we'll talk tomorrow. See how much you can remember, so I have a place to start."

Burton rubbed the worry lines on his forehead and finally nodded. "Yeah, okay. Tomorrow I'll be fresh as a daisy."

"What time? Morning?"

Burton shook his head immediately. "I'm not an early riser. It takes me a few hours to get the motor running. Morning isn't a good time."

Which, if Zachary had him pegged right, meant that he would be too hungover in the morning to be any help. By noon, maybe he'd be feeling well enough to handle an interview.

"Fair enough. After lunch? One o'clock? Do you want to meet here?"

Burton looked around at his surroundings. "If they're open, yeah."

"I'll find out." Zachary didn't want to waste his time trying to flag down a waiter. They all seemed to be occupied, even though the lounge wasn't anywhere near full. They should have been past the dinner rush. Maybe they reduced their staff once the rush was over. Zachary went to the cash register at the bar.

"What time does the lounge open tomorrow?" He handed the bartender a bill to pay for his drink.

"Not until one o'clock."

"Great. That's fine." Zachary held up his hands when the bartender indicated the register. "No change. Thanks."

He went back to Burton, who, while no longer looking so anxious, was very somber. They finalized arrangements and parted company.

3

He went home to Kenzie's house rather than to his apartment. They were still splitting time between the two places, but Kenzie's was far nicer and better stocked with food and other necessities that Zachary tended to forget about until he really needed them. So most weekdays they spent there, going back to Zachary's for the weekend. Or sometimes they spent time apart. Each of them sometimes needed their own space. Zachary carefully monitored the amount of time he was away from Kenzie to make sure that he wasn't asking for more space than she was. He didn't want to be accused of being selfish or not invested in the relationship.

"So, did you take on the new client, and is he crazy?" Kenzie asked, after greeting him with a brief kiss.

They settled in the living room, close to each other on the couch. Kenzie shut her TV program off with the remote.

"I took the case. He didn't seem particularly crazy. Anxious, yes. But crazy?" Zachary shrugged. Was it crazy for a man to want to reconnect with his history and to visit his childhood home? Zachary didn't think it was that unusual.

He told Kenzie about the meeting, leaving out any names or identifying information. Kenzie wrinkled her brow.

"You don't think it's strange that he wants you to find this house that he can't even remember?"

"Well... no."

"I could understand it if he had fond memories of the place and wanted to revisit those feelings. But when he doesn't remember anything about it and, by everything he's said so far, it probably wasn't a good atmosphere for him, why would he want to find it again?"

"Because it's something that he's lost. It's something concrete that he can look at and touch, when he doesn't remember anything from that time."

Kenzie pursed her lips, considering it.

"Why do people research their family trees? Or have their DNA tested to see what their heritage is? People like to know... their stories. Their origins. Even if it isn't something that they can remember. Maybe... especially if they can't remember."

"Is that how you feel? Do you want to do your family tree and go back —" she stopped herself and didn't suggest that he might want to go back to his childhood home. "Go back to somewhere you used to live?"

"No. I was ten when I left there... I remember it all very clearly. I wouldn't want to go back there, even if it did still exist."

Kenzie nodded.

"But I do want to reconnect with my siblings," Zachary pointed out. "I haven't seen them for a long time, and the little ones wouldn't remember me at all. But I would hope... that they would still want to see me even though they don't remember me."

"Yes, of course. And would you want to see your parents again?"

Zachary caught his breath. He felt like he'd been kicked in the chest, suddenly unable to draw in any more oxygen. Would he ever want to see his parents again if he had the opportunity? He had pleaded to go back to his mother. He had begged his social worker to see if she had changed her mind and might take him and the others back again. For years, he had fantasized about going home again, escaping whatever situation he was in and living some happily-ever-after with his family.

"Zachary..." Kenzie rubbed his back. "Sorry, was that the wrong thing to say? I just wondered how you felt about it. I didn't mean to upset you."

Zachary tried to shake his head and draw another breath. The world felt like it had frozen around him. Or maybe that he'd frozen inside himself.

"It's okay. Think about the good things. Think about being here with me. About Tyrrell, and Heather, and Joss. You were so happy to meet them again. Think about how nice it's been to have contact with them again."

Zachary managed a tiny nod, but still couldn't breathe. Kenzie continued to rub his back, not trying to rush him back. Not like those who pinched or slapped him to try to 'get his attention' when he got lost in memories. Zachary forced a little air out, then breathed in shallowly. It was a few minutes before he felt the tension melting, the memories releasing him.

"Getting a drink," he told Kenzie, trying to rise.

"You just stay there. I'll get you a glass of water." Kenzie got up. "You need anything else?" She didn't ask him if he needed his Xanax. She would let him ask for it.

"No. Just... dry."

Kenzie had cold water in a filter jug in the fridge. She poured him a tall glass and handed it to him on her return. Zachary sipped the icy cold water. It was just what he needed.

"When I was a kid... I still wanted to go back to them. I thought I could make everything right again. Glue the family back together again. But by the time I was an adult..." He shook his head. "I knew that would never work and that... the kind of people they were... I wouldn't want to live with them again."

Kenzie looked into his eyes. "Things must have been pretty bad."

"When I was little, I didn't really know... it's just the way things were. I held on to times when things were better... kind of pretended that things were good most of the time. But as I got older, I realized... how bad they really were. And my mom..." Zachary took a deep breath, trying not to let the memories overwhelm him again. "I told you how she was when she decided to get rid of us. She was..." Zachary breathed in and out again, strangled. "I can't imagine anyone treating a child like that. I thought I was grown up and that I deserved it. For a long time. But now... when I look at Rhys, or other people's kids... I can't imagine it. Rhys is a teenager, and I would still never talk to him the way she did to me or hold him responsible for... making a mistake like that."

"Yeah. You have to realize... she was unreasonable."

"There were six of us, and I know I was in trouble a lot," Zachary started, jumping to his mother's defense even after pointing out himself how wrong she had been to treat him that way. "I get how she might feel overwhelmed… burned out…"

"That's no excuse for abandoning six kids. Or for calling you the names she did."

Zachary bit his lip and nodded. He took another sip of the water, welcoming the chill. "So… no. I think that even if one of them came looking for me… I don't think I would want to meet them. Never again."

Kenzie nodded. She put her hand over his, soothing him. "Anyway… I didn't mean to bring all that up. I just didn't understand why the house would be so important to your client."

Zachary chewed the inside of his cheek, thinking about it. While it had seemed natural to him, on a closer examination, he wasn't sure it was as logical as he had asserted. Why did Burton want to find his house instead of finding his parents? Did he come from a background like Zachary's? Had they been abusive or negligent? He might not even remember any of that. He could just be following a feeling. Drawn to the house, but not to his abusers.

"I don't know. If he was apprehended when he was five, he probably didn't have a great life. Or maybe his parents were killed. He might know that without remembering it, if it was traumatic."

Kenzie nodded. "Things to think about," she said lightly. "Follow the clues."

Zachary nodded. He deliberately leaned back into the soft upholstery of the couch, trying to relax all of his muscles. He didn't need to worry about his biological parents. They weren't going to show up out of the blue. He could just focus on the case without exploring the similarities to his own life. In the meantime, he was with Kenzie, and he should focus on her and their relationship.

"I wonder how Rhys is doing," Kenzie mused. "When is the last time you saw him?"

"Just after… everything happened." Zachary shrugged uncomfortably. "I don't want to get in the way. I'm not sure how Vera feels about me seeing him. She said it's okay, but I don't want to push my way in where I'm not wanted."

"It wasn't your fault that Rhys saw Noah—Luke—shot. You were trying to protect them."

"Yes. But maybe I could have made different choices than I did. His grandma has the right to be upset about it. It's one thing that he was there, in the middle of everything. That would be bad enough. But the fact that it triggered flashbacks to his grandfather being murdered…" Zachary sighed. "I don't know if she can forgive me for that."

"I think *you're* the one having problems forgiving yourself for that. From what you said before, it sounds like Vera was pretty good about it."

Kenzie was uncomfortably close to the truth. Zachary did blame himself for Rhys's increased emotional distress. He had been trying to help, but he should have been smarter. He should have known that the traffickers would be able to track Luke.

"You should message him," Kenzie said. "It can't hurt to just keep in touch, let him know you're thinking about him."

"If it makes him think about that night, and about Grandpa Clarence being shot, then it could hurt. It could make things worse when he is starting to recover."

"Then ask Vera what she thinks."

"Mmm." Zachary made a noncommittal noise. He'd have to think about it. Even though Vera had treated him with grace and kindness, he didn't relish having to call her up to ask for a progress report on Rhys. It felt like having to go to a neighbor to tell them that you ran over their cat. Even if they took it well, it still felt awful. "Maybe I'll just wait for Rhys to contact me."

4

Ben Burton wasn't looking quite up to snuff when Zachary found him in the lounge for the second day in a row. He was already nursing a drink, and his eyes were bloodshot and shadowed. He nodded as Zachary approached the booth, the same one they had sat in the evening before.

Zachary smiled. "How are you this afternoon?"

"Just fine." Burton's voice was gravelly. He rubbed his forehead and shrugged at Zachary, realizing that Zachary could see the condition he was in. "A few more drinks under my belt and I'll be better."

"Do you have a drinking problem?" Zachary asked baldly. There was no point in tiptoeing around it.

Burton rubbed a hand through his hair. "I drink," he said. "Some people have a problem with it. Do you?"

"Are you going to be able to hold it together? To answer my questions and to pay the bills?"

"It doesn't affect me. I can drink all day long. It doesn't make any difference."

Zachary doubted that was entirely true. He sat down across from Burton. "If you want me to work with you, you're going to need to be available. And coherent enough to give me the information I need from you."

"I told you it doesn't affect me. Do I sound drunk? I'm here like we arranged. I'm talking. I'm making sense. I could drive now if I had to. There isn't a problem."

Zachary shook his head but didn't bother trying to convince Burton otherwise. He knew how pointless it was to talk an alcoholic out of drinking. There had been a lot of people in his life who had drunk too much. It was nothing new. At least with a client, he could simply drop the case if Burton became abusive or wasn't able to give Zachary the information he needed to track down Burton's childhood home.

"You getting a drink?" Burton asked, his eyes sliding over to the bar.

Zachary nodded. If he was going to be talking, he would need something to combat the dry mouth that went along with his meds. He didn't order a Coke this time, but water. It arrived with ice and a wedge of lime on the glass. Burton eyed it dubiously.

"Don't know how you can drink the stuff."

"It isn't exactly hard."

"If it was hard, I'd drink it," Burton joked. "Don't know how anyone can go without ever drinking. At least last night, it was a Coke."

"I'm good with water for now." It wasn't like Zachary had to worry about the calories. His doctor was still on his case to put on more weight. But he didn't want to be drinking cola all afternoon, or however long it took to get what he needed from Burton.

"So, you've had a little bit of time to think about what impressions you have of when you were younger." He jumped right into the interview. "And to remember some of the stories that you told other people."

Burton nodded. He sipped his drink thoughtfully, staring out the window into the afternoon light. He turned his head away from it and rubbed his eyes. "So, I'm pretty sure it must have been here. I always felt like this was where I came from. I don't remember specifics, but this was where I felt like I belonged. I didn't belong *there*. And... the other kids knew that wasn't where I belonged either. You know how sometimes kids can just sense... that you're an outsider. You never quite get into any of the groups or develop those friendships that the other kids have." His mouth turned down in a frown.

Did Zachary know? He knew what it was like always to be the new kid. The outsider. But Burton had been adopted when he was five. Before any of them had started school. He'd been there for his entire school career. He wasn't a newcomer. But he'd still been an outsider. Why?

"I've been there. Did you feel good or bad about being from here?"

"I don't know. Just… like I didn't fit in. Like an alien from another planet. And that was why. Because I wasn't from around there."

"Do you remember some of the places that you went to when you were young? A park? Grocery store? Neighbor's house?"

"Yeah… I guess there must have been other places. I remember walking down the street. The sidewalk, I mean. I feel like I was by myself, but I must not have been if I was five or younger. There must have been someone with me. Maybe walking behind while I led the way."

"And what did you see when you looked around?"

Burton closed his eyes. "I don't know. A dog. Big German shepherd. I like dogs. I must have liked them back then too."

"Probably. Do you know who was walking the dog? Was it a neighbor, someone you knew?"

Burton shook his head slowly, eyes still closed while he tried to visualize it. "I don't think so. A man. Not someone I knew. Talked to me. Maybe… ruffled my hair and called me buddy. You know how people do. Men don't really know how to talk to kids."

"Did he talk to your mom or dad? Were they there with you?"

"I don't know. I don't remember anyone being with me."

"Did he let you pet the dog?"

A smile grew on Burton's face and he nodded. "Yeah. He let me pet it."

"Did he tell you its name?"

"That's asking a lot…" Burton shook his head. "Maybe. Maybe it was the dog who was named Buddy."

Zachary didn't press the point. He knew that every question he asked could alter Burton's memories. When people were asked to remember things that they couldn't or were told that something had happened to them when it hadn't, their brains built the missing memory to fill the gap. And people became convinced that the retrieved memories were real. A brain wasn't a bank vault. You couldn't take memories out, examine them, and put them back unchanged. Every time Burton told his story, his memories would shift slightly.

"What do you like to do?"

"What do I like to do?" Burton's eyes opened. "What do you mean?"

"You enjoy some activities and not others. What would you rather be doing right now?"

Burton grinned. "Drinking in my room."

"But you're drinking here. So what is it about your room that you miss?"

Burton's eyes flicked over to one of the wall-mounted TVs, thinking about it. If he liked to drink and watch sports, he could do that while he was sitting there talking to Zachary. If he preferred something else…

"When I was younger, I liked bugs," Burton offered abruptly. "That's something you can't say about everyone."

"No." Zachary could remember playing outside with his siblings, catching bugs, putting them in jars or racing them on the sidewalk. Or dousing anthills with water to watch all of the ants come swarming out. Other things that were not quite so nice. He couldn't say that he liked bugs, but he'd been interested in them when he was a kid with scraped knees. They were something to play with for a kid who didn't have the latest toys and games. "Did you want to become an entomologist?"

"A what? No, I didn't want to do it professionally. I just… was really interested in bugs. Got books about them. Read about them at the library or watched kid videos about them. Just… they were really interesting."

Zachary nodded. "So, where did you collect them or watch them?"

Burton rolled his shoulders. "Anywhere. In the back yard. In the park. When we went out for a walk. When I was in school, if the teacher screamed at a spider or something, I was the one who would put it outside. I wasn't ever scared of them or squeamish."

"Did you catch them in the back yard of your old house?"

He watched Burton's eyes, alive and glistening instead of looking dissolute as he had when Zachary had walked up. It was something that interested him, and maybe there was a flicker of recognition or memory there.

"I don't think… not in the back yard," Burton said slowly. "Maybe… in the basement? Sometimes bugs get into the house. Spiders, centipedes, ants. Lots of kinds of creepy crawlies can live in the dark corners of the basement."

"Yeah. Did you catch them or just watch them?"

Burton's hands made an involuntary movement. As if, just for a split-second, he was reaching out to catch something. "I'd catch them. Put them in jars. At my house in Colchester anyway. Maybe here. I don't know."

"That's okay. We're just going over things, seeing what pops into your mind. Did you have a friend that caught them with you?"

"No, none of my friends were ever interested in anything like that."

"Any siblings?"

Burton shook his head. "I told you I didn't have any siblings. I was an only child."

In his adoptive family. Zachary wasn't sure about in Burton's biological family.

5
———

"What kind of car did you have?"

"When I was a kid? Let's see… mostly station wagons, probably. Maybe an SUV or van. I wasn't a big car guy. Not like some people who can tell you every vehicle they ever had since they were born. I don't know what my parents drove most of the time. Mom and dad vehicles. Nothing hot."

"Yeah." Zachary nodded, smiling. He'd ridden in a lot of mom vehicles. "And you always wore a seatbelt, right?"

Something flashed across Burton's features. He touched his shoulder. "Yeah. Of course."

"What was that?"

"What?"

"What did you think of when I asked if you always wore a seatbelt?"

"I don't know. Just… how uncomfortable they were to wear when I was a kid. I hated having my freedom restricted. I wanted to be able to move around. Lie down on the seats. Look out whichever side I wanted. But you can't, with seatbelts. You have to just… stay put."

Zachary nodded. He made a couple of notes in his notepad. Had Burton worn a seatbelt before he was adopted? Or was he allowed to do those things that he had mentioned? Had he ridden in a car that didn't have seatbelts or where wearing them was not enforced? An old car? Broken down? Parents who didn't care? Or just something that Burton had always hated to do?

"What did you see when you looked out your bedroom window?"

"Back yard. Grass, garden. Back fence. Nothing special."

"You grew up looking at that sight every day."

Burton nodded his agreement.

"Did you like it? Do you remember ever being interested or excited about it?"

"No." Burton's head wobbled back and forth. A negative head-shake, but something else too. Not just back and forth. There was too much up and down movement. The kind of 'tell' that some people had when they said something that wasn't the truth.

Zachary wrote a note about the bugs, waiting for Burton to think through the lie. Did he know he was lying, or was it something that his body knew, but his conscious brain would not release?

"I was… kind of scared of looking out my window when I was really little. Like… I might fall out of the window and land on my head." Burton rolled his eyes. "I got over it. Eventually. I'm not afraid of heights or anything."

"But you used to be?"

"I guess so. But kids are scared of a lot of things. And you grow out of them as an adult."

Sometimes. Certainly not all the time. And some people added fears and phobias as they grew up and gained experience. Especially when traumatized.

"What else were you afraid of?" Not bugs, clearly. Not dogs.

"I was afraid of a lot of things. A real mama's boy. But I grew out of them."

"What kind of things?"

"Things that might be too hot… fire, stoves, things like that…"

Zachary breathed, then took a few sips of his ice water, trying to anchor himself in the sensations and not to be drawn into a flashback to the fire.

"The dark. But all little kids are afraid of the dark. And things hiding under the bed or in the closet. You know how it is. Kids make things up to entertain themselves, and then get scared of them, like they were really true."

Zachary nodded. What kid hadn't spooked himself at one time or another?

"Uh… I don't know. Doors slamming. Sirens. Not *scared* scared, but… they get me here," Burton drilled a knuckled into the center of his chest, and Zachary could feel the heavy pain of anxiety and dread himself. He noted that Burton had used the present tense. He claimed to have outgrown his childhood fears, but he had just used the present tense. Things he was still afraid of.

"Do you take anything for anxiety?" The night before, Burton had said that drinking didn't really have much effect on meds.

"None of that stuff works. You want something to make you better…" Burton indicated the drink in front of him. "That's what makes you feel better."

"But it's a depressant. It will make you feel worse afterward. Make you swing lower."

"There's an easy fix for that." Burton leaned forward as if he were about to tell Zachary a secret. "Just don't stop drinking." He leaned back again and laughed loudly. He took a couple more gulps from his glass to demonstrate the point.

Just stay in a permanent state of drunkenness, and then you didn't have to worry about hangovers or crashing afterward.

"How old were you when you started drinking?"

"What does that have anything to do with? We were talking about when I was a little kid. When I lived here. Believe me, I didn't drink when I was five!"

"So how old were you when you started?"

Burton shook his head. "Who knows. A teenager. I don't remember when my first drink was."

"Were you copying someone else? Acting grown up?"

"Are you saying that my parents drank in front of me? They didn't. I knew they were against drinking alcohol, but that didn't make any difference. I didn't do it to act like a grown-up. I just…" He considered, a crease forming between his eyebrows. "I knew it would make me feel better. Even the most naive kid can't avoid seeing people laughing and drinking on TV. See how much better it makes them feel. Even if you don't know anyone who drinks, TV still tells you how much fun it is."

"And you drank to feel better, back when you were a teenager."

"Yeah. That's right. So what?"

"You told me you had everything you wanted growing up. Your parents provided for everything you needed. They were good. Not abusive. So why did you need something to make you feel better?"

"Because I had some trauma? Some child molester messing with me? There wasn't anything like that. Just… it's a chemical thing. A problem in the brain. That's all. It isn't the way that you were raised that makes you happy or anxious. It's just… the way your brain is wired."

Zachary had heard many different explanations for mental illness, and that was as good as any. "Sometimes, it's just the way you were born," he agreed. "In your DNA. But sometimes it is caused by trauma or abuse."

"And you think I must have gone through something awful before my mom and dad adopted me. But that's not the way it was. I don't have any memories of being abused before I was adopted." He took a drink and stared at Zachary. "And I would remember that. Trust me."

His certainty didn't convince Zachary. Quite the opposite, in fact. A lot of people would have been intrigued by the suggestion. They would have spoken softly and thought back, trying to put a thumb down on the shifting shadows of memory to test if it were true or not. But Burton was certain. He wouldn't even countenance thinking about it. That said something about him. And it wasn't that he had never been through trauma or abuse. The brain protected itself. It could wall away secrets for years. Decades. But that didn't necessarily mean they were gone forever.

The mind and the body still remembered.

6

"Do you remember any of your birthdays?"

Burton nodded. "Sure. I've had some pretty good ones. Not like my parents are rich and always got the latest and greatest, I mean. But I had good birthdays. They put effort into making it nice for me."

Zachary nodded. "What was your best birthday present ever?"

"No question." Burton didn't have to think about it. "My ninth birthday. A dog. Just a mutt, nothing special. No breed in particular. A Bitsa, my dad used to say. Bitsa this and bitsa that."

"A dog. You must have been over the moon."

"Oh yeah." Burton looked nostalgic. A good memory. Lots of good times with that Bitsa dog.

"What was the worst birthday you ever had?"

"The worst? Hell, I don't know. Like I said, they always tried to make things nice for me."

"How about before you were adopted?"

Burton looked blank. He shook his head. "I don't know. Don't remember any before that."

"What do you think they were like?"

Still nothing. No changes to his facial expression, not even a twitch. "I have no idea. I probably didn't have any before I was adopted. Why have a birthday party when your kid is too young to know what's going on and won't ever remember it? You might as well put your resources into something else."

The best birthday present Zachary had ever received, and the first, had been a camera. Mr. Peterson, his first foster father and the only one Zachary kept in touch with, had given it to him for his eleventh birthday. His first birthday in foster care. Zachary had been elated to get a present. It was a second-hand camera, but Zachary had kept it for decades. It wasn't until the second fire, the one that burned his apartment around the time he had first met Kenzie, that he lost it. He'd lost all of his possessions. He had been able to replace the essentials, but he still mourned the loss of that old camera.

His birthdays before that hadn't been anything to remember. They barely even rated a mention.

"Most people still celebrate those early birthdays, even if the child isn't going to remember them."

Burton shrugged. "Well, we didn't."

It wasn't a tentative statement. He was certain that he hadn't celebrated birthdays. Not just that he didn't remember them.

"How about other celebrations?" Zachary inquired, bringing up his least-favorite holiday. "Christmas?"

"Nice times with my parents… but before that? I don't remember."

"Nothing? No tree? No lights or presents?"

"I don't remember any."

"Maybe your family wasn't Christian. What about… those Jewish candles?" Zachary's brain wouldn't produce the name, even though he knew it. "Or the songs or the…" Zachary made a spinning motion with his fingers, trying to remember the word for the toy top. "Uh… dreidel?"

"Nah," Burton scowled and shook his head. "I'm not Jewish. I wasn't anything like that. Jewish or Muslim or some other thing. I don't know if they were Christian or not. I don't really have a *faith*."

Zachary accepted this. People didn't need to be Christian to celebrate Christmas. But Burton was quite sure he wasn't something else. So probably not raised in some strange cult or sect. If his birth family didn't celebrate, it was probably the result of poverty rather than religious beliefs. Their search would, Zachary was pretty sure, lead them to the less affluent areas of town. Hopefully, that didn't mean that Burton's old house had been bulldozed to make room for another development or parking lot.

Zachary sipped his water and swished it around his mouth, trying to combat the dryness that came from his meds and from talking to someone in a stressful situation. He wasn't the one in the hot seat, but he still had memories of his own that he would rather not have to bring to light, and he was worried that any similarities in Burton's memories might bring them back. He turned his mind to what other things might trigger memories for Ben Burton.

"Some of the other things that tend to bring back feelings and emotions when we aren't sure of the memories they are attached to are food and music. Do you have any particular favorites? Or things you hate? Foods or songs that have strong emotions attached to them?"

"Can't stand fish," Burton offered, after due consideration. "And I'm probably the only kid ever who didn't like mac and cheese."

Zachary smiled. One of his favorites as a kid. "How could you not like mac and cheese? Next thing you'll be telling me you don't like French fries."

"French fries I like," Burton said, pointing at Zachary, a gesture that suddenly brought Rhys to mind. Mute though he was, Rhys had never learned American Sign Language, but made do with a mixture of gestures, facial expressions, texts, and pictures on his phone. It worked okay, but was always a challenge. He frequently pointed at Zachary when he got something right. *You got it.*

Zachary cleared his throat and tried to continue with the conversation without getting sidetracked.

"But not mac and cheese."

"Nope. Can't abide the stuff. Even the smell of the cheese sauce." He gagged and shook his head. "No way."

"Anything else?"

"I don't know. I'm not that picky."

"And how about music. Anything take you back? Or induce strong emotions?"

Burton stared off into space for a while, then shook his head. "No. I like loud music. I mean, I like it shaking the walls. Nothing quiet. If it's one of my favorite songs, it needs to be played at top volume."

"What do your parents like?"

A brief shadow, and then it was gone. The memories were there. But reaching them was going to be challenging.

"Have you talked to your parents about what they remember from when they first adopted you? Something that the social worker might have told them, or something that they thought just from your behavior?"

"I called them last night. They know that I'd like to know more about my history, but they don't think it's a good idea, and they don't know that I'm here looking for my house."

"Why don't they think it's a good idea?"

"I don't know. Just because… they don't want me to get upset, I guess. They don't think that it will lead to anything that will make me happy."

"So they don't think that you had a very good life before you went to them."

"Yeah, I guess," Burton agreed. He motioned for another drink. "But they don't *know*."

"Kids don't usually come up for adoption for happy reasons. Not five-year-olds."

"But it could just mean that my parents or whoever was taking care of me died. It doesn't mean that I had an unhappy childhood."

"Do you think you had a happy childhood?"

Burton waited until he had another glass in front of him. He took a few swallows. "Okay. So I probably didn't have a happy childhood. But I still want to know. I want to walk through that house. Or at least to see it again. I need—I just really would like to see it again."

"Do they think that you were neglected or abused?"

"My mom will say things now and then. Like how I used to not be able to sleep without a light on. Like it's significant. But lots of kids are afraid of the dark."

"It's only natural to be afraid of what we can't see."

"Exactly."

"What else did she say that she thought might be significant?"

"I don't know. I was skinny, but I ate a lot. I didn't fill out until I was older. But lots of five-year-olds are skinny. They have legs like sticks at that age. It's not unusual."

"Right."

"When I talked to her last night, she said that she didn't think the social worker wanted them to know about where I came from. That it was better if

I just started off fresh, like I hadn't lived anywhere else before that. So that's how they raised me. Like I'd always lived there and there was no history. But I *knew* that they weren't my natural parents, so what was the point of that?"

"Were they very different from your natural parents?"

Zachary again glimpsed something in Burton's eyes that was just out of his reach.

"They were…" Burton blew out his breath and slumped down. He took several long swallows, almost reaching the bottom of the glass. "I don't know. I have no idea. It's just not there."

"What do you like about your mom?"

"She's very loving. She… smells nice. She's soft and… she gives great hugs." Burton's pale face turned pink, and he laughed at himself. "So does that mean that those are the things about her that were like my birth mother? Or that those are the things that are different from her?"

"What do you think?"

Burton didn't answer the question, diverting. "They remembered the name of the social worker. I don't suppose she's still around anymore, and she wouldn't remember anything about my case, but it's a possible line of inquiry."

Zachary looked at him for a minute, then nodded. "Do you have her details?"

Burton gave him the name and the general description of the woman that his mother had been able to provide. Age, what she looked like. She was probably still alive, but would she remember anything about one case out of the hundreds she had probably dealt with during her career?

"What else?" Burton asked briskly. "There must be channels to go through. I filled out one of those online forms to request my adoption records, but they still protect the identity of the parents if you were born before 1986, unless they've signed a release, so they'll only give me non-identifying information."

"That might still produce something helpful. Sometimes there is actually trackable information included. Profession, ethnicity, other information that we can use to narrow things down. So if they release something to you, let me know."

"It was a few weeks ago. I don't know how long it will be before they send me a letter."

"It takes a while. But it might be getting close now. And there's a possibility that we can hurry things along if I can find someone who knows someone in the department."

"You can't do that."

"Not officially, no. But sometimes, just talking to the right people can move things along."

Burton nodded without enthusiasm and drained his glass. "Are we about done here?"

Zachary looked at his notepad, considering the information he had so far. Nothing that was going to provide the key to the search. But he could start brainstorming and come up with some suggestions as to where to go next.

"Soon. Have you spent any time driving around town?"

"Why?"

"In case you might recognize something. If you're that drawn to the city, you may recognize landmarks once you get out there. You might be able to find your house just by looking. I might be able to narrow down the neighborhoods to check out. It's not that big of a city."

Burton rotated his cup in a circle of condensation on the table. "I don't have a driver's license."

"It was revoked?"

Burton nodded.

"How did you get here?"

"That's really none of your business, is it?"

Zachary held up his hands. "Okay. No, it's not. We should schedule some time to go out driving together, then."

"Sure. But not today. I'm about done in today."

Zachary pressed the button on his phone to check the time. Burton had said that he wouldn't get up until noon, and he was done in after an hour with Zachary. Because of the emotional toll, or because there was something physically wrong with him? Did he have some illness pushing him to dig into the past before it was too late? Or was he just finished with talking with Zachary?

7

Zachary had carefully selected a few neighborhoods to take Burton to. He figured from the way that Burton had talked that he had grown up in one of the poorer neighborhoods. And it wasn't an apartment building, not if there had been a basement. Add to that the fact that Burton always referred to it as his old house, not his old home or apartment or just where he had lived. He had specified a house.

That didn't eliminate duplexes and fourplexes, unfortunately. There was nothing to indicate whether it had been a single-family dwelling or a larger building. Zachary pictured some of the areas of town, thinking of a young boy walking down the street with his mother trailing behind, of him meeting a man walking a dog, and maybe being allowed to pet the dog. Poor, but not crime-ridden. Somewhere it was safe enough to walk without fear of being shot in a drive-by or mugged on the way to the store or park. It was okay to stop and talk to a stranger or a neighbor who was also out for a walk.

There wasn't much else he could work out from what Burton had told him. Liking loud music and not quiet. Hating fish sticks. Was there a fish and chips shop close by? Or were they from a grocer or corner store? Mac and cheese could be sold almost anywhere, which was probably why Burton hated it. Food deserts existed even in Vermont. Neighborhoods where it was virtually impossible to get fresh food and the residents had to rely on highly processed foods for survival if they were not able to drive far enough away to find grocery stores and produce stands.

Burton's love of dogs and bugs didn't tell Zachary anywhere about where he had lived. Dogs and bugs were everywhere.

Burton was waiting in the parking lot of the Best Western smoking when Zachary arrived. He put the cigarette out and tossed it to the side. Zachary pulled in and unlocked the doors. Burton climbed in, reeking of cigarette smoke. Zachary cleared his throat a couple of times and nudged buttons to roll the windows down a crack, even though it was still chilly out. He turned the heat on, blowing toward Burton to clear as much of the smoke as possible. Burton didn't apologize, either not noticing or not caring that it bothered his host.

"How are you doing?" Zachary asked in a neutral tone.

"Didn't sleep. Couldn't sleep… thinking about things."

"What things?"

"What we were going to find today. If I'll ever know anything about who I am and where I came from. If coming here was just one big mistake. My parents can't understand why I would come back here. No one understands it."

Zachary cocked his head slightly as he drove. "Have you talked to any other adoptees? I think it's actually pretty common to want to know where you came from. People often search for their biological families. Even people who aren't adopted, but who don't know who their father was, or who grew up apart from siblings." He shrugged with one shoulder. "I don't think it's that hard to understand."

"Maybe it would make more sense if it wasn't about the house. Maybe they'd understand more if it was about finding my biological parents."

"But it isn't?"

Burton shook his head, staring out the window. "Maybe eventually, someday. I can't say I never want to see them again… not without knowing something about what happened. Why I was adopted in the first place. There's a big difference between a parent who put you up for adoption because they couldn't take care of you anymore, and being taken away from your family because you were… being hurt."

"Makes sense," Zachary agreed. "So you think that the house will lead to some clues about what happened? Whether they are… people you want to see again or not?"

"I guess."

Zachary glanced over at Burton following the unenthusiastic reply. He really didn't seem to have any goal beyond finding the house. Finding his family was secondary to seeing the house. Standing where it had all started. Something about the place drew Burton.

"If you had to say what direction it was now, which way would you say to go?"

Burton scowled. "I have no idea." He looked at the street signs and the intersections. "I don't know my way around here. None of this is familiar."

"But if you had to point in one direction, directly at your house, where would it be?"

Burton considered for a moment, then finally pointed ahead and to the right. Zachary projected the path of Burton's finger in his head, thinking of a map of the city and what Burton could be pointing at. He did have a neighborhood in that direction that he had been considering, so he would start with that one.

Did Burton know subconsciously which direction his old house was in? Would a five-year-old have absorbed that information? Could he have a picture of the city in his head and know the approximate placement of various landmarks, the most important of which would have been his home?

It was possible. If he had good visual-spatial memory. He thought he had remembered the name of the city. It was entirely possible that the details of where his house was were stored in his brain somewhere, even if he couldn't access them directly.

"We'll go to Eastside," Zachary suggested, watching Burton's face for any flicker of recognition.

Burton didn't appear to recognize the name of the neighborhood. Not like the name of the city. So maybe it wasn't where he was from. What were the chances that they would just be able to get into the car and find it on their first attempt? Not very good. More than likely, their driving around looking for a familiar neighborhood would be fruitless. Maybe there would be something in his adoption records that would be helpful.

They were both quiet. Zachary drove, watching the road and the traffic and pondering what else Burton might be able to remember, if Zachary only knew how to shake it loose. Everything was stored in there somewhere. Burton stared out the window, his eyes searching for some familiar landmark or feeling.

The landscape around them began to change. They got away from the commercial areas into residentially-zoned neighborhoods. Nice houses at first, but gradually getting down to older, more dilapidated houses. Burton's body language became more attentive. He sat forward and leaned toward his window, trying to catch sight of something that his brain wouldn't give up.

There were not a lot of people out for walks or other business, but there were a few. Zachary watched for someone walking a dog, wondering if it would unlock something for Burton. Anything around them could trigger him, could take him to a memory that would provide the information they needed.

Burton's nose was almost glued to the passenger side window. Like a dog who wanted out or a toddler flattening his face against the glass. Zachary touched the brake, slowing a little, giving Burton a long look at each house that they passed.

"Maybe," Burton muttered, studying them all. "Maybe, this could be the right area. I just… don't know."

"Don't force it," Zachary advised. "Don't try to remember. Just look at the houses, like you never saw them before. The harder you try…"

Burton nodded. He tried to relax in his seat, but that didn't happen. He touched the window with his fingertips, resting them on the glass as he searched.

"Turn up here," Burton said, pointing to the right at the intersection.

Zachary obeyed, but he took a scan around the intersection before turning to identify any marker that might have been familiar to Burton. What would a five-year-old have noticed in that intersection? There was a corner store, not one of the big chains, but a little neighborhood place. Had he gone there for candy? Had his dad picked up beer there? Did his mother buy his mac and cheese there? Zachary turned.

Burton's head swiveled back and forth. He hit his knuckles against the door in frustration. "No. This isn't it. This isn't right."

"What did you see? What was the feeling?"

"Nothing, it just seemed like… I might have been here before. But none of this makes any sense. It's not right."

"That's okay. We didn't expect to find it in ten minutes, did we? Let's just drive around, get a feel for the neighborhood. See what else might feel familiar. Don't worry if we don't find it today. We're just taking a chance."

Burton nodded, but his jaw rippled as he clenched and ground his teeth, clearly upset about it.

"This is going to take time," Zachary reassured him. "You don't have a lot of memories, so we don't have a lot to go on. But that doesn't mean we won't succeed."

"There's no way we're going to find one house in the whole city. Not without knowing anything about it."

"We might. And we'll figure more out along the way. Just keep watching. Notice when things are familiar. Take it slow."

Burton said nothing else for the next half hour. Zachary wound in and out through the residential streets. It didn't look like he had picked the right neighborhood on his first try. But there were others. He hadn't expected to be right the first time.

"Stop. Pull over!"

Zachary slowed, then guided his car into a parking space along the curb. Burton unlocked his door and was out the door before Zachary even came to a complete stop. Burton looked back the way they had come. He jogged back down the sidewalk, looking at the houses. He ran past one, then returned. He stepped out into the street and turned to look back at it from the same vantage point he'd had in the car. He stepped closer, and stopped on the sidewalk, studying it. Zachary let him look at it by himself for a minute and, when he didn't come back to the car, Zachary got out, locked up, and joined Burton on the sidewalk.

"Is that it?" He studied the bungalow. Dirty white with brown trim. Nondescript. Some shrubbery around it. The lawn not yet green.

Burton paced back and forth to the two front corners of the lot, looking at it, studying it from every angle. Zachary pulled out his phone and took a picture of the front of the house.

"Do you want to go around? Check the side and the back?" Zachary suggested.

Burton hesitated. "Do you think it's okay to go onto someone else's property?"

Interesting, Zachary thought, that he was so concerned about doing the right thing. His behavior up until that point suggested that he didn't care about social conventions. He didn't care if Zachary saw him as a drunk.

That was Zachary's problem. He wasn't concerned about getting into the car smelling of smoke, not even making weak excuses about how stressed he was. He slept halfway through the day. But he was worried about going onto someone else's property. Because the house looked like the one he had lived in? Or was he just a naturally law-abiding person and was concerned about trespass?

"If someone comes out, we can explain ourselves," Zachary said. "I don't think you need to worry about it."

"What if... *they're* here?"

"After this many years? I don't think you need to worry. People don't stay that long in one place, especially in an area like this. They come and go every year or two."

"So you don't think they're there?"

Zachary highly doubted it was even the house they were looking for. It had just happened to catch Burton's eye, to trigger some sort of memory. "No."

Burton stepped onto the lawn, then balked again.

"Do you want me to drive you around to the back?"

Burton nodded. "Yeah. Let's go around, instead of cutting through. More respectful."

Zachary led the way back to the car. Burton was hesitant to leave the front of the house, but eventually slid back into the passenger's seat and pulled his door closed.

Zachary had noted the house number in case it wasn't recognizable from the rear. He circled around to the alley and drove slowly down the alley until they reached the house. Zachary got out and Burton followed. The back yard was completely enclosed by a high fence. Too high for Zachary to see over comfortably. Easier for Burton. He peered over for a minute, then shook his head.

"This isn't it."

"That's okay," Zachary assured him.

Burton punched the fence, making Zachary wince. "I thought this was it!"

"What were you thinking and feeling, when you were looking at it?" Zachary made motions for Burton to get back into the car. Burton stayed there, staring at the back of the house.

"I thought... I don't know. I just thought I had succeeded."

"And how did you feel about that? Were you—" Zachary cut himself off before he could finish the question. He didn't want to suggest an emotion that might color Burton's answer. If Zachary suggested that he should be happy or excited, it might completely change Burton's analysis of what he had been feeling.

"I was..." Burton shook his head, a tiny movement, confused. "I felt anxious. Worried." He looked at Zachary, meeting his eyes for maybe the first time since they had met. "Why would I feel that way?"

"It's okay. You felt however you felt. Do you know what you felt anxious or worried about?"

Burton thought about it. "I'm not sure. That it was my house. That I was going to get caught there. I don't understand, though, why it would be a bad thing to find it. I want to find it. Don't I?"

"Consciously, yes. But sometimes we have mixed feelings." Zachary couldn't count all of the times that he had contradictory feelings about a person or situation. It would probably be stranger for him if he only had one feeling. It seemed like different parts of his brain and body were always fighting against each other. He felt a certain kinship with people with multiple personalities. It would feel like a relief to him to be able to assign each set of feelings a different name. To be able to say 'Tom feels like this and Joe feels like that' instead of trying to figure out which feeling was really him, which one won out in a situation.

"I didn't feel good," Burton mused. He looked at Zachary's car. "Are we going back now?"

"We don't have to. We can drive around some more. If you think that we've done all we can in this neighborhood, I have others that we can check out."

Burton nodded. "I think we've seen everything there is to see here. It obviously isn't the right area. Maybe we'll have better luck somewhere else."

Zachary didn't point out that it had been close enough that Burton had thought that he'd found the house. There were good reasons to think that it might still be the right area. They hadn't gone down all of the streets. But he understood Burton didn't want to stay there. They might have better luck somewhere else. Or Burton might just want to rid himself of the oppressive feelings that the 'wrong' house had brought him. They got back into the car. Before driving away, Zachary wrote down the address of the house they had stopped at.

Just in case.

8

There were a couple more houses that Burton had Zachary stop at. Zachary took pictures of each one and wrote down the addresses. It would be up to him to examine the houses and the neighborhoods to identify the similarities among them. Then he would have a better idea of what they were looking for. If Burton actually did remember something and wasn't just on a wild goose chase. Zachary believed from watching his changes in expression that Burton did have memories of his childhood and his childhood home, even if he couldn't access them on demand.

After stopping at one last house, Burton was too agitated and moody to carry on. Smoking and pacing around at the last house hadn't seemed to settle him at all. Zachary was getting anxious from his own client's behavior. It would be pushing his luck to stay with Burton much longer. He was winding himself up for something, and Zachary didn't want to be in the way when he decided to blow.

"I think we've done enough for the day. I'll drop you back at your hotel."

Burton shook his head in irritation. He looked around and pointed to a bar in a low, dark building with several restaurants and retail shops. "I'm going there."

Zachary didn't think that Burton was going there to make inquiries as to whether he had ever lived in the area. He had been several hours without a drink, and he wanted to remedy the fact.

"I'll drive you back to your hotel. You can drink there."

"I don't want to go back to my hotel. I want to drink here."

"Why? You'll be more comfortable at the hotel. And when you're done, you can just take the elevator up to your room and go to sleep."

"I'm not going back there," Burton growled. "I just told you that. I'm not going back there; I'm going to drink *here*."

"Does it have something to do with your memories?"

"What?"

"This place. Does it trigger something? Are you going in to have a look around or ask some questions?"

"No. I'm going in to have a drink. It's the closest place to drink, and I'm not waiting any longer."

"I can have you home in fifteen minutes. Better if you drink at the hotel."

Burton didn't argue any further; he just started walking toward the bar.

"How are you going to get back to the hotel?" Zachary reminded him.

"I can take a cab."

"That will cost money and you'll have to wait around. I can take you now."

Burton swore at him. Zachary didn't chase after him as he headed for the bar. He wasn't going to try to physically coerce Burton back into the car. He was bigger than Zachary and, if he wanted to drink in a bar, there was no reason he couldn't.

Zachary glanced at the lock screen of his phone. He still had a couple of hours before Kenzie would be getting home from the medical examiner's office. He had time to get a few things done before she got home and he would need to turn his attention away from the case and give her some face time. He flipped through his notepad and decided to see what Heather had found him on skip tracing the social worker.

He tapped her icon on his favorites list on the phone. Like Joss, Heather was one of his older sisters. But there were few similarities between the two. She had come back into his life after Tyrrell, looking for Zachary's help on finding the identity of the man who had raped her when she had been a teenager. A cold case that had not been easy to break since the police had destroyed the forensic exam kit collected after her assault.

One of the things that changed in Heather's life after the case was closed was that she needed something to do with her time. She no longer wanted to hide from the world and everything in it, living a quiet, isolated life. She wanted to work, to do something useful, but after decades of not having a job, finding something that would satisfy her was a challenge. So Zachary had taken the opportunity to train her in some of the basics of investigator work. Things that could be done from her computer at home or through discreet phone inquiries. Heather had taken to the job with an unexpected passion and was doing a lot of Zachary's routine investigative work while he pursued the bigger, riskier cases.

She answered the phone after the second ring. "Hey, little brother!"

"Hi, Feathers. I'm just checking to see if you had any luck tracing Aurelia Pace."

"Well, it's an unusual name. That makes it easier."

"If she signed up for services using her name and not just an initial."

"Yeah. Well, most of the time, I couldn't find an Aurelia. So either she used an initial, or she used a husband's name."

"Or a different last name. Got married or divorced."

"Right. All of the usual. But I did find a couple of good prospects."

"Great. Do you want to shoot them my way?"

"They should already be in your inbox. Mailed them to you a few minutes ago."

"Awesome. Thanks for your help, Heather."

"Thank you. I'm having a lot of fun with it."

"Good. Let me know if I push too much stuff onto you. Otherwise, I'm going to assume that you're okay with the amount I'm giving you, and I'm just going to keep giving you more."

"Load me up. I'm fine."

"Okay, remember you asked for it!"

"We should get together sometime soon."

Zachary thought of the last awkward dinner at Mr. Peterson's house, and wasn't sure he wanted a repeat. Lorne Peterson's house was one of the few places he felt welcome and calm, and he didn't want it to become a place he avoided going.

"Uh… yeah. Sometime soon."

"You okay, Zachy?"

Zachary cleared his throat. "Yeah, I'm fine. I'm just not sure that all of us together…"

"Not all of us. You and me. We don't always have to do everything together as a family. I find it easier… if it's just one-on-one. Having everyone in the room is exhausting. It's fine for holidays like Easter and Christmas, but I can't do it all the time."

Zachary breathed out a sigh of relief. "Me neither," he admitted. "Especially with Joss. She's pretty… intense."

"I thought the two of you were getting along together better."

"Better. But she's still… not easy to be around. And putting everyone together, there are just too many things to try to do at the same time."

"I know. Joss is kind of… an acquired taste. Small doses."

Zachary laughed. "Yeah. That's a good way of putting it. Okay. You and me can get together for coffee or a visit. You could come to my apartment if you want."

Heather was the first person he had actually invited there. Kenzie and Mario had taken it upon themselves to come see him and spend time with him at his home but, outside of them, it was the first time he had actually asked someone over. He held his breath for a moment, thinking about it and how it felt, and then released the air, letting it dribble out slowly.

"That would be nice, Zachary. Thanks. I'll see what Grant's schedule is like, and some day when he's busy with other things, I'll come for a visit."

"Okay," Zachary agreed. "That sounds good."

After the call with Heather, he clicked immediately on his inbox before he could be distracted by anything else. There were always so many things trying to pull him away from his work. He found Heather's email and focused in on it. He had set up his mail window so that he couldn't see the subject lines of the various emails, which helped him to avoid being pulled in by the promise of something more interesting or exciting.

Heather's work was neatly summarized and presented. Zachary looked at the time clock on the computer and decided there was still plenty of time to call Aurelia Pace. Hopefully, one of the numbers Heather had dug up would work.

He dialed the first, scripting the call in his head. He wanted to put Aurelia at ease, but still to be able to request information from her that she might not remember or be willing to part with. Adoptees had more rights than they had thirty years ago, but some of the restrictions that the government put on things still made things too difficult for adoptees to get the information they needed.

"Hello?" The phone was answered by a male voice. Maybe a bad sign. He pictured Aurelia Pace as a single woman. There was no reason to think that she couldn't be married, but he pictured her as either single, divorced, or widowed. Men tended to die before their wives. So even if she were married, chances were he had died before her.

"Yes, I'm looking for Aurelia Pace."

"Wrong number."

"Sorry, has there ever been an Aurelia at this number?"

"How would I know? Not a name I've ever heard."

"No one else has called this number looking for her?"

"No. Just you, buddy."

"And can I make sure I dialed properly? Is this…" Zachary recited the number.

"Yeah, that's the number you called. And there's no Aurelia here, okay?"

"Okay. Thanks for your time."

Zachary ended the call. He tried the next number.

"Hello?" A woman's voice this time. Older. Not shaky, but not a young woman's voice. Zachary breathed a sigh of relief. This would be her. This was the right one.

"Is this Aurelia Pace?"

"This is Aurie."

"Ms. Pace, are you the same Aurelia Pace who used to be a social worker?"

There was a pause before she answered. "I don't know of any other Aurelia Pace," she said cautiously.

"So you were a social worker."

"Yes. Who is this?"

"My name is Zachary Goldman. I'm a private investigator and I've been hired by a man you placed for adoption years ago. He's trying to track down some information about his past, and I was hoping that you would be able to fill in a few blanks."

"Information about adoptions is private."

"Yes. I will have you talk to Mr. Burton. He will confirm to you that I'm acting on his behalf. You can release information to him about his own history."

"Well, it isn't that simple. The law prevents me from releasing anything confidential."

"But there are some things that you would not be prevented from telling him. He knows nothing right now, so any information that you could provide to him would be greatly appreciated."

"Biological families have rights too. I can't share information about them."

"But you can share information about my client."

There was a long pause as she considered this. "Maybe," she said finally.

"If you want to set the parameters for the discussion, that's fine. And of course, if something is confidential, you can tell us that. We won't push you to provide information that you're not allowed to share."

"If I even remember anything about this client of yours. Why isn't he going through the proper channels? There's a form he can fill online. It's very easy."

"He has done that and is waiting for the reply. And that will, of course, be non-identifying information."

"Which is the only thing I can provide. I can't tell him anything that identifies who his parents were."

"You can talk about some of the circumstances."

Another pause as she considered this. "Some of them," she conceded finally. "If I can remember. It's been a long time since I was doing adoptive placements. A lot has happened since then, and I don't remember a lot of the cases very clearly."

"All you can do is your best."

She didn't voice any other objections, and Zachary waited for her to fill the silence. People didn't like it when there was too much time without anything being said. They liked to fill it, to have a back-and-forth discussion. Too much silence was uncomfortable.

"I suppose," Aurelia said eventually. "Where are you?"

9

When Kenzie got home from work, Zachary was examining the pictures he had printed off. Kenzie took a quick look at what he was doing.

"Looking at buying a house?" she teased.

"If I was, I think I could do better than these. I hope so."

"So, what are these?" Kenzie reached for one of the photos, pausing with her fingers an inch away, looking at him to see whether he would object. Zachary shrugged, and she picked it up.

"These are houses that provoked a response in my client. Houses that he initially thought might be his childhood home."

"Oh, how interesting." Kenzie lined the houses up in a grid, looking over them. "So you're trying to figure out what was the same between all of the houses. What it is that he sees that makes him think of home."

Zachary nodded. "But it might not be one thing the same between all of them. Some of them might have triggered a response because of... the colors, and others because of the windows. Or the porch or the fence. We don't know that it's one thing among all of them."

"Hmm." Kenzie looked at them, considering Zachary's words. "And we can probably assume that some of them have several things together that made him think of home. The right color and the right windows, but not the right porch."

"Yeah."

"Interesting. What have you got so far?"

Zachary laid his scratchpad down where Kenzie could read it, his face warming as he looked at his messy writing. If she could read any of it, she was doing better than most of his school teachers.

But Kenzie didn't complain about his writing. She looked over the list and then turned her attention back to the pictures, seeing if she could contribute anything to the puzzle's solution.

"Single-family homes. Mostly bungalows," she observed.

Zachary nodded. "I had a pretty good idea going into it that it wouldn't be apartments. He has possible memories of a basement."

Kenzie nodded. "And no duplexes."

Zachary closed his eyes for a moment, trying to center himself. He added this note to the list. He had been aware of it, but had not put it into words.

"What's wrong?" Kenzie asked.

"Nothing. I put it down."

"Yes… but I thought…" Kenzie trailed off.

She was very good at reading him. Too good, sometimes, so that it felt like she could get right into his brain. And there was danger in anyone being able to read his thoughts.

"Color schemes are all dull," Zachary said, pointing to one of the points on his list. "Mostly beiges and browns."

Kenzie looked at the pictures, then back at Zachary. He had been using the skills that he had developed in reading faces and body language to figure out what Burton remembered or was emotionally affected by, so why should it surprise him that Kenzie could do the same with him?

"It's nothing."

"If you don't want to talk about it, okay. But don't act like nothing happened," Kenzie said gently.

Zachary hesitated. He looked at the pictures of the houses. "With multiple-family dwellings, it can be harder to get away with abuse. Neighbors hear through the walls, report… what they might overhear."

Kenzie was still. "Oh. Yes. Hadn't thought about that."

She looked back at the pictures as well. Zachary waited for her to continue that line, to drill down to ask Zachary about his experiences, but she didn't. They were working a case, and maybe she recognized that it wasn't the right time to discuss his demons.

"You have the fences," Kenzie commented. "Lots of chain-link enclosed yards."

Zachary nodded. "Yes. More secure than a wooden fence. Strong, good visibility, easy to lock. There are not many plants. This place probably wasn't landscaped. A few shrubs, maybe, close to the house. But if you want good security, like the fence provides, then you don't want them close to the windows. You don't want people to be able to get access to windows while hidden by shrubbery."

"Just because it wasn't landscaped then, doesn't mean it isn't landscaped now," Kenzie pointed out. "It's been a lot of years since he lived there."

"Yes. Hopefully, that won't stop him from recognizing it when he sees it."

"You're going to need more than just his visual recognition, aren't you? Is that going to be good enough for him? He doesn't want proof that it was where he lived?"

Zachary hadn't thought that far ahead. "I don't know. If he feels an emotional connection, then maybe not. I don't know whether seeing the house is what he wants, or whether he needs to know what happened to him there. I don't think he knows. I don't think he will know until he sees it. He only has one goal right now."

"I guess if he sees it, then you can do a title history to see who has owned it."

"If his family owned it. But they might not have."

Kenzie conceded the point. "It's really interesting. I wonder how he's going to feel when he sees it."

"I asked him how he felt when he saw one of these houses that was close…"

Kenzie raised her eyebrows inquiringly.

"He was anxious and afraid."

"Hmm." Kenzie nodded. "So he's not chasing a happy feeling. Looking for a place where he felt peaceful and contented."

"No, I don't think so." Zachary considered how much to reveal to Kenzie about his client. He owed Burton some degree of confidentiality, of course, but as long as he didn't give Kenzie any identifying information about him, his privacy was assured. "He's not in the best shape emotionally.

Drinks a lot. He says that his adoptive family was very loving, gave him everything he needed, but he went badly off the rails."

"And you think that's because of what happened to him before he was adopted?"

"It's possible. Plenty of kids from loving homes still experiment and get dragged down by addiction, but he's quite a mess. He only has vague memories and feelings about what happened before he was adopted, but his facial expressions and body language… they don't lie. And they say that the memories are not happy ones."

Kenzie nodded, accepting his analysis. "What's your next step?"

"Tomorrow, we're going to meet with the social worker who placed him with his adoptive family. I haven't told him yet, but I've set up a time with her."

"You're meeting her without him?"

"No, I just haven't let him know yet. He's not doing anything while he's here, other than drinking and looking for this house, so he'll be available. But I don't want to tell him too much ahead of time. I don't want to make him any more anxious than he already is."

"You don't think you need to prepare him ahead of time?"

"I think it could send him on a binge, if he isn't already on one. Best not to chance it."

10

The pictures were cleared away. Their dishes from dinner were in the dishwasher. Zachary sat on the couch, staring at his phone screen, swiping at random.

"Everything okay?"

Zachary looked over at Kenzie. "I thought maybe I should touch base with Rhys."

She nodded. "I think it would be a good idea. He has to be wondering how you are, why you haven't been talking to him."

"Vera said she didn't think it would make him worse, if I called."

"How is he doing?"

"He's back to school, but his teachers say he is distracted. Not getting his classwork done. Vera said he's not telling his therapist much. He says everything is fine now."

Kenzie sighed. "Kids. Teenagers are not well-known for sharing their troubles with their parents or caregivers. And when you start with someone who is already non-verbal…"

"Non-speaking," Zachary corrected. "Or mostly."

She looked at him for a minute, then shrugged. "Does he usually talk to his therapist? Or have good communication with him?"

"Vera made it sound like it was less than usual. I didn't ask any details."

Kenzie nodded. "Well, pop him off a message. I don't see what harm it could do, especially if Vera said to go ahead."

Zachary looked back at his phone, shifting back and forth between screens with his thumb, as if he didn't know what to do. He was just concerned about Rhys and didn't want to make things any worse than they already were.

"Just bite the bullet," Kenzie suggested. "But it's up to you. I'm going to take a break. I have some things to catch up on."

She got up and left the room, leaving Zachary to himself. He suspected she didn't have anything to do that she couldn't do sitting beside him, but was leaving the room to give him privacy to work through his problems on his own.

And she was right. That was exactly what he needed. He opened his message app. It was at Rhys's name already. Zachary glanced through the last few words and pictures that he and Rhys had last exchanged. All before the shooting. Nothing since. Rhys had come to him for help, and Zachary had done his best, but had ended up scaring Rhys. Maybe permanently traumatizing him. Could he ever forgive himself for that?

Bite the bullet.

Zachary tapped out a brief message. *Just checking in to see how you are doing.*

He watched the screen for a reply. There was no guarantee that Rhys was looking at his phone or was able to answer him right away. He might be doing chores or be in therapy, though it was pretty late for that. He might be working on homework, unable to concentrate on his classwork during the day. He might have already gone to bed, overwhelmed by the anxiety he'd had since the incident.

Or maybe he didn't want to talk to Zachary. Or was unable to bring himself to reply. He'd had enough problems with communication before, usually choosing to use images and concepts rather than linear language. Ever since his grandfather had been shot.

Like Luke.

Although Luke's injury had been superficial and his grandfather's fatal, it had been similar enough to throw Rhys into flashbacks and cause ongoing issues.

Even though Zachary was staring at the phone screen, he had ceased to see it, and was surprised when the phone vibrated in his hand. He looked down and saw Rhys's reply.

It was a picture Zachary had seen before. The three women in the Salter family. Rhys's grandmother, aunt, and mother. All smiling at the camera. Rhys with them, looking solemn and unhappy.

Rhys usually smiled when he greeted Zachary, but the rest of the time, his face was naturally sad. Mouth turned down. A look of grief in his eyes. He had been through so much in his short lifetime, and it had left a permanent mark.

Zachary's chest hurt, looking at that picture. He knew now what he hadn't known when he'd seen it the first time. The secrets those three women and Rhys's silence had hidden. The ongoing pain and trauma that Rhys suffered as a result. They weren't the happy women he had taken them for the first time he saw that picture. The happy faces were just masks, hiding all of the ugliness underneath. Zachary touched his phone screen as if Rhys might feel it and be comforted.

I'm so sorry, Rhys. I never meant to hurt you.

He felt Rhys's hand around his forearm in the clasp Rhys had given him when he had visited last. Strong and forgiving. Rhys didn't hold it against him. But Zachary did.

Another message came through from Rhys. This time, a picture of Luke. Zachary immediately recognized it as a still taken from a video Rhys had made of Madison and Luke. Madison had been cropped out, only her shoulder still visible.

Zachary knew what Rhys was asking. He wanted to know how Luke—who Rhys knew as Noah—was doing. Had he recovered? What had happened to him?

Zachary wasn't sure how to respond.

Rhys would want to know that Luke was okay, that he hadn't died like Grandpa Clarence, but how would he feel about the fact that Luke was free? He hadn't been charged for his crimes and hadn't paid the price for what he had done to Madison.

The minutes ticked by as he thought about how to word his reply. Another message from Rhys bubbled up under the picture of Luke. A big cartoonish question mark. Zachary sighed.

He's okay. Recovered from the shooting with just a scar.

Rhys sent a thumbs-up.

Zachary breathed a sigh of relief. *How's school?*

Rhys sent back a gif of some celeb shaking his head slowly. Zachary wasn't sure who it was. He didn't watch a lot of TV that might be popular with the younger generation. But he understood the sentiment.

Any way I can help?

As he waited for Rhys's response, Zachary looked again at the picture of Rhys with his family and the picture of Luke. Even though Rhys had told his therapist that everything was fine, he was clearly still caught in the emotional vortex that the shooting had triggered. He was obsessing over what had happened, maybe remembering things that he hadn't been able to recall before. Zachary ran this thumb along the edge of the phone, trying to compose his thoughts in a way that would resonate with Rhys.

I know about flashbacks, he typed finally, though he knew that the language was awkward and someone else would have been able to be more eloquent than he was. *I still have a lot of them myself.*

Rhys posted a series of dots, which Zachary thought meant that he was trying to compose an answer. He waited, watching the screen for the next image or text to appear.

Eventually, a picture of Winnie the Pooh and Christopher Robin was added to the stream.

Even if we're apart, I'll always remember.

Zachary stiffened, alarmed. He quickly thumbed in a response. *Are you thinking about suicide?*

This time, Rhys's response came quickly. A red circle with a slash through it. Zachary took a deep lungful of air, strained.

If things are bad and you need help... it's okay. You remember when you told me to go to the hospital.

Yes.

But that wasn't what Rhys had meant. Zachary studied the picture of Pooh and the words written over it. He looked at the previous couple of exchanges, thinking. The picture wasn't about being apart or saying goodbye. It was the memories. *I'll always remember.* Rhys was thinking about Luke. About his dead grandfather. He couldn't get the images out of his head. Just like Zachary couldn't shake his flashbacks, even after so many years had passed.

It sucks, he typed, *having to remember things that you don't want to.*

Yes.

Have you talked to your therapist about them?

Another big red circle with a slash through it. Zachary had already known the answer when he asked.

He can't help you if you don't tell him.

:-L

Zachary had to look that one up. A quick internet search told him the emoticon signified frustration. A feeling he could understand and relate to. *Do you need a new therapist? Does he listen to you?*

:-L

Grandma would get you a new one if you need one. I can give her some names.

After a minute, Rhys sent a gif of a man raising and lowering opposite hands. *Maybe.*

I'll talk to her. You can still decide.

OK.

Zachary blew out a long breath. He didn't think he'd been holding it, but he felt like it was a long time since he had taken a full breath. He was worried about saying the wrong thing to Rhys and making him feel worse or decide to cut off communication.

Okay. If we find someone you can connect with, maybe he can help you feel better. Work through some of the memories.

There was no response from Rhys.

Sorry again, Zachary messaged. *Really sorry about Luke getting shot and bringing back those memories.*

Rhys sent back a picture of a baby with a scrunched-up expression and the name, *Luke?*

Oh. Noah. He's not going by that anymore.

:-O

Zachary smiled at the expression of surprise. *For the flashbacks, do you know how to anchor?*

Rhys sent a picture of an anchor.

It can help. You focus on your senses. Identify five things that you see, five things you hear, etc. Like I did with you in the car.

Helps U?

Yeah. Sometimes. I'm still working on it. My family tries to help me. Remind me to do it. Kenzie too.

Rhys sent back a picture of Kenzie with a red heart outlining her face.

When they were communicating face-to-face, Rhys always asked after Kenzie with a kissing sound. It never failed to make Zachary blush, however hard he tried not to react.

He turned his face toward Kenzie's bedroom and called out to her. "Kenz? Do you want to say something to Rhys?"

She returned to the living room and sat down, reaching out for Zachary's phone. "Of course. How's he doing?"

"Things are tough. But he's hanging in there."

"Good." Kenzie's eyes flicked up, seeing her picture in the message feed, but she didn't scroll up to see the rest of the conversation. Slouching down into the couch, she tapped out a message. She looked up from the phone after sending it and looked at Zachary. "So you're okay too? Wasn't so bad after all."

"Just had to bite the bullet, like you said. I was worried…" He trailed off. Kenzie already knew what he'd been worried about.

Kenzie looked back down at the phone as Rhys sent her a message back. They exchanged a few more messages, and then Kenzie handed Zachary his phone back. "Yeah, he seems a bit down, but okay."

Zachary nodded. "Sometimes people put on a false front and tell you they're okay when they're not. But Rhys… he's pretty good about not glossing over how he feels."

"Yeah. You know, I think part of it is his communication difficulties. He doesn't have the words to waste like we do. He'd better get the message out as succinctly as he can, because it's so hard for him."

"Yeah, you're probably right." Zachary looked down at the phone and said his goodbyes to Rhys, sensing that he was done with the conversation. *I'll talk to Grandma.*

A dog waved its paw at Zachary. He shut off the screen, turning his full attention back to Kenzie. "Okay. I'm done that. And done work. So I'm all yours."

She slid closer to him and put her arms around him. "Excellent. Just what I wanted."

11

Zachary tried several times to reach Burton, but there was no response to his calls and texts. Either Burton was still passed out, or he had decided he was finished with Zachary. Hopefully, he had made it back to his hotel. Zachary considered going over to check on him and have a talk, but decided that his attention probably wasn't wanted. Burton had made it clear that his alcohol consumption was no one's business but his own and that he would deal with Zachary on his own terms. So if he wanted to reach Zachary, he could be the one to make the next move. If Zachary had to cancel or reschedule the social worker, then he would.

After Kenzie headed off to work, Zachary had an appointment with his own therapist. He took a couple of minutes at the beginning of the session to tell Dr. Boyle about Rhys and to ask her for some recommendations for therapists who would take the time to learn how to communicate with Rhys, and not just assume that he either didn't want to communicate or was not able to.

"He sounds very interesting," Dr. Boyle observed. "He hasn't learned sign language or how to use a communications device? There are so many options; I would think that he would have succeeded in finding something that worked for him."

"He has… it's just kind of unconventional. His mutism seems like it's more than just a problem with speaking, but even putting language together in the usual way. His grandmother says that he does okay with multiple-choice or short-answer questions at school, but he doesn't write in full sentences and he couldn't write an essay or something like that. When he and I are talking, he doesn't type in sentences. It's all... concepts rather than structured sentences."

"Fascinating. I'd love to meet him myself, if you want to include me on the list of recommendations."

Zachary hesitated to add Dr. B's name. "How does that work, when you have two patients who know each other? I mean... with confidentiality and all."

"You would both have complete confidentiality. I wouldn't repeat anything that either of you said to the other."

"But what if... I had concerns about him or something he said, or vice versa. You'd have to bring it up, wouldn't you? Or take some kind of action."

"If you're not comfortable with me counseling both of you, that's fine, Zachary."

"It's just that... well, we both discuss personal stuff sometimes. Anxieties. Mental health stuff. Relationships."

"I don't want to do anything that would make it harder for you to talk with me. That's fine. You have a few names that you can give Rhys. Hopefully, one of them will work out."

Zachary nodded. "Yeah. If he goes all the way down the list and doesn't have any success, maybe then. Because I want him to get the treatment he needs too."

Dr. Boyle nodded. "You're a good man."

"Well," Zachary's face warmed. "I can see myself in him. I can feel his pain."

"Yes." Dr. Boyle gave a little frown. "I am a little concerned, though..."

Zachary's heart thumped harder. He didn't like Dr. Boyle's tone or that frown. "Uh... what?"

"It sounds like the two of you are very close."

"Well... friends, yes."

"You are discussing mental health issues and relationships. That's very intimate to be discussing with a teen."

"He doesn't really have anyone else who understands..."

"Yes, I get that. But you need to be very careful. This kind of situation can lead to inappropriate relationships. You're much older than him and you're discussing very personal issues. You don't want to end up..."

Zachary swallowed. "It isn't that kind of relationship. No. We're not talking about sex." His face grew hot just at the suggestion and he knew he was turning beet red. Would Dr. Boyle think that meant he was lying?

"Not now, maybe. But what would you do if he wanted advice? Or expressed an attraction or made an unexpected advance?"

"I wouldn't get into that kind of relationship with him. I wouldn't."

"Have you thought about how you would react? Because emotional closeness can cross boundaries. If you haven't made plans ahead of time, thought about how to handle it or made sure that you're never in a compromising situation, it can be difficult to make good decisions in the heat of the moment. You know your impulsivity is an issue that often works against you."

"His grandma makes sure that we only meet at the house. She's asked me not to take him out anywhere. For burgers or anything. We only meet when she is there."

Dr. Boyle smiled and nodded. "That's good. That's a good rule to have. I'm glad that she's already anticipated any possible issues."

Zachary nodded. His face was still burning and he didn't try to explain to her that Rhys didn't always follow his grandmother's rules and had shown up at his apartment by himself twice. Just the kind of situation that Vera and Dr. B would want him to avoid. And instead of sending Rhys immediately home, Zachary had made some less-than-optimal choices.

He wouldn't let that happen again. He'd told Rhys that he needed to follow his grandmother's rules. If Rhys ever did that again, Zachary would take him straight home. That was the only proper thing to do.

"All right. Let's move on with your session," Dr. Boyle said. "Our time is short now, but I'm glad to hear how you're helping Rhys out. You have a very compassionate heart."

Zachary shrugged and looked away.

"So, do you have something particular you want to bring up today? Or did you want to let me know how things are going with Kenzie?"

He and Kenzie had gone in for several couples sessions now, and it was getting easier for Zachary to talk about their relationship in front of Kenzie or to deconstruct how things were going when Zachary met with Dr. Boyle alone. Which was good, because the first time they'd done a couples session, the anxiety had been so brutal, he had thought he was going to have a heart attack and die.

"I guess… talking about things with Kenzie works. If you think I need to."

"What do you think?"

Zachary looked down at the carpet where Dr. Boyle's desk met the floor. Talking about their intimate relationship, he needed something to focus on other than Dr. Boyle herself.

"I think… things are pretty good. We're close. But… we still have problems. You know."

"With you dissociating?"

Zachary nodded. He was glad that his face was already red from their discussion about Rhys, so she couldn't see him coloring again. It didn't just embarrass him to talk about his physical relationship with Kenzie. He felt completely inadequate. He should be able to have intimate contact with her without either getting overwhelmed by flashbacks or losing himself and mentally floating away from his body, making Kenzie feel like she was in the room by herself.

Zachary had hoped that after a session or two with Dr. Boyle, things would be fixed. He would be able to go on and carry on a normal relationship with Kenzie. What was even more embarrassing to him was that he had not had problems with dissociation while he'd been married to Bridget. He didn't want Kenzie to think that it was her fault. It was Zachary's problem and had been triggered by an assault that had triggered the emergence of a whole slew of repressed memories.

"I know you're disappointed by that," Dr. Boyle observed.

"I wanted… I hoped that we'd be able to work through things, and I'd be… I'd be normal."

"These issues didn't just develop overnight. I know it seems a little like that, because you weren't having them with Bridget, but they were already there, they were just under the surface."

"Why couldn't they stay there? Or why can't I… repress them again?"

"Even though you want to, repressing them is not healthy. That was the only way you could deal with them when you were younger, but you've grown and developed since then. You have other tools in your toolbox, and you have the ability to work through them instead of just shoving them down."

"So you think it's good that I'm having problems."

"Well… not exactly. But yes, I think it's better for you to be able to talk about the issues and work through them in therapy than not to deal with them. Repressed memories just continue to fester and to pop up here and there as other kinds of problems."

Zachary stared at the carpet, thinking about this.

"Have you ever had an unexplained reaction to something?" Dr. Boyle asked. "You get really angry when someone puts their hand on your shoulder, or you hear a song or smell a scent and feel like something bad is going to happen?"

Zachary nodded. "Yeah. I've had that happen."

"That could be due to repressed memories. Your body and brain have a reason to react to a stimulus like that, but you have no idea what it is. You don't remember what happened to you and don't know why that trigger is there. You may learn to anticipate it, and avoid that trigger to avoid it happening again, but that doesn't mean you've dealt with the memories,;you're just avoiding them."

"I have a client who is trying to find where he used to live. He can't remember a lot from that long ago, but I can see him reacting to things when I ask him a question or make a suggestion. I know he's not lying to me about not remembering. He just… can't reach it."

"Exactly. Sometimes things are locked away so tightly it can take years to identify them and work them out."

"So… you think it will take years for me to sort things out with Kenzie? Because I don't think she's going to wait that long."

"No, that's not what I meant. Your memories have surfaced, and that means that we can deal with them. While they were still locked away, we couldn't deal with them, could we?"

"Well, no. Not if I didn't even know they were there."

"And it may take a long time for your client to be able to access his memories. Or it may need… a big trigger to bring them to the surface."

"Like I had."

"Hopefully, not like you had."

"Yeah." Zachary wouldn't wish what he had gone through on anyone. Burton was better off drinking and not remembering. Better if he just went home and quit looking for his past.

12

It was nearly two o'clock before Zachary got a call from Ben Burton. Zachary determined not to ask Burton any questions about where he had been or how much he had drunk the night before. Zachary had enough issues of his own; he didn't need to take on Burton's too.

But he was grateful that he had never become addicted to alcohol. Unlike Tyrrell, who had been an alcoholic before he'd managed to pull himself out of the hole. Or their parents. Joss, too, had dealt with alcohol and drug addiction. Zachary was lucky to have avoided that particular issue. He mostly avoided it due to his meds, but he had remembered how ugly his parents had gotten when they drank, and he didn't want to be like that. Didn't want to be like that with his family, when he had still hoped to have a family of his own. He wouldn't ever want to treat his children the way his parents had treated him and his siblings.

But would he ever have children? It became less and less likely. First getting married to Bridget, who had insisted she never wanted to have children but was now pregnant with twins, and then getting into a relationship with Kenzie that he couldn't seem to stay in mentally. Yes, he could still perform physically, but what woman would want to have children with a man who checked out like that? And if he still had so many emotional problems, what were the chances that she would ever trust him around children?

What if one of them triggered an involuntary response? What if his impulsivity put one of them in danger?

What if he couldn't be a good father?

Burton called at two o'clock. "Driving around looking at houses isn't getting anywhere," he growled without preamble.

"I have an appointment set up with the social worker who placed you, if you can get yourself together for a three o'clock meeting. I was just about to cancel it."

"I'm up. I can get wherever you want."

"We're meeting at a coffee shop," Zachary told him. "She wanted something on neutral ground." In reality, he just didn't want Burton in the bar. He would probably bring a flask with him, but he would have far less alcohol available than he would if they met in the hotel lounge.

"Do you want to pick me up?"

"You can take a cab. Here's the address." Zachary gave it to him slowly, taking extra care to get the numbers in order. He didn't want Burton to have any obstacles in getting there. Zachary wouldn't have to put up with Burton getting into his car reeking of smoke. Hopefully, if Burton had to take some responsibility in getting himself there, he would be sober and more receptive to whatever the social worker might have to say.

Burton muttered something that Zachary didn't hear. Zachary could hear background noises; rubbing and banging and Burton cursing under his breath. Eventually, Burton's voice was in his ear again. "Okay, I've got a pen. Can you give that to me again?"

Zachary got to the coffee shop before the meeting time they had arranged. He looked around for anyone who appeared to be a retired social worker sipping a cup of coffee while waiting for him, and didn't see anyone who fit the bill. There were only a couple of people who were there by themselves, and they were intent on their phones. One had a phone in one hand and a notebook under the other, scribbling occasionally in the notebook. Too young to be the social worker. A student, maybe.

He ordered himself a coffee and sat down at a table where he could watch the door for the other arrivals. The social worker was the next to arrive. A tall woman, mature figure, long graying hair that had probably been done up in a bun when she had been on the job. Now softer around the edges. Someone who was no longer required to see the worst that society had to offer every day. Zachary waved a hand at her.

"Ms. Pace?"

She walked over to him and Zachary stood up to shake her hand. "Aurie. And you must be Mr. Goldman."

"Zachary."

She gave him an appraising look. He remembered the many social workers and other professionals who had dealt with him while he was in foster care. Many different faces, and yet all the same face. The same looks in their eyes as they examined him, coming to conclusions about what kind of a boy he was.

Mostly wrong.

Sometimes horribly accurate.

"Yes. Have a seat. I'm just waiting for my client."

She made a motion to the counter and went over to get herself a pastry and a cup of tea, and returned to sit with him.

They made small talk while waiting for Burton. Awkward, Zachary watching Aurelia Pace break the pastry into bite-sized pieces, getting flakes all over her napkin and the table, occasionally looking at her face, wondering what she must think of him. It was an unusual situation, a private investigator contacting a social worker to ask about one of her old cases. He hoped that they would be able to get something out of it. Something Pace said could lead them to the house or could provide Burton with part of his story.

It was quarter past three by the time Burton pushed through the door and made his way over to the table. He didn't bother to get a cup of coffee at the counter. He slid into one of the free chairs and looked Pace over with interest.

"You're the social worker?"

She put her hand out. "Aurie. Aurelia Pace."

"Aurie," he repeated. "I would have known you as Mrs. Pace? I don't remember you."

Pace withdrew her hand and continued to worry her pastry. "Why don't you tell me who you are?" she said. "We need to establish your identity before I say anything at all."

"Ben Burton. I don't know who I was when you knew me. What my name was before."

She just looked at him. Burton flushed. He reached into his back pocket and worked out a wallet. He removed his driver's license and tossed it across the table to her. "My parents are Elsie and Jack Burton. They live in Colchester. I was about five when I was adopted."

She checked his identification and slid it deliberately back to him. Zachary could see the beginnings of recognition on her face. Zachary remembered seeing Tyrrell for the first time when they had been reunited. Seeing his eyes and knowing him. No matter how he had changed, Zachary knew those eyes. They had been the same when Tyrrell was small. Everything that had happened since the fire had not extinguished that twinkle.

If Pace recognized Burton, then she remembered placing him. Remembered his case and what his history had been.

"Robert," she said finally. "That was your preadoption name."

Burton's jaw worked. His name. Somebody knew his name. Now he knew it too. "Robert what?"

"I told Mr. Goldman that I could only give non-identifying information. I gave you your first name. I can't give you your last."

Burton's eyes were angry, but he kept his temper and didn't even raise his voice. "And they lived here? *I* lived here? In town?"

She nodded.

He relaxed slightly. A confirmation that his memories—or the feelings he'd had—were correct. Confirmation that he wasn't crazy.

"What happened? How did I end up being adopted?"

"Are your parents still living? Your adoptive parents?"

"Yes."

"Then you already know the details from them. Your profile was shown to them. They had been waiting for some time and knew that it was unlikely they could get a child that was any younger unless he was severely handicapped. There were a couple of meetings before placement so they could see whether you all clicked, whether they thought you could all function as a family." She paused, looking at him. "Are they still together?"

Burton nodded. "Yeah. They are."

She smiled slightly. "So many couples end up divorcing. I hoped that it would work out. But you never know."

"Why? Because I was so difficult? My mom said that I was an easy child.

Quiet and well-behaved." He pulled a flask out of his pocket, unscrewed it, and took a few gulps. "I didn't start developing problem behaviors until later."

Burton was putting it all out there. Not pretending to be a mature, well-adjusted man. He was what he was, warts and all.

"Quiet and well-behaved doesn't necessarily mean well-adjusted," Pace said, taking it all in stride. She'd seen humanity at its very worst. She wasn't going to be shocked by a man drinking and being antagonistic. Zachary imagined that a lot of her former charges had ended up self-destructing. He'd seen that in foster care. While there were good homes and kids who managed to rise above their less-than-stellar beginnings, all too often, they just ended up crashing and burning—ending up on the street homeless, addicted, starting a brand-new cycle of abuse. Or obliterating themselves with a gun, razor blade, or some other method.

"But I want to know the other side," Burton said. "I want to know why I was in foster care in the first place. What happened?"

"Your biological parents were unable to take care of you."

"Why?"

She considered the question silently, swirling her tea. "You were apprehended for abuse and neglect," she said finally.

Just as Zachary had expected. But it wasn't much information to go on. No specifics.

"What were they like? My biological parents? Did you meet them?"

"I did not."

"But you knew about them. What did you know about them?"

"They had a dysfunctional relationship. They were unable to care for you."

"That's not telling me anything."

"As I said, I can't say anything that might identify them. They are accorded confidentiality under the law, even though you are an adult now."

"You must be able to tell me something about them. How old were they? What about professions? What part of town did we live in?"

Pace's eyes slid over to Zachary. "She was young. He was not. He worked in a variety of casual labor jobs. She didn't disclose how she earned money, if she did. Probably through illegal means."

Burton considered this information, his expression grim. "And where did they live?"

"Why does that matter?"

"Because I want to see the house. I want to go there."

She shook her head and waved this idea away. "It probably isn't even there anymore."

"Then it won't hurt anything to tell me where it was."

She considered this seriously. She looked at Burton, then looked at Zachary. "I'm sure it's not there anymore."

"Then…?"

She brushed her crumbs into a careful pile, and then off the table onto her napkin, which she laid back down on the table. She was chewing on her lip.

"Peach Tree," she said eventually. "Peach Tree Lane."

A lovely sounding name, but Zachary knew the area it was in. There were no peach trees. Not anymore. He didn't know if there ever had been. Burton's shoulders dipped down in relief. He knew something concrete. He knew a street. Not just the city anymore, but the street that his house had been on. Even if it had been bulldozed and replaced with a condo building or a gas station, at least he could go back there, stand where it had been, close his eyes and imagine himself there.

"What else can you tell us?" Zachary asked.

"There isn't much more to tell. That's it."

Burton shook his head at Zachary. He had what he'd come for. The street his house had been on. He didn't need anything else.

If it had been him, Zachary would have wanted more. Not the details of the abuse, maybe, but something. Something about what he had experienced in those first five years. What had made him the way that he was.

"Why didn't you meet his birth parents?"

Pace shook her head. "It wasn't in the cards."

That was a load of crap. If she'd said that Burton was already in foster care when she had first met him, Zachary might have believed it. But Pace's answer was too vague. Not the kind of thing that would have gone into an official report. There had been a reason she hadn't met his parents. A real reason.

"Why?" Zachary repeated.

"Mr. Goldman, I told you that there were things I would not be able to tell you. I'm sorry that I can't answer all of your questions or tell you the reasons that I can't answer. I'm doing the best I can."

"You were the one who took me to my parents?" Burton changed the subject, returning to an inquiry he already knew the answer to.

"Yes. I drove you to your new home. Handed you over to your parents. They seemed like lovely people. I hope I did not misjudge them."

"No. They were always good." Burton pondered for a moment. "Maybe not prepared to handle a rebellious teenager, but before that... they did everything right. I don't remember having anything to complain about."

She nodded, satisfied. She didn't ask Burton why, if his adoptive parents had been so great, he needed to dig into his past. She hopefully knew, after being in the business, that the one thing didn't necessarily have anything to do with the other.

"Well, I wish you the best of luck, Mr. Burton. I hope you find what you are looking for."

Burton summoned up a smile and nodded at this.

But Zachary was watching Pace's eyes, and he could see that she was holding something back.

She was lying when she said that she hoped he found what he was looking for.

What she really wanted was for him to forget it all and go home.

13

"Peach Tree Lane," Burton said exultantly when they had said goodbye to Aurelia Pace. "Peach Tree Lane." He said it like he could taste the words, and they were just as sweet as the name. Did they resonate with him? Did he remember that was where he had lived as a child? Five was not too young to teach a child his address in case he was ever separated from his parents or something happened to one of them.

"Yes," Zachary agreed. He tried to picture it in his mind. He hadn't spent a lot of time in that area, but he knew the neighborhood generally. He frowned, trying to remember any areas that had been developed in the last few years. Despite what Pace had said, he couldn't remember any redevelopment.

That didn't mean that a house hadn't been bulldozed and replaced with a duplex or a fourplex. Just that there hadn't been any major revitalization. Pace knew more of the story than she was willing to admit, so she might know exactly what had happened to the house.

Zachary couldn't help being suspicious. Maybe it was just because he'd been lied to by social workers in the past. They had told him things, promised him things, just to keep him quiet.

"Today, we celebrate," Burton said cheerfully, pulling out his flask and downing the rest of the contents. "Come with me. Have a drink on me. You can do it just this once."

Zachary shook his head. He found it particularly unpleasant when people pressured him to drink. Burton was an alcoholic and naturally wanted to celebrate by drinking. He didn't mean it to be offensive. People who drank so much seemed to think that *not drinking* was somehow a slap in the face, a holier-than-thou attitude that they needed to fight back against.

Zachary didn't care if Burton wanted to drink. He could spend the night drinking yet again, and not wake up until noon or two o'clock. But Zachary had no interest in joining his binge.

"I have other work to do tonight," he said. "You'll have to do the celebrating on your own."

He was surprised that Burton didn't want to head over to the house immediately. He would have thought with how eager the man was to find his childhood home that he would want to waste no time in getting there. But he wanted to celebrate first, putting it off another day—what a waste of time.

"I'll drive you back to your hotel, and then I need to get back to work."

Burton waved his offer aside. "You don't need to do that. I'm not a cripple. I can get around."

"It's not a problem to drop you off."

"No. I'll see you tomorrow. We'll go to Peach Tree Lane together, right? You'll go with me?"

"Are you sure you don't want to see it by yourself? You want an outsider there?"

"I…" Burton rubbed his forehead, frowning. "I don't know if I could… go there myself. I mean, physically, sure, I can take a cab. But… I feel like you understand this quest, and how important it is for me. So… is that okay? Will you come?"

Zachary nodded. "Of course. Touch base tomorrow and let me know when."

Zachary looked around, unsure where he was. The walls around him seemed familiar, and yet not familiar at the same time. He stood up and walked around, looking at the hallways and decor, looking in classroom doors, walking down up the main stairs to the dorm rooms, before it finally occurred to him that he was at Bonnie Brown.

He'd spent a lot of time there while he was in foster care, so he didn't know why he hadn't recognized it immediately. He'd been in and out of Bonnie Brown regularly, especially every year around Christmas, when his anxiety and depression made it too difficult for any foster family to manage him. And there were other times when he had to be moved, but they didn't have a family lined up for him yet, and he'd find himself in Bonnie Brown again.

It was a pretty dismal place, especially to an outsider but, for Zachary, it had represented stability. A predictable routine, strict rules that he knew, and familiar halls never adorned with Christmas candles or lights or other fire hazards.

Zachary spun in a slow circle, looking around. It had been decades since he had been there, yet it looked exactly the same.

A matron walked toward him, two children with her. Zachary looked down at them curiously. Two boys. Dark hair and eyes and pale skin. They were twins. Younger than most of the kids at Bonnie Brown, but they did occasionally house younger children, especially if they were prone to violence or self-harm.

"You can only take one," the matron told him.

Zachary looked at the two boys, not understanding. Take one? "You can't separate them," he countered. "They're twins."

Though, of course, they had separated him from his siblings. And even though they had promised to keep them in sibling groups, they had broken up Joss and Heather within a year. Tyrell and the younger children had stayed together longer. But just because social services said they would try to keep brothers and sisters together, that didn't mean that they did.

Twins, though? They should let twins stay together.

"You can only save one of them," the matron said solemnly. She looked down at the two boys, a hand on the shoulder of each. Waiting for Zachary to make his choice.

"Save one? Why? Why can't they both be saved?"

"Which will it be? This one?" She raised one boy's face up with a finger under his chin. "Or this one?" She showed him the other.

"No, no. We have to keep them together."

"They cannot both survive."

Zachary tried to reach out to take both boys from her. He was there. He could help both of them. He didn't need to listen to her.

But he found himself grasping at empty air. He pushed his hands forward farther, trying to reach them, but he could no longer see them and couldn't feel them. He stretched his arms out and windmilled them around, looking for the lost boys.

"No! No, wait!"

"Zachary."

There was a hand on his arm, trying to hold him back. Zachary shook it loose, still trying to feel for the twin boys. He had screwed up. She had told him that he had to choose one of them, and then when he'd refused, he'd lost both of them. He could have saved one and he tried to take back his wrong choice.

"I will, I will, just let me!"

But he couldn't see them or feel them and he was no longer at Bonnie Brown. Zachary blinked, trying to see around him. He was enveloped by darkness. Had the power gone out? Where was he?

"Zachary." A light turned on suddenly, power apparently restored. Zachary covered his eyes. They teared up and he tried to blink to get them used to the brightness.

He looked around him in confusion. At first, he didn't recognize Kenzie's bedroom. Then he did, but it didn't make any sense. How had he gotten from Bonnie Brown to Kenzie's house? He continued to reach out, looking for the boys in the now-illuminated room. They weren't hiding in the shadows. They weren't under the blankets or pillows.

He suddenly felt bereft, as he had when he had first been taken away from his family. Longing to hold his brothers and sisters in his arms. To comfort and be comforted. To cuddle them close and hum a lullaby until they all felt safe again.

"Zachary." Kenzie's hand was on his arm again, and this time Zachary didn't shake it off. He covered his face, eyes welling up with tears.

Why hadn't he saved them? Why hadn't he been able to save one of the children?

Even as he gradually understood that it had been a dream, Zachary's heart still ached. It was as if he had lost everyone all over again. He turned toward Kenzie and hugged her close.

"No," he murmured. "No, no, no."

"It's okay. It was just a dream. You're okay."

"It was… but it wasn't…" Zachary sniffled. "Why couldn't I save them?"

"It was just a dream. You didn't do anything wrong. It's not real."

"No. My family… everyone… why couldn't I save them?"

"You did." She squeezed him and rubbed his back. "You did, you saved all of them."

"No."

"Yes. You did. They're all okay. Nobody else got hurt. Okay? You're okay. They're okay. It was just a dream."

"They're okay," Zachary breathed.

"It was just a dream. I know it can feel real. But it was just a dream."

Zachary dragged in a couple of deep breaths, trying to calm himself. He kept repeating Kenzie's words. It had just been a nightmare. A disturbing dream, but just a dream. The feelings were not real.

"I tried," he murmured.

"They're okay, Zachary." Kenzie nuzzled his neck and kissed him. "You're okay. It's all over."

Zachary shuddered. He remembered the eyes of the twins, though the clarity of the dream was starting to leave him now. The deep, dark, sad eyes. He had wanted to save them. He had thought that he could save them both. And they had slipped away from his fingers.

"Do you think it would be okay…?"

"What?"

Zachary breathed in through his nose and blew his breath out in a long stream between pursed lips. "Do you think it would be okay if I called Tyrrell?"

"It's the middle of the night, Zachary. Call him in the morning."

Zachary closed his eyes. He could just go back to sleep. He would fall asleep for a couple more hours, and then when it was a decent hour, he would call Tyrrell just to chat and make sure he was okay.

He leaned back. Kenzie lay back down with him, cuddling up close to him, kissing him on the forehead and cheek and stroking his hair. "Better? Okay now?"

Zachary breathed slowly. "You can shut the light off."

She moved away from him for a moment to switch off the lamp, then lay against him, holding him. In a few minutes, her breath had lengthened out and he knew she was asleep once more.

He tried to match his breathing with hers, convinced that if he could mimic a calm, sleeping rhythm, he would be able to fall back asleep just like she had. But he knew better. He'd tried that trick a hundred times, and it had never worked.

He waited a few more minutes, making sure that Kenzie was deep asleep, and then he slid out of bed.

"Hello? Zachary?"

"Hi, T."

"Is everything okay? What time is it?"

He could hear Tyrrell moving around, sitting up and checking the time.

"Sorry. Kenzie said I shouldn't call."

"No, it's okay, Zach. Of course you can call, any time. I've told you that before. Day or night, it's okay."

"I couldn't get back to sleep."

"Yeah? What happened?"

"Nothing. Just a dream."

"What about?"

Tyrrell knew not to ask whether the nightmare had been about the fire. They both still dreamt about it, but Tyrrell bringing it up might trigger a flashback for Zachary.

"About... I don't know. I was at Bonnie Brown."

"Yeah?"

"And there was... there were twin boys, and they told me I could only save one of them."

"Save them from what?"

"I don't know. I just know I had to choose."

"What did you do?"

"I tried to save them both."

Tyrrell chuckled. "Of course you did."

Zachary had to laugh at it himself. It was, after all, typical Zachary. Immediately looking for a way out when he faced a rule he didn't want to follow.

"Then you couldn't get back to sleep."

"Yeah. Kenzie's gone back to sleep and I don't want to wake her up again tossing and turning."

"So does that mean you're up for the day? Or are you going to try the couch?"

"Probably up for the day."

"You're crazy, man. I would die without sleep."

"Not just one night. And I did sleep a couple of hours."

"But I know you don't sleep the rest of the time either. There's a disease where a person can't sleep, and it eventually kills you. You should be dead ten times over by now."

"I usually sleep. A couple hours, anyway."

"Not enough for me."

"I guess I should let you go back to sleep again. I just wanted to hear your voice."

"Hang out with me for a couple more minutes. I want to make sure you're okay."

"I am."

"So, dreaming about these boys, is that because of a case you're working on right now?"

Zachary considered. "Yeah, maybe," he said. "I don't really know if that's what triggered it. I have a client who's looking for the house he grew up in. No twin brother, though."

"Looking for his house?"

"Yeah. He was adopted, and he remembered that this is where he used to live. He wants to see his house again."

"Huh. Well, why not?"

"Would you go back? If you could?"

"I don't know. I did my best to put that behind me."

Zachary wondered why he never had. He had suppressed other things. Why did he have to keep reliving the fire?

"Tell me about your kids," Zachary suggested.

Tyrrell's voice was warm as he talked about his kids for a few minutes, telling Zachary about the last time they had visited and what they were each doing in their lives.

"You miss them," Zachary said.

"Of course I do. I see them whenever I can."

Zachary didn't say anything. He couldn't ask Tyrrell if he would ever choose between his children.

It had just been a dream.

It wasn't about Tyrrell, or his kids, or Burton. It hadn't been about Zachary missing his siblings or growing up without them. It wasn't about returning to Bonnie Brown.

It was just a dream.

"Good thing none of us were twins," Tyrrell commented.

Zachary thought about how difficult it had been for his mother, having so many children so close together. She had never dealt with it well. Zachary could remember the newborns. Tyrrell, Vinny, Mindy. How amazing it had been to look at the new lives that his parents had brought into the world. The overwhelming feeling of potential and of his love for them.

Maybe they, as kids, had tried to make up for the lack of love that their parents showed.

For his mother, another baby was just another problem. More trouble. More tears. Another mouth to feed. She would be in bed for the first few weeks. Zachary had thought this normal, and it wasn't until he was an adult that he realized it wasn't. Mothers didn't just hand over their newborns and take to their beds for weeks after birth. But it had been normal in his family, and Zachary and the older girls had taken the babies and cared for them the best they could, rotating through the duties of feeding and changing and trying to keep the little ones quiet so that their mother could sleep, until she finally got out of bed and started to see to her responsibilities again.

And there was something else niggling at the back of his mind, but he couldn't think of what it was. He couldn't quite seem to reach it. Like an itch in the middle of his back.

"Tyrrell?"

There was no response on the other end of the phone. Zachary sat down on the couch. He readjusted the pillows and pulled a blanket over him and lay partly reclined, listening to Tyrrell breathing.

14

Kenzie rubbed her eyes and ran her fingers through her mussy hair, looking at Zachary.

"Where were you? I woke up and you were gone."

"Just here. I didn't want to keep you awake."

"You should stay. You don't have to leave if you're having trouble sleeping."

"You're working today. You needed to get your sleep."

"Well, so do you."

"Not as much. And if I need to stop and take a nap in the middle of the day, I can."

"And when is the last time you did that?"

Zachary didn't answer. If Kenzie thought about it, she knew the answer to the question. He had done little but sleep after the assault. He would get up late in the morning, try to do some work, and fall asleep in the middle of it. His brain just shut down, not letting him function. It had taken some pretty intense work with Dr. Boyle before he'd been able to start to regulate his sleep schedule again. As regular as it could be.

He preferred not being able to sleep to sleeping all the time.

"Do you want coffee, or are you going to shower first?" he asked Kenzie.

Kenzie yawned and considered. "I think I'd better have the coffee first, or I'm going to fall asleep in the shower. You want one?"

Zachary passed her his mug. "Yes, please."

"How many have you had?"

Zachary looked at the mug in her hand, considering. "I think… two."

"You need something other than coffee for breakfast."

"A granola bar?" Zachary suggested.

He knew the sugary granola bars weren't the healthiest choice. But he was usually too nauseated to eat in the morning. Kenzie had tried enough different breakfast possibilities on him to come up with a limited list of acceptable choices, one of which was chocolate chip granola bars.

So she nodded without arguing about it and went into the kitchen.

"Are you feeling okay this morning?" she asked when she returned and they were both sitting down with their mugs. "That nightmare really seemed to bother you."

"Yeah." The horror and grief of the nightmare had faded over the hours that he'd been up, puttering away at the pile of computer work and billings that were always piling up. "It's fine now. I'm not sure why it bothered me so much."

"It wasn't… a dream about Archuro this time?"

"No." Zachary described the dream to her. She listened with a frown.

"Huh. I wonder what triggered that."

"Current case, I think, but I don't know about the part about choosing between twins."

"Oh." Kenzie took a sip of her coffee.

Zachary frowned. "What?"

"Twins. I can only think of one reason you'd be thinking about twins right now."

Zachary analyzed the expression on her face. She wasn't happy about it. Few things would put that expression on her face other than Bridget.

Bridget was expecting twins. Or at least, that was what Zachary assumed from Gordon's mention of "the babies" rather than "the baby." Hopefully, "the babies" only meant twins, and not triplets or more. He couldn't imagine Bridget, who had steadfastly refused to consider having children when she and Zachary were married, agreeing to carry more than two babies to term. It must have taken some convincing for Gordon to persuade her to keep twins.

"I hadn't even made that connection," he told Kenzie.

"Are you worrying about her having twins?"

"Yes. I didn't think it was keeping me up at nights, but… it's hard to get it out of my mind."

"You think she can't handle it?"

Zachary shook his head, trying to put it into words. "Well… what do you think?"

"She's not exactly the most stable person."

"Kenzie…" he protested.

"She's fixated on you. She says she wants you to leave her alone, blows up if she even happens to see you somewhere, and pops back into your life acting like she's concerned about you or because she wants a favor."

"She's just… we were together for a long time and it was a very emotional relationship. And I made a lot of mistakes; she's right about that." It wasn't a new argument. And it was something probably best left for their next session with Dr. Boyle.

"Well, maybe having twins will take her focus off of you. She'll be distracted by other things."

Zachary nodded. "Yeah. Maybe it will be good for her."

But he still worried. How was Bridget going to manage it? He couldn't help returning to his thoughts the night before of how his mother had been after she gave birth, and how impossible it would have been for her to handle twins. Bridget had sophisticated tastes. She liked the company of adults, attending events and going to museums and fundraisers. She didn't even like children, as far as Zachary could tell. He'd been the one in the relationship who was baby hungry, who'd been happy when she had a positive pregnancy test.

Only the test had been wrong.

And that had been the beginning of the end of their marriage. Not just the revelation that she had cancer, but the fact that he had been happy about the possibility of a baby, and she had unilaterally made the decision to terminate.

"Gordon has money," Kenzie said, her eyes on Zachary's face. "They can afford all of the nannies and maids they need."

"Yeah." Zachary crumbled the granola bar into the bowl that Kenzie had given it to him in. "She'll have lots of help."

15

Burton was up earlier than usual, surprising Zachary by calling him before noon.

"Are you free? What time could we go to see the house?" he demanded.

"I'm pretty open today. But remember, Ms. Pace said that it might not be there. She thought it might have been redeveloped."

Burton snorted. "That was just so I wouldn't go look. I don't know why she didn't want me to go. I don't care what anyone says about it, I'm going to go back."

"Okay. You could be ready in an hour?"

"Yeah. I'm ready any time."

"All right. I'll give you a call when I get there."

But as it turned out, he didn't need to call Burton when he got to the hotel. Burton was already outside the Best Western in the parking lot, chain-smoking. He tossed his cigarette aside when he saw Zachary, and climbed into the car, immediately filling it with the smell of cigarette smoke. Zachary rolled the windows down farther than he had on the previous occasion, glad that he was wearing a jacket and that it was warmer than it had been recently. Burton made no comment about the windows and made no apology for the cloud of smoke that clung to him.

Zachary had checked to make sure he knew where Peach Tree Lane was before leaving his apartment, and also had his phone in its dash mount with the maps app on display in case he had any trouble finding it.

"I can't believe I'm finally going to see it," Burton said, sitting forward in his seat and staring out the window like it might come into sight at any minute. "You must think I'm crazy for being so attached to a place I can't even remember. But… I have to see it. That's all I can say. I really, really need to."

Zachary nodded. "I actually don't think it's that strange. Why do people build monuments? Some places are important in our lives. Sometimes, we just need to stand where our ancestors stood. Or where we came from."

Burton nodded. For a while, he just watched out the window. He broke his gaze to look over at Zachary. "Thanks for agreeing to come with me. I know I could have just taken a cab, but I… could use your support. I didn't want to do this alone."

It was too bad that he hadn't brought his parents or a friend along with him. Zachary felt like a poor substitute for the emotional support that Burton needed. But maybe he had burned too many bridges with his previous behavior.

"We're getting close now," Zachary said, pulling off of the main road into the development. He glanced around. "You might start to recognize some of the landmarks in this area. I don't know what they looked like twenty or thirty years ago, but a lot of these places look like they've been standing for a good while."

Burton nodded. He didn't say what he recognized, if anything. His face was very pale, a stark contrast to his hair and eyes.

Zachary slowed, looking at the street signs and at the crossroads marked on the GPS map. Two more blocks. They seemed interminably long. Much longer, he was sure, for Burton, who was sitting so far forward on his seat that Zachary worried what would happen to him if they were in an accident.

"Just coming up to it now," he warned.

At the next intersection, he turned onto Peach Tree Lane. Burton rolled his window down all the way and hung out the window like a dog, looking at each of the houses with ravenous eyes.

Zachary slowed the car to a crawl. He didn't want to be responsible for Burton getting hurt if he suddenly decided to jump out of the car, or be unable to stop the instant Burton saw what he was looking for.

"Is this it? Is this it?" Burton called out, gesturing.

Zachary hit the brakes. Burton jumped out. He looked at the house they had stopped at.

Chain-link fence. Bungalow. It hadn't been replaced with a duplex. Nor had it been knocked down and replaced with a new single-family dwelling. The structure was clearly more than thirty years old.

It was run down. Faint blue paint, cracked and peeling. A couple of windowpanes broken and taped over with cardboard. The front lawn was brown and probably wouldn't grow unless it were reseeded. There were no peach trees ready to bloom. In the front yard, there were a couple of old, rusted tricycles. A family lived there. Or had lived there at some point.

Burton stood on the sidewalk outside the yard, looking in.

"Is this it?" Zachary asked.

Burton didn't answer. Zachary took a picture of the house, then took a couple of pictures of the corners of the yard.

"Do you want to look at the back or ask if you can go inside?"

Burton looked back at him with wide eyes. Zachary gave him time to think it through. He knew it had to be pretty difficult for Burton to work through. If Zachary had been able to go back to his home, or had even gone back to the lot where it had once stood, it would have been impossible for him to talk about it or do anything. Not for a long time.

Zachary looked around the neighborhood. It was the type of area he had envisioned. Low income, an older area. Not quite a slum. There were people in yards or on the sidewalk. Not behind closed doors, afraid of gangs.

People were watching them. Neighbors watching to see what was going on. Curious about the strangers staring at a random house along the street. Debt collectors? Cops? Salesmen? Missionaries? They didn't quite fit any of the usual scenarios.

Eventually, a man came along the sidewalk to talk to them. Taller than Zachary but shorter than Burton. Lots of tattoos, piercings, and a straggly beard. He was heavyset. Someone who sat in front of the TV a lot, or maybe on a motorbike or driving a truck or bus.

"Help you, guys?" he challenged.

Zachary gave Burton a few seconds to explain and, when he didn't, but kept staring at the house, Zachary filled the biker dude in.

"My friend used to live here. He wanted to see it again. He just needs… some time to process it."

The man's eyes narrowed, thinking about this. He shook his head. "Lived here when? What's the problem?"

"When he was a child. Very young. He's been trying to find it for some time. To reconnect with his heritage."

The biker looked around, his bushy brows pushed together. "Reconnect with his heritage? What kind of crap is that? What's the point in that? Seeing the house he lived in? It's not like a foreign country or different culture. It's white trash growing up in a white trash neighborhood."

"No, this isn't what I grew up in," Burton said. He looked around him, taking in the rest of the neighborhood for the first time. "This is nothing like what I grew up in."

The man gave a short laugh. "Well, good news for you. Congratulations. Don't know why anyone would want to come back to a trash place like this."

Burton put his hand down on the chain-link fence and looked at it, like his hand was something alien. Did he remember the fence from another perspective? How tall it had been when he had been four or five years old? Was he remembering his little-boy hand grasping the links of the fence, trapped like an animal behind it? Burton stared, mesmerized.

"You guys should move along," the biker advised. "You've seen what you came for. So get out of here. Go back to your fancy houses and leave us alone."

Zachary bit back a sharp retort. It wasn't like they were hurting anything, standing there looking at the house. But he'd dealt with guys like this before. It would be very easy to trigger a negative reaction, and Zachary had no desire to end up in some kind of physical altercation with the stranger. He was the one who was off of his own turf. The police would not be sympathetic to someone who had trespassed on the hospitality of another neighborhood and stirred up trouble.

"If you could give him just a few more minutes," Zachary said. "I know it doesn't seem like much, but this is the only piece of his past that he has. He just needs a few minutes."

"Well… wrap it up quick. I don't want to have to warn you again." The biker gave a curt nod, and left them alone again.

Zachary breathed out slowly. He studied Burton, wondering how long it would be before he could suggest moving on.

"Do you want me to take a picture of you here?" he suggested.

Burton looked at him, eyes hollow. "What do you think happened?" he asked.

Zachary raised his brows. "I don't know what happened. Do you… remember something? Have an idea?"

"No," Burton growled, as if Zachary had been pestering him about it. "I don't remember."

"You have… a bad feeling about it?"

Burton nodded jerkily.

"Do you want to go around the back? Talk to the owner?"

"They don't live here anymore. Tell me they don't live here anymore."

"I wouldn't expect so. People in neighborhoods like this… they don't stay for decades. A year or two maybe. I'm sure your birth parents don't still live here. Do you want me to make inquiries? We shouldn't stay too long; I don't want to cause any trouble."

"What would you say?"

"What do you want me to say? Do you want me to tell them who you are and to see if you can go inside? Or do you want me just to get some general background? How long they've been here, and if they know who owned it before they did?"

"I don't know."

"Do you want to go in?"

"No. I don't think so."

"Okay. Why don't you just wait here, then, and I'll go see if there is anybody home?"

Burton nodded jerkily.

Zachary breathed slowly and evenly. While Burton's reaction made him anxious, it wasn't like it was his own house. It wasn't part of his past. He could do what he had set out to do, helping Burton to find what he needed—just inquiring for a client. He pushed back the catch for the gate and let himself into the yard. He closed the gate behind him and made sure the latch caught. If they had a dog or a child, they wouldn't be thanking him for letting it out of the yard.

He walked up the broken sidewalk blocks to the door and knocked politely. A woman opened the door. She had dark hair and eyes and was around Zachary's age, some fine lines on her face, especially around the eyes. She hunched her shoulders, looking at him fiercely.

"Who are you? What do you want here?"

"I'm just helping out a friend, ma'am." It wasn't the time to be announcing that he was a private investigator. "He used to live in this house a long time ago."

Her eyes went to Burton, still standing outside of the yard, then back to Zachary. "So what? Why do I care about that?"

"I just wondered how long you've lived here. If you know any of the history of the house?"

"The history?" She shook her head, scowling. "What would I know about the history of a place like this? I live here. My son lives here. His children. We don't know anything about the house."

"I understand. Have you lived here long?"

"What does it matter? A few years, that's all."

"Do you know who lived here before you did? The previous owners?"

"Same owners, probably," she told him. "I don't own this pile of sticks. I just rent."

"Oh, of course. Sorry. And the owners haven't changed?"

"I told you I don't know. I only live here. I rent. I don't ask anyone questions."

Zachary nodded.

The woman looked past him again. Zachary heard a squeak and, turning around, he saw Burton coming in through the gate. He left it ajar and walked up to join Zachary.

"I told him, I don't know anything," the woman said to Burton, raising her voice. "You call the owners."

"Could I see inside?" Burton asked, his voice gravelly like he was hung over again. "Could I just take a minute or two to look around? Then we won't bother you anymore. I'm sorry about all of this. I just need to see it."

"You don't need to see anything." She motioned to him. "You've seen the outside. You don't need to hang around here and you don't need to see inside."

"Just for a minute," Burton begged. "Please."

"I don't know who you are. I'm going to call the police."

"We're not doing anything wrong," Zachary pointed out.

"I could pay you," Burton offered, taking another step forward, crowding so much that Zachary was forced to take a step back, away from the door.

He was going to tell Burton that they should go before the woman decided to make trouble for them, but the woman was looking at Burton, her eyes narrow and suspicious, and was no longer trying to shoo him away.

"How much money?"

Burton looked at Zachary. Zachary wasn't sure what to offer. What was an appropriate amount to pay someone for a look around the inside of their house? He'd never had the opportunity to ask before, despite all of his private investigation experience.

Burton pulled out his wallet and looked in it. He tweezed out a wad of bills between finger and thumb and held it toward the woman. She reached out eagerly to take it, but at the last moment, he pulled back, keeping it away from her. "Let me in first."

16

And just like that, they were into the house. No police were called. The woman allowed them both to enter and then closed the door behind them. The windows were covered with blinds and, with the door closed, the interior of the house was dim. The low wattage bulbs were not up to the task of lighting it properly. Many of them were still turned off or were burned out. Zachary could understand if it had been the middle of summer and they were trying to keep the house cool but, in the cool spring weather, it felt dismal and oppressive.

Burton looked around, his eyes wide. Zachary tried to imagine what he was feeling and thinking as he looked around. How similar did it look to what it had been thirty years ago? Probably a different paint color and carpet. Different furniture. But the bones of the house were still the same. Burton walked around the main floor, looking at the living room, kitchen, and bedrooms. He poked his head into the bathroom but didn't go inside.

"Do you remember which room was yours?" Zachary asked, when he walked around each of the smaller bedrooms.

Burton shook his head and brushed past Zachary like he was an irritating child.

Zachary followed him back out to the kitchen and to another door. The door to the mudroom and back door, Zachary assumed. And to the basement. Burton opened the door and stood at the top of the stairs, facing the back door. Zachary waited, thinking that he would probably step out into the backyard, where he had undoubtedly played when he was a child. Maybe there would be things back there that were familiar to him.

But Burton didn't step out the back door. He turned his body slowly and looked down the stairs.

It was a narrow stairway. Not well-lit. To a child, it had probably been scary. Though maybe his parents had installed brighter bulbs and the walls had been freshly painted an ivory or cream color instead of the odd beige and brown that decorated them now. Beige on the top and brown on the bottom like wainscoting.

Burton looked back at Zachary, wide-eyed like the child he would have been back then. *Would you go down with me?*

Zachary took a few steps into the back entryway so that he was close behind Burton.

"Thanks," Burton murmured.

They both stood there for a moment, looking down the stairs, while Burton worked up the courage to go down the dark stairway into the unknown.

Then he started walking like it was perfectly natural and there was nothing to be afraid of. Because of course, there wasn't. Even if it had been a frightening place full of imaginary monsters and too real spiders when he had been a small boy, there was nothing that posed any threat to him as an adult. Zachary followed him down.

Neither had to hold on to the handrail as a five-year-old boy might have done, clinging to it all the way down and taking one uncertain step at a time.

Zachary tried to shake off the feeling that there were ghosts there, specters of the past. Of course people had lived there, had come and had gone, Burton among them. But there was nothing sinister about that.

They got to the bottom of the stairs. There was a doorway right in front of them, one on the same wall as they turned into the basement hallway, and then a closed door at the end of the hall when they turned the corner. Burton paid little attention to the first two rooms. Zachary glanced in as they walked by. A combination bathroom and laundry room, followed by a storage room with shelves lining the walls and boxes stacked high.

They looked at the third door. Closed. Zachary waited for Burton to either decide he didn't feel like going any farther or to open the door. Eventually, Burton reached out and touched the door. Not the doorknob, just the door itself, as if he didn't quite believe that what he was seeing was real.

"Are you okay?" Zachary asked quietly, wondering if he was having flashbacks. Did he remember this place, or was he so tentative because he didn't? Maybe none of it seemed familiar and he was disappointed.

Burton turned his head slightly to look over his shoulder at Zachary. In the dim light of the basement hallway, his face looked skeletal. Zachary tried to look relaxed and confident. Like any normal adult would be. There wasn't any reason for him to have second thoughts about the basement. He was a grown-up and he had no history there. No bad memories. Whatever had happened to Burton there, the abuse and the neglect, it hadn't happened to Zachary. He had his own memories, some of them accessible, and some of them not.

Eventually, Burton lowered his hand and grasped the doorknob. He turned it.

"It's unlocked," he said, surprise in his voice.

"Do you want to go in?"

Burton pushed the door open and let it go. It was dark on the other side. He reached around the doorframe, grasping for a light switch.

He apparently found one, and in a moment a couple of bare bulbs in the beams above them came on, filling the space with more dim light.

Zachary looked around. It was furnished as a den or entertainment room. A ratty old couch that should have been taken to the city dump. A TV that had probably been expensive ten years before, but now looked small and old. An ancient videotape player was hooked up to it and some Disney VHS videos scattered nearby. The carpet on the floor was thin and Zachary could feel the cold concrete beneath it. No subfloor or underlay. It didn't even go all the way to the walls; it was just a big piece of carpet discarded from some other project that someone had laid down there on top of the concrete to make the room more comfortable. But it didn't do much to make the room cozy.

The walls were still bare concrete, and a chill poured off of them. The windows were covered with black garbage bags, eliminating any light or view of the outside.

Burton stood there looking around, searching for all of the details in his memory. He shook his head at Zachary. "It's not right. It's been changed."

"People do change things over the years. Replace things, renovate, try to make things more comfortable for themselves."

"It was… I don't know what you call it. Not a crawlspace, but…"

"Unfinished?" Zachary offered.

"Unfinished. But…" Burton shook his head. "There was no floor."

For an instant, Zachary had a vision of a bottomless pit in the basement. A dark, terrifying hole. But he shook his head, reframing it, understanding what Burton was saying.

"Just a dirt floor? The concrete hadn't been poured?"

Burton nodded slowly. "Yeah."

"Were there rooms, or was it all just one big area?" If there was no floor, then they wouldn't have developed the utility room or storeroom. They wouldn't put up studs for the dividing walls until there was a concrete floor, at least.

Burton looked around, his eyes uncertain. "Maybe. I don't know."

"Was there storage down here? Maybe it was just a cold room. A root cellar."

Burton sat abruptly. Zachary wasn't expecting it and reached to grab him and help him to the floor, thinking he had stumbled or fainted. Burton sat there on the thinly carpeted floor, looking around him with wide eyes.

"This is… this is not right," Burton whispered. He swallowed, looking up at the ceiling and the covered windows, down at the floor, around and around. "Where is… where is the furnace?"

Zachary glanced around and listened for the hum of the furnace. "Over here." He walked to a folding door that looked like it was a closet and opened it up. The large furnace was situated behind it, fan whirring loudly. Burton crawled along the floor on his hands and knees until he was at Zachary's side. He looked up at the furnace. On his knees, he probably had a similar perspective to that he'd had as a boy. Looking up at everything.

He pushed past Zachary, crawling past the ragged edge of the carpet onto bare concrete once more. He looked at the furnace, all around it, a prominent frown line between his eyebrows.

He reached and craned his neck around the furnace, trying to see around all sides of it. It was a few inches away from the wall, so there was a small space behind it. Burton touched the wall, touched the sides of the furnace, like a blind person trying to recognize his surroundings. He reached behind the furnace, into the space between the furnace and the outside wall, and Zachary heard something shift.

17

Burton's hands were big and clumsy compared to what they would have been when he had been a small boy of five. He knocked it down, then finally managed to get his fingers around it and pulled out a skinny glass jar. Something that might have previously held olives, pickled onions, or maraschino cherries. He held it close to his eyes, studying the dusty, cobwebby jar. He held it up to show Zachary.

"What is it?" Zachary asked, afraid at what he might see if he examined it too closely. What looked like pieces of brown, dried leaves filled the first inch of the jar.

Burton held it in front of his eyes again, then looked at Zachary.

"Bug jar."

"Oh!" Zachary laughed. "Of course. You said that you caught bugs in the basement." Looking around the room and picturing it the way that it had been when Burton had lived there, with only a dirt floor, he could believe that there had been plenty of centipedes, beetles, and earthworms for a young boy to catch, if he weren't squeamish.

Burton put his bug jar carefully to the side where it would not get knocked over, and looked back at the wall. He held his hands flat against the wall and held his nose just an inch or two away from it.

"Look," he breathed.

Zachary got closer, but he couldn't see anything on the wall and Burton was blocking him from getting any closer.

"What? I can't see."

Burton backed away until he was out of the little closet. He picked up his jar and motioned for Zachary to go into the closet and have a look for himself. Zachary was much smaller than Burton and it was easy for him to fit into the space. He looked back at Burton, unaccountably worried that Burton was going to close the door on him and imprison him in the small closet.

He hated closets.

He swallowed and crawled in on his knees, wanting to get in and out quickly. He pulled out his phone and turned on the flashlight utility. Shining it at the wall, he looked for what Burton had seen.

Then he saw it. A crayon scrawl across the concrete, almost hidden behind the furnace.

Bobby

Aurelia Pace had said that Burton's name had been Robert. Bobby. He had left his mark there thirty years before and it was still there.

Zachary's eyes slid down to the word beneath Bobby to read his last name.

A different crayon. Maybe it had been red at one point, before all of the dust and dirt had caked around it.

Allen.

18

"Bobby Allen," Zachary said. "That was your name." He couldn't help the smile that spread across his face. Burton now knew his full name. Robert Allen.

They had set out to find the house, but Zachary knew that it had been more than just the house that Burton was looking for. Maybe Burton himself didn't know, but he was looking for his identity. Who he was. And now he had his name.

"Bobby Allen," Burton repeated softly, looking stunned. "My name was Bobby Allen?"

Zachary nodded. He watched Burton to see if he wanted anything else from the furnace closet and, when he didn't appear to need anything more, Zachary squeezed back out through the door and closed the folding door over the opening once more.

"It doesn't feel real," Burton said, sitting on the carpet, not looking like he had any intention of ever moving from the spot. "I was here. Me." He picked up the bug jar and held it in his hand like a treasured artifact, looking down at it with wide eyes. "I caught bugs here. I wrote my name on the wall. This was me. I was *here*."

"Yes."

He could see Burton *becoming*. Changing from the two broken pieces into one. Not one little boy who had lived in a different city and another little boy who had been adopted and raised by the Burtons, but one person who was both. Like Zachary's dream of the identical twins. Burton was suddenly more than he had been when he entered the house. His history went back further. Another five years. He was now whole instead of missing that piece.

Burton looked like he was going to sit on the floor for a long time. The woman who had let them in did not come down the stairs and shoo them away, and Zachary hoped she would not. If the strange men wanted to sit in a cold, dimly-lit basement, then let them sit there. Burton had paid well for the privilege. They were out of the way, not underfoot.

Zachary sat down on the end of the couch closest to Burton. He didn't want to sit on the hard floor.

"Do you remember more?" he asked. "Being here again, and looking around, and knowing your name, does that help unlock anything?"

Burton frowned. His eyes moved back and forth, searching. "There is more… but I can't quite reach it. It's closer, but I still can't quite grasp it."

"Maybe it will come over time, as you've had a chance to think about it. You might want to consider therapy. They can help you to remember and can help with… emotions it brings up. Because it does. It isn't like just reading a story in a book. All of the emotions come back."

Burton's eyes flicked over to Zachary curiously. He nodded. "Maybe. I've been in therapy before. Can't say it ever helped me very much."

"I know. But it can, if you put the effort into it and find the right therapist."

Burton waved this suggestion away. He reached into his pocket to pull out his flask, looked at it, and slid it back away again. He held the bug jar in both hands and looked around the room, eyes wide, drinking it all in.

"I am Bobby. Bobby Allen."

They stayed in the basement of the house for a long time. Zachary took pictures of everything he could think of. He had taken a few pictures upstairs, but Burton did not seem to be interested in the main floor. He was in his element. Downstairs, where he had hunted bugs and scrawled crayon on the walls. He didn't drink the whole time they were down there.

Eventually, they made their way back upstairs. The lady of the house looked at them with dark, puzzled eyes, and shook her head. "What were you doing down there for so long?"

Zachary shrugged. "Just taking some time, collecting memories. Thank you for your hospitality."

She frowned again and herded them to the front door.

"Did you want to see the back? Before we go?"

Burton shook his head. He followed Zachary out, moving slowly, somewhat reluctant to again leave behind the place where he had been a child.

"You won't forget it now," Zachary encouraged. "And you can have whatever pictures you want of it. Do you want me to take one of you standing in front of it?"

Burton considered, then nodded. It might seem a strange thing to do, but this was the only part of his pre-adoption history he had, so Zachary could understand him wanting to memorialize it in some way. It would help when he looked back later.

They got back into the car. Zachary could see the biker dude who had stopped them down the street, watching them go.

As they left the neighborhood, Burton's flask came out again and this time he gulped down several swallows as if he were dying of thirst. Zachary pressed his lips together and said nothing. Drinking wasn't going to solve anything. But who was Zachary to say anything about dysfunctional behavior? Burton was who he was, and he would have to work his way out of that trap himself.

"You want me to drop you back at your hotel?"

"Could you stay for a while? Have supper with me?"

Burton didn't say how he was feeling, and his face was an unreadable mask. His voice didn't quiver or sound vulnerable when he said it, but Zachary suspected he was probably feeling pretty unstable after finding what he had been looking for.

"Uh… yeah, I can manage that," he agreed after consideration. "I'll need to make a couple of phone calls. Then we can break bread."

Burton nodded. He let out a pent-up breath. "Thanks."

"Yeah, you bet. It's a bit of an emotional rollercoaster, huh?"

Burton didn't answer, staring out the side window.

Zachary explained to Kenzie about Burton needing someone to stay with him for a while after being in the house and, while he could hear tones of disbelief in Kenzie's reply, she didn't argue. They both worked hard, and sometimes that meant overtime, night surveillance, or having to break a date to take care of something urgent. While choosing not to stay with Burton wasn't likely to cause any harm, only Zachary could decide whether it was important enough to take time away from Kenzie.

"You're off tomorrow, right?" he asked. "We can spend some more time together tomorrow. Maybe go out to brunch together."

Kenzie liked her pancakes and eggs.

"No," she sighed. "I've been called in for tomorrow. Ernie is down with the flu."

"Oh, I'm sorry. I didn't know. Well… maybe I should come home, then. I'll tell my client—"

"No, go ahead and have dinner with him. The guy's been through a big, emotional thing. You and I will still see each other tonight. And we'll get some more time together over the weekend."

"Are you sure? You're not upset?"

"No. A little disappointed, but you aren't going to be that long. You don't anticipate it taking all night?"

"No. I'll make sure he knows that I have somewhere else to be once we're finished eating. Who knows if he'll even eat."

"Oh?" Her voice was curious.

"I haven't seen him eat yet. Only drink."

"Oooh." This time, she understood. "Well… be careful. Who knows what the guy could do if he goes on a real binge after an emotional experience like that."

"He says it doesn't affect him, and I haven't seen him act drunk, even with the amount he's consumed. So I think it will be fine."

"Still be careful. You never know. Even someone who is used to drinking a lot can get belligerent or violent."

"Yeah. You're right. I'll be careful."

"Okay. See you tonight."

19

Burton did, as it turned out, eat some of his calories in solid form. He ordered a burger and fries once he and Zachary had sat down together and had a chance to peruse the menu. Zachary ordered a small steak and a baked potato with sour cream. Burton looked surprised at that.

"You're such a skinny dude, I thought you'd order a salad."

Zachary shrugged. "I lost some weight recently. I'm trying to put it back on." He didn't have a lot of appetite due to some of his meds, but it was better later in the day when they started to wear off and he wasn't so nauseated. Small amounts of calorie-dense foods were his best bet to get back up to a healthy weight.

"Have you been sick?" Burton inquired.

"Sort of, yeah." Zachary didn't bother telling him it was mental health related. He had a feeling Burton would just scoff at that.

Burton nodded his understanding.

"So how are you feeling?" Zachary asked. "Now that you've had a little time to process."

"I don't know. I don't really want to talk about it. I just don't want to be alone."

"Fair enough. Did you call your parents? Are you going to tell them about it?"

"No. I suppose I'll tell them sometime, maybe. If it comes up. I'm not rushing to do it. Wouldn't make much sense right now anyway. I don't really know anything, just where I lived. They won't care about that."

Zachary nodded. They watched the games showing on the various TVs mounted around the lounge and didn't talk much. When their food arrived and they dug in, Zachary brought up his next question.

"Is that it, then? When you came to me, it was to find your house. Now we've found it. Are you satisfied? Ready to go home?"

Burton considered this. "I guess… yes. That's all I really wanted to do. We're not going to be able to find my biological parents. Social services won't give any identifying information."

"I could find more. We have your name and address. There is plenty I can do with that." He was, after all, a private investigator. That was what he did.

"Oh." Burton was quiet. He took several big bites of his burger, chewing slowly, thinking it through. It was a lot to take in at once. It had been a big step for him to see the place where he had once lived and to find out his name. He was still integrating that experience. Zachary didn't want to dump him if he were still interested in finding out more, but he didn't want to push Burton into anything either. They were emotional decisions, and he didn't want to be accused later of taking advantage of the situation.

"You think that's enough to find my biological parents, even though they don't live there anymore?"

"Yes. Enough to find out their identities. And I'm pretty good at finding people once I know who I'm looking for." Not everyone, of course. Sometimes people took great pains to hide from those who might be searching for them. But were Burton's biological parents hiding from him? Probably not. Had they been involved in something that would have required them to completely change their identities? Most people couldn't manage to leave their old lives and identities behind. Even people who went into WITSEC didn't always choose to stay there, finding it too difficult to be completely cut off from everyone and everything they had known.

He could find Burton's parents.

He was pretty sure.

Even Heather, with her brand new skip-tracing skills, would probably be able to find them. It wouldn't take that much skill. Just access to the right databases.

"You think I should find them?" Burton asked.

"I'm not going to tell you whether you should or not. It's totally up to you. The answer is going to be different for everyone. Depends on the circumstances. If you're happy with what you have and just want to walk away, then you can do that. There's no reason you have to go further. But if you want to, you can."

"When do I have to decide?"

"No particular time. You can come back to it in a few years, if you want to. The longer you wait, the greater the chances that they will be gone, but…"

"Gone?" Burton asked, frowning. "Gone where?"

"Sometimes when people go looking for their parents, they find out it's too late. They already passed on. Sometimes just a few months or a year before they started searching. If you wait for your adoptive parents to die before you take up a search, like some people do, then the chances are much higher that your biological parents could be dead as well."

"Oh. Well, my adoptive parents are still in pretty good shape. I think I've got a few years."

"Remember that they are wealthier and have better access to good health care. People who live in neighborhoods like the one you saw have shorter lifespans."

"Yeah, I guess."

"You can wait if you want to. You don't have to jump into anything."

Burton nodded. "I think I'll at least sleep on it. I don't think I'm going to look for them, though."

"Okay. No problem. Just wanted to make sure that I knew what your thoughts were."

Zachary kept an eye on the time so that he could get home to Kenzie.

"You look like you're falling asleep over there," Kenzie commented, digging her toes into Zachary's leg. She was sitting lengthwise on the couch reading a book with her feet against his leg, and he was sitting facing the TV, though he wasn't sure what was on it anymore. His mind had been wandering and his eyes slowly shutting.

"I'm awake."

"Not for long. And you only got a couple of hours of sleep last night. You want to head to bed?"

"Only if you're ready."

She hesitated.

"I can stay up for a while," Zachary assured her. "I'll at least watch the end of this show." He glanced at the TV to see what was on. "Uh…"

"Top Gear," Kenzie told him with a smile. "Are you into fancy cars now?"

Zachary cleared his throat. He looked at the time on his phone before saying that he just hadn't changed to the program that he wanted to watch yet. It was twenty minutes into the show. "Well…"

"Admit it. You were sleeping."

"Not actually asleep… but maybe… daydreaming a bit," he waffled. He looked at the TV screen, remembering one of the children he had met during his investigation at Summit Learning Center. What had his name been? It took Zachary a minute. Ray-Ray. He wondered how the little guy was doing. Hopefully, better now that he had been pulled from the abusive program. He smiled.

Kenzie kneaded his leg with her toes. "Just a few minutes longer then," she said. "I don't want to have to carry you to bed."

Zachary grinned at the mental image. But Kenzie did help with moving dead bodies around at the medical examiner's office and he had been surprised at how easily she had shifted Luke's weight when he had been unconscious. She probably could carry him a short distance. But he wasn't about to test the theory.

He looked down at his phone to take a look through his social networks. Maybe that would keep him alert until Kenzie was ready to put down her book.

It didn't work. He awoke with a start, his whole body going rigid, ready to defend himself or run for it. Kenzie laughed. She moved beside him, pulling her feet back and turning her body to put them on the floor.

"You okay?"

Zachary looked around, blinking, getting oriented. He tried to shake off the cobwebs. "Sorry. I guess… I did fall asleep."

"You dropped your phone. I think that's what woke you up."

Zachary looked down and found it on the floor at his feet. "Oh. Yeah." He picked it up, then rubbed his eyes. "Sorry. I'm awake, now."

"Well then, walk yourself to bed. I'm going to brush my teeth and then I'll be in."

"Okay."

She waited.

Zachary moved rustily. "Did something happen?"

"What do you mean? You just fell asleep."

He shook his head, unable to escape the feeling that something important had happened and he had missed or forgotten it. He must have been dreaming and, like the night before, the vestiges of the dream, the feelings it brought, had stayed with him.

He turned his phone on and looked down at the screen. Maybe it was something he'd been reading before he fell asleep and dropped it. Something had just stuck in his brain. But nothing in the feed on the screen was familiar. Probably it had reset when the screen powered off, or Zachary had drifted off while scrolling and hadn't seen what was next. He pressed his home button and saw that he had a message. Tapping it, he saw it was from Rhys.

It was a gif of Marge Simpson talking to her sleeping husband. "Homer, are you up?"

Zachary looked at Kenzie. "Go ahead. I'll just be a minute. It's Rhys."

"Get into bed first, in case you fall asleep again. Then all I have to do is pick your phone up."

Zachary agreed and shuffled to the bedroom, trying not to wake his body up too much, and yet to be alert enough to talk with Rhys for a minute before bed. He would probably fail at one of them, either waking himself up too much to go back to sleep, or unable to stay awake for the conversation with Rhys. More than likely, he would be unable to go back to sleep. He got comfortable and messaged Rhys back.

Up for a few more minutes. Are you okay?

Rhys sent a thumbs-up. Zachary waited to see if there was more. A few seconds later, Rhys sent a picture of Kenzie.

She's here. Just getting ready for bed.

Another delay while he waited to see what else Rhys wanted to talk about. Since he had initiated the conversation, Zachary had to assume that he had a reason to want to talk.

Then a picture of a black actor whose name Zachary couldn't remember, with the caption "I was just wondering…"

Zachary typed a question mark and waited for Rhys to say what he was wondering about. Zachary had given Vera the names of the therapists that Dr. Boyle had suggested, so Rhys wouldn't be wondering about that. Something else about his flashbacks? How to manage the emotional stress? Admitting that he needed more help and should probably be admitted to the hospital?

Rhys sent another picture, and Zachary found himself looking at Luke's face again. Clearly, Rhys was having difficulty moving beyond the shooting.

Luke is okay, he assured Rhys. *You don't need to worry about him. He has recovered.*

Rhys sent back an image of a dog nodding eagerly.

Yes. He's okay. It's true.

There was only silence from Rhys. Zachary watched the screen, waiting for something further. Finally he tapped out another message.

Are you okay, Rhys?

A large green checkmark appeared on the screen.

Zachary was still puzzling over the conversation when Kenzie returned from the bathroom and climbed into bed.

"How is he?" she asked.

"He says he is okay."

"You don't sound sure, though."

"Yeah. I'm not sure if I'm missing something. He sounded like he was concerned about Luke, but he… I don't know. The responses just don't sound right. Like I'm missing the point."

"Well, it's an easy thing to do, with the way that Rhys communicates. Do you want me to take a look at it and see if I can think of anything?"

Zachary considered. He scrolled back through the short conversation, but didn't see anything there that Rhys would be embarrassed about him sharing with Kenzie. He handed her the phone.

It only took a few seconds for Kenzie to scroll through it. She considered for a moment, looking up at the top of the opposite wall where it met the ceiling. After a few minutes of silent contemplation, she looked back at the phone. She scrolled back farther, which Zachary knew meant she was into the last conversation he—and she—had had with Rhys. She handed him the phone back, frowning slightly.

"You're not getting it either?" Zachary guessed.

Kenzie shook her head. "Well... I'm not sure. I have a thought, but it's a little out of left field."

Zachary shrugged. "If it might help..."

"I noticed he hasn't asked you about how Madison is. He only asks about Luke."

Zachary nodded. "Yes... that's true."

"He originally came to you about Madison, because he was concerned with her well-being, right?"

"Yes."

"Then why isn't he asking about her? Making sure that everything is okay with her and she hasn't gone back to the life or gone off the rails somehow?"

"I don't know. He's asking about Luke because he's the one who got shot. It was seeing him all bloodied up that triggered Rhys's flashbacks to Grandpa's shooting. So that's what's stuck in his mind, what he's constantly worried about."

"Unless that isn't what he's worried about. Or asking about."

"What, then? He's worried that Luke might get Madison away again? We engineered everything so that Luke would never know where Madison had gone, and that she didn't know he survived. Luke couldn't lure Madison away again."

"No, that wasn't what I was thinking."

"What, then?"

"I wonder if Rhys had a crush on him."

Zachary's mouth dropped open. "What?"

Kenzie shrugged. "It's a possibility."

"But Rhys isn't..."

"You don't know. He's at the age that people are figuring themselves out, deciding what they are attracted to. Just because he's never said anything to you to indicate he might like boys, that doesn't mean he doesn't."

Zachary stared down at the phone in his hand. That put a whole different perspective on things.

"What do you think?" Kenzie asked.

"Maybe."

She seemed surprised at his acquiescence. "Maybe?"

Zachary nodded slowly. "When we get together, sometimes I ask him whether he has a girlfriend. You know, he teases me about you, and I ask him about his love life. Just one of those things that guys do."

Kenzie nodded.

"And he's always been very adamant. No girlfriend." He imitated the X gesture that Rhys would use and shook his head. "It's never 'maybe' or anything to indicate that there's a girl that's caught his eye, even if he's too shy to pursue her. Until Madison."

"And that might not have been romantic interest. She was missing and he was concerned about her."

"And he'd been watching her with Noah—with Luke. Because he was interested in Madison, or because he was interested in Luke?"

Kenzie shrugged. "You can't tell unless you ask."

Zachary looked back at his phone, scrolling down to the bottom of the conversation. "I don't know if I want to do that. It's not any of my business. And I don't want to start a deep conversation right when we're going to bed."

"Then tell him you'll talk to him tomorrow. Or drop in on the weekend. Then you can ask him when it's a better time for you."

Zachary blew out his breath. "You don't think that would be rude?"

"Ruder to just ignore him. And you really do need to get to sleep. You'll just fall asleep mid-conversation if you try to pursue it tonight."

"Yeah, I guess."

Zachary tried to think of how to compose his message so that it sounded casual but not like he was disregarding Rhys's feelings or not wanting to talk to him.

Falling asleep, Rhys. Can we talk tomorrow? I'll check to see how Luke is and let you know.

He got a big smiley face back from Rhys, which made him feel better.

Okay. Goodnight.

Rhys sent him back a picture of a snoozing kitten. Zachary shut off his phone and put it on the nightstand.

Kenzie wanted some time to snuggle, which gave Zachary the opportunity to relax his body and to try to get back into the right frame of mind to go to sleep. His brain worked on the possibility that Rhys was interested in Luke, examining it from every angle. He couldn't find anything that would disprove Kenzie's theory, and Rhys's response to Zachary's promise that he would check on Luke in the morning had been... very large, yellow, and smiley.

He listened to Kenzie's deep breathing as she started to doze. He rested his face against her head, breathing in the smell of her shampoo.

20

The next morning, it was Kenzie who woke up first, which was very unusual. She wrapped her arms around Zachary and pulled herself closer to him.

"Hey. You're still in bed. What's wrong, are you sick?"

Zachary took a couple of long breaths, feeling relaxed and happy. It was rare for him to wake up in such a calm, focused mood. "That was a really good sleep."

"It must have been. You're never still asleep this late."

They cuddled for a few minutes, but Kenzie had work, so she eventually pulled back from him and rubbed her eyes. "I'd better get up and get ready, or I'm going to be late getting into the office."

"It's not like the bodies are going anywhere. They're already late, so what does it matter if you are?"

Kenzie laughed. "It's not the clients I'm worried about, it's the coworkers. And the boss. And they are, unfortunately, all very much alive."

Zachary turned and slid his feet off the bed. "You go ahead and get ready. I'll get breakfast ready."

"Sounds good."

Zachary picked up his phone and left the bedroom. He used the main bathroom so that Kenzie could have the ensuite to herself, and went to the kitchen to start getting the coffee and toast on. He noticed that his notification screen was full of messages. He focused in on them.

Burton.

Over and over again.

He tapped the message at the top of the screen, which was the most recent one. Burton was incoherent, rambling on about something that was obviously a continuation of all of the other messages that he had sent to Zachary. Zachary went to the app and scrolled up so he could read the messages in a logical sequence.

Burton must have had a lot to drink. In the middle of the night, he had started texting Zachary about how he had changed his mind and he needed to find out more about his past. The truth and not the lies that the social worker and his adoptive parents had told him. He needed to know what had really happened, who his parents were, and where they were now. He didn't necessarily want to meet them, but he wanted information. Where they were and what they had done with their lives.

Zachary read through the thread a couple of times. While there were parts of Burton's texts that he couldn't quite figure out, he got the gist of them.

He sent back a text of his own, telling Burton to let him know when he was up and they could talk.

A minute later, the phone started to ring. Burton. Zachary hadn't expected him to be awake already. Or still. He silenced the alarm and looked at the screen for a minute, trying to decide whether to talk to Burton or not. But Burton already knew that he was awake and using his phone, so it would be rude to just send him to voicemail because he hadn't been prepared to talk quite so soon. Zachary tapped the answer button and held the phone up to his ear.

"Ben. Hi. I wasn't expecting you to be up."

"I've been texting you all night," Burton told him with some pique. "Of course I'm up."

"You should probably get some sleep."

"I will. But I didn't want to miss your call."

"Sorry, I'm usually up a little earlier."

"Doesn't matter. Doesn't matter. What I need is for you to tell me that you're going to find them. You said last night that you could. I didn't think I wanted to, but it's been bugging me all night long. I couldn't go to sleep until you said you would find them."

"Sure. I'll look for them," Zachary agreed. "I told you I could if you wanted me to."

"I didn't want to. I didn't want to know who they were or what they were doing. But it won't leave me alone. I can't forget the basement. I want to know where they went. Where did they go?"

"I don't know. I'll look into it." Zachary tried to sound calm, hoping that it would settle Burton down. He'd clearly had plenty to drink in the time he'd been waiting for Zachary to wake up. And hopefully, that meant he'd go straight to sleep once he was satisfied, and he wouldn't keep calling Zachary throughout the day for an update. He'd had more than one client figure he had a monopoly on his time and that his was the only case Zachary had to work on.

"You're going to find them, right? You said you could."

"I can't promise I'll have that for you today, but I will get started on it today, okay? I'll track down their names first."

"Their names," Burton agreed. There was a bang, and Zachary winced, wondering what Burton had run into or dropped. "You'll get me their names, and then I'll know who they are. I'll know their very own names."

"Yes."

"Okay."

There was a pause. Zachary waited for Burton to say goodbye or hang up the phone.

"You know, Zachary…"

"What?" Zachary suspected he knew what was coming next.

"I love you, man." Burton's voice shook with emotion. "You're the best, you know that? You're the best private detective in the world. I mean it, man. I love you."

"You too," Zachary said with a laugh, and he ended the call.

He made himself a cup of coffee and went over to his computer, beside the couch where he'd been using it the night before. After a couple of sips of coffee, he put it on the side table where it was out of reach unless he leaned over for it, so that there was no danger of bumping it by accident and baptizing his computer or staining Kenzie's furniture or carpet. He started typing.

"Zachary?"

Zachary looked up from his computer at Kenzie, standing a few feet away from him, looking at him expectantly. She'd obviously asked a question, and he'd been too focused to even hear it.

"Uh, sorry, what?"

"You didn't make anything?"

"Uh…" Zachary looked at her, taking in her still-damp hair and work clothes. She was between him and the kitchen, and it was a minute before he realized she was asking him if he'd had any breakfast. "Just a coffee. I'll grab something a little later."

She nodded, still looking at him.

Zachary looked back down at his computer to follow the next lead.

"Zachary."

He looked back up at her, slightly irritated. She could see that he was focused on a case. "What?"

She rolled her eyes up at the ceiling, shook her head, and went into the kitchen. Zachary turned his eyes back to the screen. He could hear her, in the back of his consciousness, putting toast into the toaster and banging her mug down on the counter. It still took a while longer before he looked up from his computer, suddenly realizing what she was upset about. He put the computer to the side and hurried to the kitchen. Kenzie was sitting at the table with her toast and coffee, looking at a textbook.

"Kenzie, I'm sorry. I got distracted. I didn't even realize… I'm sorry. I told you I'd make breakfast and I got completely sidetracked! You should have said something."

"I thought I did."

"No, I'm sorry. It was all my fault. I should have finished making it before I left the kitchen, and I didn't. That was really inconsiderate."

"Being sorry doesn't get the breakfast made. I thought that I had a few extra minutes for my shower because you were getting it ready, and now I feel rushed."

It only took two minutes to make coffee and toast. But Zachary could have done that for her. He should have done it, like he'd promised.

"I really am sorry."

She shrugged irritably. "Go back to your work."

"Burton called, and I wanted to get started on his search, and I completely forgot I was supposed to be making you breakfast."

Kenzie took a deep breath. When she spoke, her words were perfectly enunciated and flat, and he recognized that she was using one of the communication patterns that Dr. Boyle had talked to them about. "When you get distracted by something like that, it makes me feel like I'm not important."

"You are. I didn't do it intentionally. I didn't mean to choose the work over you; I just got distracted."

"But obviously it was more important to you than getting breakfast for me."

"No. The call from Burton just pushed it out of my mind."

"You had enough presence of mind to still get yourself a cup of coffee."

Zachary looked down at his hands, which were empty. He looked around the kitchen, but didn't see the cup of coffee that he had made for himself. Kenzie sighed.

"It's in the living room. On the side table."

"Oh." Zachary went back to retrieve it, then sat down at the table with Kenzie, determined to make her his sole focus until she left for work. He sipped his coffee, but it was cold.

Kenzie shook her head, allowing a slight smile at his grimace.

"I forgot I made it," Zachary said.

"Well, that's something."

21

At his own apartment, Zachary continued to search through the published historical records for the five years that, as far as he knew, Burton had lived in the house on Peach Tree Lane. There was no listing for an Allen family on Peach Tree Lane. He couldn't account for every year, so maybe they had been there during the intervening year or two. But he could remember being there, and he had written his name on the wall, so he had to be older than two or three when he lived there. He should have been there during the time he was four or five. But during that time, there were no Allens listed at that address. Only a couple by the name of Weaver. And census records didn't indicate that any children had lived in the household.

Zachary sat back, rubbing his gritty eyes and trying to puzzle it out. Burton clearly remembered the house. He knew about the bug jar by the furnace, and that was proof enough for Zachary. Burton could have pretended all kinds of memories of that house, but he couldn't conjure a glass jar out of the air. Or his name on the wall. The social worker had said that his name was Robert, and Zachary had stood there and watched Burton find the name Bobby on the wall. He hadn't written it there himself and it was clear from the dirt and cobwebs on the wall that it hadn't been a recent addition. A child named Bobby had lived in the house.

He moved backward and forward through the records. Perhaps Burton had not been five when he had been adopted. Maybe that was only an estimated age for a child whose birth had not been registered. He could have been four or six. If he were very small for his age from neglect and malnourishment, like Zachary himself had been, then he might be seven and mistaken for a younger child. But Zachary couldn't see them being wrong by more than two years. If he had been eight years old, he would have been able to tell them that, and it would have been obvious from his maturity level even if it were at odds with his size. The doctors would be able to tell from his bone and tooth development. And similarly, he couldn't have been younger than four. A three-year-old did not look like a five-year-old, even if he were large for his age.

But even adjusting for a mistake in ages, he couldn't find any record of an Allen family. He couldn't find a record of any family with one young child who had lived in that house during the right period. It was possible they hadn't registered as voters, answered the door to census takers, or had driver's licenses. But he found it hard to believe that they hadn't been listed in any directory, consumer database, credit history, or social security registry.

He went into the kitchen and made himself a fresh cup of coffee, working through the possibilities.

If the Allen family didn't exist, and Burton wasn't some kind of scammer, then Allen could not have been his last name. It could have been his middle name. He might have been called by both, or he might have been intending to write his full name but got interrupted and never returned to the project. There were a number of possibilities, but Zachary was pretty sure by then that there was no Allen family.

He returned to his desk, sipping the coffee.

That left him with the Weavers. They had been living in the house at the right point in time. Not listing the fact that they had a young child on the census was not a huge oversight. People made mistakes filling out forms. The census taker didn't hear, forgot to check a box, or there was an interruption and the adult who was doing the interview had never finished answering the question in full.

Robert Allen Weaver. It was a nice, strong name.

Parents Elizabeth Weaver and Samuel Weaver.

Zachary noted them down. The census had a woman in her twenties and a man in his forties, which fit with the social worker's statement that

Burton's mother was young and his father was older. His profession was listed as a delivery driver. Elizabeth listed as unemployed, which the social worker had not believed.

Now that he had the names, he dug deeper.

There had been no further calls from Burton, and Zachary assumed that he would be sleeping for a good long while with the amount of alcohol he'd consumed. That was fine with Zachary. He needed some time away from the computer screens, and he knew just where to go.

He timed his visit for around the time Rhys should be getting home from school, and watched the house for a few minutes, not wanting to bother Vera before Rhys arrived. If Rhys were late, then Zachary being there waiting for him would just emphasize the fact for Vera and make her more anxious. Zachary didn't know if Rhys had any after-school activities. He didn't usually, but that didn't mean he didn't have a tutoring session or an appointment with his new therapist, or something else that Zachary hadn't thought of.

He kept an eye on the door while he checked his social networks and email inbox.

There was a tap on his window that made him jump, and he turned his head, expecting to see a cop or an irritated dog walker who wanted to know why he was sitting there in his car like some creepy stalker.

But it was Rhys. He spread his hands wide and raised his brows. *What are you doing here?*

Zachary opened his door. "Just waiting for you. I didn't want to bother Grandma."

Rhys waited while he climbed out and locked up, then walked with him up to the front door. The door was unlocked and Rhys let himself in.

Vera was in the living room reading a book. She looked up and smiled at them.

"Zachary. I didn't know you were coming."

"I didn't arrange anything ahead. I hope that's okay."

"Of course. You know you're welcome any time. How was school, Rhys?"

Rhys rocked his hand back and forth. *So-so.*

"Looks like you have plenty of homework to keep you busy."

Rhys shifted the loaded backpack, rolling his eyes.

"Okay, well, relax and have a visit with Zachary, and you can hit the books after supper."

Rhys nodded. He led the way, not to his bedroom, but to the kitchen. He motioned for Zachary to sit down and had his head in the fridge, on the hunt for something good to eat. With the fast metabolism of a teenager, Rhys ate at least twice as much as Zachary, and it was no surprise he got home from school hungry. Zachary watched while he assembled a sandwich, slathering the bread with mustard and mayo and stacking the fillings high. He sat down across from Zachary and grinned.

"Looks great."

Rhys pointed at Zachary and raised his eyebrows inquiringly.

"No, not for me. I... just ate."

Rhys jerked his head back, lifting his chin and giving a little shake. Clearly expressing his doubt about that fact.

Zachary shrugged uncomfortably. "Okay, maybe it's been a few hours, but I'm not hungry."

Rhys nodded and took a big bite from his sandwich.

Zachary took out his phone and laid it on the table in front of Rhys, with the picture of Luke on the screen.

Rhys nodded and looked at Zachary eagerly to see what he had found out. Zachary looked at his face, reading the signs there. Pupils dilating slightly. Leaning forward in attention. Breathing a bit louder and faster.

"You like Luke?" Zachary asked, pointing to the picture.

Rhys nodded.

"I mean, you *like* like him?" Zachary asked. His face warmed and he looked away, as if something else had distracted his attention. Just because Rhys was a teenager, that didn't mean Zachary needed to talk like one. There were probably better ways to ask Rhys what his feelings were. But nothing helpful had come to Zachary's mind.

Rhys nodded again.

"Oh!" Zachary rubbed the short whiskers on his chin. "Well, some detective I am!"

Rhys grinned and took another bite of his sandwich. As he chewed it, he made a motion back toward the living room, where Vera was still reading. He made a locking gesture at his lips.

"I'm not going to out you," Zachary promised. He'd known too many kids who had been kicked out when their parents had found out they were gay or something other than cis and straight. Things were improving, but Vera was the older generation and knew what it was like to be part of a minority. She had previously expressed to Zachary that she didn't want him to meet with Rhys in public because people might think the two of them were having a romantic relationship, when Zachary had been mistakenly identified in the media as being gay.

Zachary pursed his lips, thinking about that. Rhys cocked his head, looking at him questioningly.

"Are you sure she doesn't already know?"

Rhys's eyebrows went up even higher. He shook his head, frowning.

"Just… something she said once," Zachary said. He tried to remember what her words had been when she asked Zachary to only meet with Rhys at home from then on. But the words were elusive. It had been a very bad time for Zachary, and a lot of what had happened during that time was fractured and incomplete. He shrugged in irritation. "I don't remember exactly what she said. I just wonder… if she at least suspects."

Rhys shrugged as well. He made the locking-lips gesture again, and Zachary reaffirmed his agreement.

"I won't bring it up. I won't say anything."

Rhys nodded. He pushed Zachary's phone back toward him, tapping the screen, even though it had turned off and the picture of Luke was no longer visible.

"Luke is good. I talked to the woman who is helping him out today. Physically, he's healed up. Barely any marks left from where he got cut, though he'll have a scar from the bullet track," Zachary traced the length of his jaw, following the path the bullet had taken. "Kenzie had been concerned about how bad his concussion was because he was out for so long, but mentally he seems to be fine. Some headaches and dizzy spells, but when you consider the drug withdrawal…" Zachary gave a shrug. "All of that is to be expected and more."

Rhys gave him a thumbs-up. Zachary nodded his agreement.

"All good."

Rhys pointed at himself and then at his eyes. *Could I see him?*

"I don't know." Zachary took a deep breath and let it out. "Let's leave it for a while, anyway. I don't want to distract him from his recovery. We really don't know yet whether he's going to be successful in staying away from drugs and the trafficking business. And I don't want you anywhere near that."

Rhys's frown became more pronounced, but he didn't argue.

"I'm sure you don't want to derail him either. Let's give him some time to figure out where he's going… who he is. Remember, he hasn't really had a chance to be his own person since he was twelve or thirteen. He has lots of 'inner' work to do."

Rhys nodded slowly, and Zachary thought he was a little more understanding this time.

"I'm sorry for not understanding," Zachary said, his face warming again. "You must have thought I was being pretty dense."

Rhys laughed and gave a little nod.

Zachary laughed too, not having expected that answer. "Well, I'll try to be a little more discerning in the future."

22

Burton called as Zachary was leaving Rhys's house. Zachary looked at the time on his phone and started the car. He answered it once it connected with the Bluetooth system.

"Hello, Ben. How are you feeling?"

Burton groaned, not even bothering to put on a front that overindulging never bothered him. "When can we meet? Have you got anything?"

"I have some information for you. We're not quite there yet, but I can tell you what I've got when we meet. When are you going to be in shape to get together?"

"I'm going to head down to the bar now. I'll be fine by the time you get here."

Zachary pictured Burton staggering down to the lounge still with bedhead and a rumpled shirt, determined to drink until he was no longer feeling any pain. "Well, hold off on getting drunk until after we meet. I want you to be coherent."

"When have I not been coherent?" Burton demanded. "I've been just fine. I haven't caused you any trouble. I got us into the house, didn't I? Didn't just barge in there like a bull in a China shop and get us arrested."

"No. You did just fine. But I want you to be able to focus on what information I have."

"I will. Just get over here."

"I'll be there soon."

Regardless of whether Burton slowed down or not, it wouldn't take Zachary more than twenty minutes to get to the hotel; Burton couldn't have too many drinks in that length of time. With his level of tolerance, he would have to drink longer than that to be feeling the effects.

Zachary's mental picture of Burton hadn't been far off the mark. The bartender was already eyeing him, even though he'd only been there for a few minutes.

"Let's grab a booth," Zachary suggested, steering Burton toward the one they had sat at previously. It felt like home—his own place in the lounge.

Burton grabbed his glass and motioned to the bartender to bring him another at the table. They got settled in their usual seats. Zachary got out his notepad.

"So, what do you know?" Burton demanded.

"You're sure you want me to go ahead? You've been back and forth on this. If you want to wait…"

"I don't want to wait. I'm here now. I want it now."

"Okay. First off, Allen is not your surname."

Burton blinked at him, eyes narrowing. "Then who is Allen?"

"I'm thinking Allen is probably your middle name. Or maybe a double-barreled first name. Bobby Allen."

Burton shook his head. "No. What is my surname, then? That doesn't make any sense."

"Weaver. Unless I miss my guess, you were born Robert Allen Weaver. Known as Bobby or Bobby Allen."

Burton continued to shake his head, not believing it.

"There was no Allen family that lived in that home in the years that I checked," Zachary explained. "If you were five when you were adopted, there is only a very narrow window for me to check for your family to be living in that house. If that was your house when you were four or five, then your family name is Weaver."

"Weaver," Burton repeated. He frowned and had a drink, thinking about it.

"Does that sound at all familiar to you?"

"I don't know."

"You would have known your last name when you were five years old. Most five-year-olds have been taught their last name."

"No... I don't think I've ever heard that before. What are... their other names?"

"Elizabeth and Samuel."

"Elizabeth Weaver. Samuel Weaver." Burton considered the names as he continued to drink. He was downing the drinks quickly. Like someone who had just run a marathon without any water. Desperate. Trying to drown the memories even as Zachary was trying to tell him the details.

"Just think about them for a minute," Zachary suggested. "Stop everything else, close your eyes, and just repeat the names to yourself. Elizabeth Weaver. Samuel Weaver. Maybe they had nicknames. Lizzie. Sam. Maybe your mother still went by her maiden name; the authorities weren't very good at keeping track of that kind of thing back then. They just assumed that the wife would take the husband's name."

Burton stared at Zachary, his eyes bloodshot and his expression stony. Eventually, he pushed his glass away an inch, placed his folded arms on the table, and closed his eyes. He swayed a little with them shut, the alcohol affecting him even though he insisted it didn't.

"Lizzie Weaver. Sam Weaver."

Burton sat there, eyes closed, thinking about it. He breathed in and out and Zachary waited for his response. Were those names buried in his memory somewhere? All kids heard their parents' names from time to time. Even if he didn't know their last names, he would still have heard his parents speak to each other, occasionally using each other's names when they were calling across the house for help or reprimanding the other. Answering phones. Talking to salespeople at the door. *Yes, I'm Mrs. Weaver.* Answering census interviews.

Burton opened his eyes. He looked at Zachary.

"Who was Allen?"

23

Zachary let the words stand between them for what seemed like a long time. It couldn't have been that long, because nothing happened in the silence. No conversations between other patrons, people coming and going, the bartender serving drinks. Zachary thought about Burton's question.

Who was Allen?

Wasn't Allen Burton's middle name?

What if it wasn't? What if the two names were for two different boys? Two children. Daring each other to write their names on the wall behind the furnace. Making their mark on their territory, like lower-order animals.

Two different colors of crayon. The names one below the other, not in a straight line. Were they the names of two separate people?

"If Allen was not your second name, then you must have had a brother," Zachary said. "Or else a friend you were allowed to have over who played with you in the basement."

He couldn't imagine any mother letting her child go over to the Weaver house to play in the dark, dank basement with a dirt floor. But she wouldn't necessarily have known. If Allen never told her what went on over at the Weaver house, then how would she know?

Burton gazed at Zachary. "A brother?" he repeated. "I don't have a brother."

"Maybe he was just a friend, then. Did you have friends over?" He had been about to add 'to play,' but he was afraid of influencing Burton's memories too much. Taking them out and molding them into something different before putting them back on the shelf. He didn't want to be accused of planting false memories.

"No," Burton seemed sure of himself. As if it were a ridiculous question. Having friends over? Not something he ever would have considered. Or that would have been allowed.

"If you didn't have friends over…"

"Then who is Allen?" Burton repeated.

Unexpectedly, he slammed his open palm down on the table with a crack like a rifle. It shook Burton's glass, the condiment bottles, and everything else on the table. People looked over at them to see what was going on, eyes wide.

"Who is Allen?" Burton repeated in a loud, confrontational voice.

Zachary made calming gestures with his hands. Downward, soothing motions that there was nothing to be concerned about or to start swearing about. "It's okay. There's no need to yell or get upset."

Burton smacked the tabletop again. Not as hard, but still distracting and frightening to the other customers. He would get them kicked out of the lounge. And they probably wouldn't let him sit down at the bar again. He'd have to move to a new hotel.

"What's wrong?" he asked Burton reasonably. "If you think I'm full of crap, just fire me. I don't have to do anything else. You have some names you can look up, or you can do nothing with them. It's totally up to you."

"I want to know who he is." He didn't yell this time, but kept it in an undertone.

"Do you want me to find out if Allen Weaver was your brother? If he is still around?"

Burton sat there, morose, thinking about it. Zachary could see the bartender watching them, making a decision as to whether to kick them out or not. If Burton could keep himself calm, he would probably be allowed to stay, but one more outburst and they would be pushing him out the door.

"Allen Weaver."

"Yes. Does that sound familiar?" Zachary had a thought. "Maybe the social worker remembered the wrong name. Maybe she placed both of you, and she gave you the wrong name. Do you think *your* name is Allen Weaver?"

"No." Burton seemed sure of that. "No. I'm not Allen. But… where is he?"

"I don't know. I could look into it, if that's what you would like."

Burton nodded slightly. Not a definite answer, but his brain telling his body what it was he wanted, nudging him along.

"Okay. Let me look into it. I don't know how much I'll be able to find. If he was also adopted, he'll have a different name now. It's hard to track kids through adoption finalizations."

"I don't have a brother," Burton said, shaking his head slowly.

"Maybe. We can look and find out. Or maybe you'll remember who he was."

"No. Allen is…" Burton stalled. "I don't know what I was going to say. Allen is…" He reached for the words. "Not there? Allen is not there?"

Zachary listened, analyzing it. Had Burton remembered the phrase? Someone telling him that Allen was not there? Or was it just part of his drunken ramblings. He smelled strongly of drink. Possibly he still had alcohol from the night before in his system. And he'd had a jugful since waking up.

"Allen is not there," Zachary repeated, making it a statement rather than a question.

Burton stared at him, his mouth tightening in anger. "Why did you say that?"

"Allen is not there. Does that bother you? You don't like me saying that?"

"No. Don't say that. You don't know anything about it."

"No, I don't. I don't know anything about Allen."

"But you can find out?"

"I can try."

"There must be a birth certificate. You have the parents' names, so can't you look it up?"

"If he was not adopted. If he *was* adopted, then all traces of the original name are wiped out and replaced with the new information."

Burton picked up his glass, but it was empty. He looked toward the bartender. The man shook his head. Burton was already being disruptive; the bartender wasn't going to give him anything else.

"There's a minibar in the room," Burton said. "Costs an arm and a leg, but at least I can keep drinking. Let's go up."

"I think you've had enough to drink."

Burton shook his head. "I'm just getting started."

While he stayed with Burton for a couple more hours, Zachary didn't really get anything helpful out of him. Burton bounced from one topic to another, abandoning anything that got too intimate or led back to questions about his brother and what had happened to him.

"There were two tricycles," Burton told Zachary. "But there weren't two boys. I would remember if there were two boys."

"Those tricycles wouldn't have been yours. They were old, but thirty years old? I don't think they've been sitting in the yard for that long. They belonged to other children, not to you."

"No. Not me."

"Do you remember playing outside? You remember catching bugs in the basement. You must have caught them outside too."

"No… don't remember that. I just remember… I don't remember, I have impressions… I recognize things. But I don't remember."

"It's okay not to remember things very well. It was a long time ago and it might have been traumatic for you. That makes it harder to remember things properly. Some things get pushed to the front and you keep remembering them over and over again. And other things… you want to remember, but can't. They just never coalesced into a memory."

"I don't have them," Burton asserted.

"That's fine. That's the way it is sometimes."

Burton downed another tiny bottle, setting the empty down beside him on the floor with the rest. "I want to know who Allen is."

24

It might take a lot of alcohol to affect Burton, but he wasn't immune to it. Zachary left him sprawled across the bed in his hotel room, snoring away, and hoped that he would be okay after sleeping it off.

He headed for home. Or for Kenzie's home, where she would be waiting for him. He hesitated when he looked at his phone, trying to decide whether to tell her he was on his way or just to show up. He settled for calling her on the Bluetooth once he was on his way.

"Hi, Kenz. I'm on my way. Just running a little later than I expected to."

"Okay. Supper will hold for that long. Everything okay?"

"Yes, just fine. Just getting my client settled for the night."

"Are you offering a tuck-in service now?"

"You tuck your clients in, don't you?"

Kenzie laughed. "I suppose so. But I'm hoping your client hasn't entered that stage of sleep yet."

"No."

"See you when you get here."

After hanging up, Zachary turned the radio on and let his mind wander while he listened to the music. He needed to let his brain just go for a while; he'd been concentrating too hard most of the day and it was exhausting.

Sometimes, not thinking about a problem was the best way to come to a solution. Zachary would let his subconscious mind worry over whatever bits of his investigation it wanted to, and it tried to put the puzzle pieces together. Hopefully, the next day he would feel a better sense of direction as he tried to find out what had happened to the elusive Allen, if he was a second child. Zachary wasn't convinced that he was. The crayoned names had looked pretty similar; he hadn't thought when he saw them that they were written by a different hand. Maybe all kids had similar handwriting at that age, or anyone writing with crayon on the wall would end up looking similar. He wasn't a handwriting expert, though he'd studied the science a little in the course of his investigations.

He had parked his car and was most of the way up the sidewalk to the house when he realized that his body had been operating on autopilot and he didn't even remember most of the drive back. He paused at the door to try to rein in his brain again. He wanted to give Kenzie the attention she deserved, especially after his goof that morning forgetting that he was supposed to be making her breakfast.

He took a couple of deep breaths, and went in.

Kenzie was in the kitchen. At his arrival, she bent over to open the oven and pulled out a loaf of crusty garlic bread that set Zachary's mouth watering. He didn't care what else she had made to go with the bread. He just wanted the fragrant, yeasty bread on his plate.

"That smells absolutely heavenly!" he told her.

"Well, good thing you weren't too long in getting here, or it would have been dry or burned."

"It smells just right." He watched Kenzie carefully remove the foil and reveal the loaf, crust shiny with butter. She started to slice it, and each piece looked even and perfect.

"Quit slobbering and set the table."

"Set the table," Zachary repeated, and went to the cupboard. No way he was going to forget what he was supposed to be doing this time. He wouldn't even forget the cutlery, which he frequently did. Kenzie always rolled her eyes over his doing jobs only halfway, such as setting plates on the table, but nothing else. Or maybe cups and cutlery and no plates. But she didn't give up on getting him to do it properly and today he would get it right. He muttered to himself as he got out everything that needed to go on the table. He might sound crazy talking to himself, but it helped him to get all of the steps done if he could hear his own voice instead of trying to keep it straight in his head.

When Kenzie was finished cutting the bread and getting the rest of the dishes on the table, Zachary looked over the place settings, again listing off plates, cups, knife, fork, spoon, and cloth napkin—because their fingers were definitely going to be greasy with the delicious garlic bread.

He raised his eyes and looked at Kenzie, waiting for her approval or criticism. At least Kenzie wasn't Bridget, who would go up one side and down the other when he did something stupid. There was no way she would have trusted him to set the table. Not with all of the specialized silverware she liked to use, with special forks for salad, pickles, or caviar. He never knew what everything was for and, even though he tried to watch her and copy what she used everything for, he would still make a mistake, and she would rip into him.

"Zachary."

Zachary blinked, swallowed, and looked at Kenzie.

"Looks good," Kenzie said, sounding like she was repeating it for the second or third time. "Good job."

"Oh. Thanks." He sat down, and then wondered if he should have held her chair for her. They weren't usually so formal but, thinking about Bridget, he wondered if he should do more to try to make Kenzie feel special. She did the lion's share of the cooking and other jobs maintaining her house and many of the things in his apartment as well. He should be able to keep up better.

He smiled, hoping it didn't look too strained.

"Relax," Kenzie advised. "You seem really tense tonight." She sniffed, "Have you been drinking?"

"No." Zachary smelled his shirt. "Burton was, but I don't remember him spilling anything."

"You might have just absorbed the fumes." She took a couple of bites of her salad. "Not that you can't drink. I'm just surprised, because usually you don't."

"No. I didn't have anything tonight either. It was all Burton."

She nodded. "Everything went okay?"

"Well… no, not exactly. I mean, nothing went wrong, but he had a lot of problems with the information that I gave him."

"He didn't get violent?"

"Slapped the table and shouted. That was as bad as it got."

"What was he so upset about?"

Zachary thought about it, tearing his bread into smaller pieces as he ate it. "We think that maybe he had a brother named Allen. Initially, I thought that was his last name, but it turns out it wasn't. It could be a middle name, but he is quite certain that it was not, and that Allen is someone else. Best bet is that he was a brother."

Kenzie nodded. "And this upset him because…"

"I think mostly because it was just a shock. He hadn't realized before that he had a sibling. He wants to know where he is, what happened to him."

"That's going to be pretty hard, isn't it? Unless his brother starts looking for him, the same as he did. There are adoption registries."

"I told him I would do what I can. I'll start on it tomorrow."

"Sounds like a plan." Kenzie put a bite of roasted vegetables in her mouth. "Are you going to eat anything other than garlic bread?"

"Uh…" Zachary looked at the other dishes on the table. "Yeah, sure. I'll have a bit of chicken and vegetables."

"But mostly garlic bread."

Zachary put another piece of bread in his mouth and grinned.

25

Zachary went through the records that he had already compiled on the residents of Peach Tree Lane, looking for families that had lived there at the same time as Burton would have been there with his family. There wasn't anyone still living on the street from that time, which didn't surprise him. As he'd told Burton before, it wasn't the type of place people would live for more than a few years. Only as long as they had to. They would get kicked out or get enough money saved up to move somewhere else. Somewhere nicer.

But he was good at tracking people, and he was able to dig up phone numbers in order to contact a couple of them. A lot of people retained their landline numbers from the eighties into the new millennium, and only recently had started dumping them because they just didn't use them anymore. Even the grandmas and grandpas were using cell phones now.

He looked at the first name on his list. According to the census numbers, Elise Perry was around the same age as Burton's birth mother. With any luck, their kids had played together and she would remember the Weaver family, and maybe know something about what had happened to them. It was odd that Zachary hadn't been able to trace Burton's parents after he had been adopted. Unless, perhaps, they had died in an accident and that was why he had needed to be adopted. It was also possible that they had moved out of state, had changed their names, or a whole host of other possibilities. It should have been easy to track them by their SSNs and credit records, but sometimes people stayed under the radar intentionally.

He dialed Elise Perry's number and waited. It went a few rings before being picked up, and he imagined that it was in her purse as she shopped or drove. But eventually, she found the phone and answered it.

"Hello?" She sounded a little breathless.

"Is this Elise Perry?"

"Yes?"

"I'm a private investigator, Ms. Perry, and I'm trying to track down a family that used to live on Peach Tree Lane. Which is where you used to live."

"That was a long time ago, Mr...."

"My name is Zachary. Goldman Investigations."

"It's been years since I lived in that part of town. I don't think I can help you."

"Did you happen to know the Weaver family?"

She didn't answer for a moment. Zachary had been hoping against hope for immediate name recognition, but if she did recognize it, she wasn't announcing it.

"I don't know. The name sounds sort of familiar, but it wasn't anyone I had anything to do with."

"They would have had kids. Did your kids play with them, maybe?"

"Weavers... I don't think... there was a couple called the Weavers, but I don't remember them having any kids. Maybe they were older than mine."

"Bobby Weaver was five when they left. I'm not sure whether Allen was older or younger."

"No, I don't think so. I don't remember any kids by those names."

"No Bobby?" Zachary was surprised. It was a common name. He thought there would have been a few of them around.

"No, not on the street. And I knew all of the kids that age."

"And no Allen?"

"I can't remember any Allens my son's age, not even at school."

"But Weaver sounds familiar."

"That's all I can tell you. I must not have known them very well, but maybe heard about them at Community Watch or something like that. You know how you can hear someone's name a few times, so they get familiar, even though you never actually met the person."

"Sure. So you don't think you even met them? Maybe a community lunch or breakfast? Canvassing for the Heart Foundation or Diabetes?"

"No, sorry. I'm not much help."

"Would your husband know, do you think?"

"I'm not in touch with him anymore. But I wouldn't think so. He was always working during the day. I'm the one who got to know people in the community. He would just get home from work and sit in front of the TV for the rest of the night. Like he'd earned his right to sit there and didn't have to be responsible for anything else."

Zachary grimaced. It was probably a good thing that the two were no longer together.

"Okay. Well, thank you for your time, Ms. Perry. Can I leave you my number in case something occurs to you later?"

"It's on my call log. I'll let you know if something comes up, but I don't expect it to. I just didn't know them. Our kids didn't play together and I don't remember what either one of them would have looked like."

Elise Perry hadn't remembered very much, but her call confirmed that Zachary was on the right track. Neighbors remembered things. Even that many years later. The names and faces came back to them—or they didn't. Her lack of memories of Bobby and Allen didn't mean that the boys hadn't lived there. Just that they hadn't played with the neighborhood children, which Burton had already told him.

He didn't have friends.

He didn't play outside.

They had kept to themselves. Maybe the parents had been religious nuts. Or paranoid about the coming apocalypse. Who knew?

The next mother on his list was May Richmond. Zachary tried the first number he had for her, and got a recording that it was out of service. He was not surprised, and it wasn't the only number he had found for her. And, of course, there might be several May Richmonds, but he was pretty confident in the information he had managed to dig up. He tried the next number on the list.

"Hello?" It was a male voice. Zachary looked down at his screen to see whether he had dialed correctly.

"Hello?" the man repeated.

"Sorry, sir. I'm looking for May Richmond. Is she at this number?"

"You can get her on her own cell."

"Is it…" Zachary slipped down to the next number on the list and read it off.

"No," the man answered, and dictated May's number to him. Zachary wrote it down.

"Thank you very much. You have a nice day, sir."

"You too."

Zachary tried May's cell phone, and she answered it quickly.

"Mrs. Richmond?"

"Yes, this is May."

Zachary again explained his dilemma, how he was trying to find people who might have known Burton's family all of those years ago. She gave a disbelieving laugh.

"I'm not in contact with anyone from that time anymore," she said. "Those were not my friends. We didn't keep in touch."

"I realize that, I'm just looking for a little bit of direction. If you don't remember anything, that's fine. I'm hoping someone will remember this family and be able to point me in the right direction. I lose their trail after Peach Tree Lane."

"I don't think I'll be able to help you, but go ahead."

"Do you remember the Weaver family at all?"

"The Weavers." Her voice held a note of disbelief. "Why would you be trying to find them?"

"I'm sorry, does that mean you know something about them?"

"I remember them," she said slowly. "They were not friends with anyone in the neighborhood. Kept to themselves. They were…" her tone was hesitant, "they were not the kind of people you wanted to be around."

"Oh?"

"They were… you know what they did, don't you?"

"No. What did they do? I thought Mr. Weaver was a trucker."

"I don't mean that. I mean… when we all heard what they'd done to that boy…"

"What boy? Bobby?"

"Yes! You must know, then."

"No. I know that he went into foster care and later went on to be adopted. But I don't know anything that happened before that."

"He was just like a skeleton when he got out of there. They say they'd abused him. Kept him locked up all the time. Didn't feed him. Beat him. It was horrible. We were all devastated that something like that could have gone on right under our own noses. You don't know. You just don't know what goes on behind closed doors."

Zachary could attest to that. A person could never assume that he knew what things were like for someone, what kind of a person they were behind closed doors. Or what kind of person they lived with behind those closed doors.

"What do you remember about it? How did anyone find out?"

"He got out one day. Escaped. Somebody didn't lock the door or pull it shut, something like that. So he ended up wandering down the street, this strange little boy that no one knew."

"And someone called the police."

"Yes. Exactly. By the time the police got there, we were all gathered around him, trying to figure out where he had come from, how he had gotten there. We thought… someone dumped him there. That he came from somewhere else and had just been abandoned there, where someone would find him. We didn't know that he'd lived right on our street. That he'd lived just a few doors down from where we found him."

Zachary nodded, fascinated with the story. "How did they trace him back to the Weavers, if no one knew him?"

"He was old enough to talk, to point out which house was his, who Mommy and Daddy were. They didn't do DNA testing back then. But when they came looking for him, the police were waiting."

"I guess that was a shock for them."

"They were not too happy about it, that's for sure."

"What happened to them? They went to prison?"

"We didn't hear much. It wasn't a story that got into the newspaper, and we didn't have internet back then. I heard rumor that they were both convicted, but I don't know what the sentences were. Less for her. She said it was all his fault, she had just been doing what she was told and she was afraid of him."

"I didn't come across any of this when I was searching. If they served prison time, that should have shown up on my searches."

"Weaver wasn't their real name. I don't remember what it was. And like I said, there was no internet and I don't think it ever made it into the papers. Maybe a line or two on a slow news day."

Zachary sat there with the phone, thinking about everything.

"That was Bobby?" he asked eventually. "The little boy who wandered off?"

"Bobby… yes it was something like that. Yes."

"And what about the other boy?"

"The other boy?"

"They had two children. Bobby and Allen."

"No. They only had one. Just Bobby."

Zachary tried to keep his breathing steady.

Then what had happened to Allen?

26

Zachary wasn't sure how to go back to his client with more bad news. Not only did he not have anyone who remembered Allen, but he didn't even know the right surname. After considering it for a while, he called Aurelia Pace.

"Aurie. It's Zachary Goldman. The private investigator."

"I remember who you are," she sighed.

"Then you probably know why I'm calling you back, too."

"You went back there, didn't you?"

"Yes, we went back to Peach Tree Lane. And Ben Burton went into the house."

She made a sympathetic noise. "Why did you let him do that? Why couldn't you let him think that the place had been knocked down and there was no point in going there?"

"I'm working for him, not for you."

"But you must know that wasn't good for him. He should never have gone back there."

"My job isn't to do what's best for my client. It's to do what I'm hired for."

She sighed. "How was it?"

"Initially... okay. He got to see the house, wander around, find a link to his past."

"And then?"

"And then… he found his name and Allen's written on the wall beside the furnace."

"Allen's?" Pace repeated in a blank tone.

"Allen. His brother."

"Bobby didn't have a brother."

"Then who else was down there with Bobby? Who else was it that wrote his name on the wall?"

There was only silence from Pace.

"You never had any clue that there was another child," Zachary said.

"No. Never. Bobby didn't say anything. His crapbag parents didn't say anything about another child."

Zachary snorted in surprise at Pace's choice of language.

"Well, they were," Pace asserted. "I don't sugarcoat it. They were evil people who should never have been allowed anywhere near children. Horrible people. It's the kind of existence that you wouldn't wish on your worst enemy."

"No," Zachary agreed. "I sure wouldn't."

Neither of them said anything for a few minutes.

"They had another child?" Pace said finally.

"Yes, apparently there was another boy."

"And no one knows what happened to him."

"No one knew he existed until now."

She swore.

Zachary thought about the dimly-lit basement. He thought about it back when Burton lived there, when there had been a dirt floor.

Zachary knew that Joshua Campbell was probably his best bet in the police department, but he was a busy man and might not have any time to see Zachary. So he decided to give Mario Bowman a call and see what he thought.

"Zach, my man," Mario greeted. "What's going on in your world today?"

"Well, I have a case that needs some police involvement."

"It wouldn't be the first time."

"No," Zachary agreed with a little laugh. He seemed to be attracting more and more of those lately.

"So what kind of case is this?" Mario asked. "Another serial killer? Breaking up a trafficking ring? What's on the menu today?"

"It's a cold case. A child who disappeared in the eighties."

"And you found him?"

"No… I think he met with foul play, and that I know where his remains might be found."

"Do you know for a fact that they are there? Is this something that you've seen and are calling the police in to 'stumble' across it themselves?"

"No. I haven't seen them. They're probably buried under concrete."

"And what makes you think so?"

"My client is his brother. The children were both imprisoned in the basement for most of their lives." Zachary hoped this wasn't stretching the truth too far. "My client managed to escape and was rescued, but his brother was never seen or heard from again. I think he died before Burton escaped, and the basement was unfinished with a dirt floor. Awfully convenient place to dispose of a body."

"Yes, but can your client corroborate that's what happened?"

"His memories are very vague. I would rather not ask him about that part. I don't want to suggest or taint anything. I'll leave that to the police. To question him properly, I mean."

Mario snickered. "So how do you know this, if your client hasn't told you?"

"He told me that the basement used to have a dirt floor. We found evidence of both children in the basement, which now has a concrete floor. I've talked to a neighbor who told the story of Burton escaping and the police coming to take the parents away. I've talked to the social worker who was involved, and she confirms that part of the story. She didn't ever know that there was a second child."

"That's not really a minor detail."

"Five-year-old traumatized child. Neglected, abused, malnourished. He probably saw his brother killed and buried. Would you confide in any grown-ups?"

"He must have had therapy. Why didn't it come out then?"

"Because kids who have been told not to tell, who have been threatened… they learn to keep their mouths shut."

Mario's computer keys tapped in the background. "You say that the parents were arrested?"

"Yes. I don't know their real last names, but they were Elizabeth and Sam Weaver when they were arrested, so there should at least be an alias in the system."

"If those records were digitized, which is touch-and-go, as you know. A lot of stuff was just shoved into boxes and stored away. Then it gets black mold into it and has to be destroyed."

"Give it a try anyway."

Mario typed away for a while. Zachary kept quiet and let him do his job. Mario knew what he was doing. If anyone could find any trace of the cold case, it was he.

"Yeah, there's a file connected with those names."

"What were they charged with?"

Mario read through whatever had appeared on his screen. "Sketchy details. Looks like only the summary was digitized. But you're right, child neglect and abuse. No mention of another child."

"Because they didn't know about him. But now we know about him, so…"

"You think we should tear up someone's basement just because you have a hunch?"

"Where would you look?"

"First, I would want to verify that this other kid even existed. Did it ever occur to you that your client might have an imaginary friend? Or even DID?"

Zachary was taken aback by that. "Like dual personalities?" He remembered how similar the writing of the two names had been. Because Ben Burton had written both? Two fractured personalities who didn't know that the other existed, or someone he had made up? "Uh… no, I hadn't thought about that."

"Do you know anything about this client's psychiatric history?"

"No."

"So he could be snowing you completely. You have no idea. He might not even be who he says he is. He might have just heard the story or read it in the paper and decided to play a part and see how far he can get with it."

"I don't think so."

"I don't either, but it's a possibility. Until you've verified his identity, you don't know who he is. And I think you need to get access to his medical records, if you can. Make him prove his case. Because he's going to have to before the PD is going to touch it. We can't just dig up someone's basement on some lunatic's tip."

"Right. Okay. He did verify his identity to the social worker, and she knew his names before and after adoption. But I'm not sure how much of this *can* be proven, though. Both children were kept a secret. No one on the street even knew they lived there. So no one but Burton or his parents could verify that there was a brother."

He could hear Burton asking over and over again. *Where is Allen? What happened to him?*

Did Burton know? Was it there, buried in his memories? Or was he shining Zachary on, enjoying playing a role?

And even if he believed it was true, was it? Were Bobby and Allen two different sides of the same person? From what Zachary understood of DID, it was usually caused by the kind of abuse Burton had been through. Horrific, ongoing child abuse. The inability to deal with reality as an integrated person. The need to dissociate to remove himself from it, just as Zachary found himself doing when something reminded him of the assault by Archuro.

"You need to find out what you can," Mario advised. "We'll need as much proof as possible before rushing into something like this."

27

Zachary knocked on Burton's hotel room door. He knew that Burton had consumed a huge amount of alcohol the day before, and who knew when he had finally stopped drinking and either passed out or gone to sleep.

"Do not disturb," Burton growled back from within. "Can't you read the sign?"

He had the door handle sign hung to keep the maid service from disturbing him.

"It's Zachary."

"I don't need any more towels."

"Ben. It's Zachary."

"What?"

"I need to talk to you. Are you decent?"

Burton started muttering to himself. Zachary assumed he was getting himself together and would let Zachary in when he was finished. It took some time, and there was a lot of muttering and walking back and forth in the hotel room before Burton finally opened the door.

He was looking pretty rough, but he was all in one piece. He motioned Zachary in, and Zachary took a few steps into the room before changing his mind. The room smelled rankly of alcohol, sweat, and vomit, and Zachary had no desire to sit in the fumes for a couple of hours.

"Let's open a window and let this place air out," he suggested, and proceeded to open one window a few inches without waiting for Burton's answer. "And we'll go somewhere else to talk." He considered. He wasn't going to go down to the lounge again, having to deal with Burton's constant drinking and possibly loud and threatening behavior. "We'll go back to my apartment." He hustled Burton out of the hotel room, grabbing the key card off of the dresser on his way out. "I don't usually have clients to my apartment, so—"

"We don't need to go to your apartment; we'll just go downstairs again."

"No, not this time. We need some privacy."

"Why?"

"Just come with me." Zachary motioned to the elevator down the hall, and Burton went along with him, dragging his feet the whole way.

Zachary managed to get him past the lounge with difficulty, and out to his car.

"At least let me stop for a smoke," Burton whined.

"I don't want the smoke in the car."

"I'll smoke it out here."

"You'll still smell like it. No."

"Sheesh, why are you being such a hard case all of a sudden? Knowing all of what I've had to go through, don't you think I have the right to drink and smoke a bit?"

"You've been through a lot of crap," Zachary agreed. "Worse than most people can even dream of. But that doesn't mean you need to drink and smoke constantly."

"Well… it kinda does."

"No. Just get in the car. We can stop and get something to eat if you want. Comfort food. Calm yourself down that way."

"Comfort foot," Burton repeated dubiously. "What, like chocolate ice cream?"

"Chocolate ice cream works," Zachary remembered Kenzie insisting that they go out for ice cream after their first couples therapy appointment. It had become a tradition, and he had to admit, he looked forward to it, despite his usual lack of appetite. "Is that what you want?"

"No, I don't want ice cream. It's not my period," he sneered. "I want… a steak and a case of beer."

"Do you cook?"

"Not really."

"Well, we want to grab something you can take back to the apartment. Our steakhouses don't do takeout. So something you can get as takeout or at the grocery store and cook yourself."

Burton sniffed. He sat looking out the window while Zachary drove toward the apartment. He was behaving like a sullen teenager. But eventually, he decided that he'd better pick something or he was going to end up at Zachary's apartment with nothing to eat. Or having to choose between granola bars and frozen burritos.

"Burger and fries," he grumbled finally. "I suppose."

"Sure. Five Guys?"

Burton nodded. Zachary detoured to the nearest fast food place and they went through the drive-through.

"Aren't you getting anything?" Burton demanded after Zachary relayed his order to the crackling speaker.

"A milkshake. I've already eaten."

Not much, but he had eaten a little before going to pick Burton up.

"Milkshake," Burton repeated.

"You want one?"

"No."

In a few minutes, they were on the road again, and then back to Zachary's apartment. When he unlocked the door and let Burton in, his client looked around at the set-up. Zachary waited for the criticisms or teasing to begin. But Burton shrugged and headed over to the couch with his fast food. "I don't know what I was expecting. Jim Rockford worked out of his trailer, right?"

Zachary shrugged. He wasn't sure what Burton had been expecting either, but he was grateful not have to defend himself and his choice of where to live. Burton didn't know anything about the apartment fire where Zachary had lost everything he owned and nearly his own life. Burton didn't know about Zachary's history or the vagaries of the private investigator business. He indicated the table.

"Eat there. I don't want ketchup on the furniture."

"I wouldn't spill."

"Use the table."

After Burton sat down, growling grumpily, Zachary sat across from him. He took a few sips of his milkshake while Burton sat and got his food arranged on the table. Zachary wasn't surprised when, after drinking the first few inches of his cola, Burton lifted the lid to pour in the contents of his flask.

"So, why did we have to come back here for privacy?" Burton demanded. "Why not just meet at the lounge? That was good enough for you before."

"How much of last night do you remember?"

Burton didn't answer at first. He had said that drinking didn't affect him, so he was conflicted whether to admit that he couldn't remember everything that had happened or bluff his way through it. Zachary waited, seeing which he would choose.

"Fine," Burton said, "I might not have a clear recollection of everything that happened last night. What does that have to do with it?"

"I just think we should give the lounge and the bar a day or two to forget about it too. Give them a break. Otherwise, you might not find yourself able to drink there again."

Burton rolled his eyes. He worked quickly on his hamburger.

"Whatever. I don't see what difference it makes."

"So…" Zachary pulled out his notepad to make notes as he needed to. "I have talked to a few people today about you and Allen."

Burton froze and met Zachary's eyes. Then he reared back, moving farther away from Zachary and leaning back against his chair, when he'd previously been sitting forward. He was afraid of what was to come.

"Allen. What did you find out?"

"I found out more about you, but not very much about Allen."

"What?" Burton was cautious, not sure he wanted to hear. Zachary determined to take it slowly. He didn't want Burton to have a meltdown and to punch him in the face. Having a flashback and seeing him as one of his abusers.

"Do you remember telling me about walking outside one day? The day that you saw a dog?"

Burton nodded. The corners of his mouth lifted slightly at the memory of the dog. "His owner let me pet him."

"Was that the only time you had been out of the house?"

Burton's forehead creased. "The only time I'd been out? No, of course not."

"How often did you go out?"

"I don't know. How often do kids go out of the house?"

"I don't think you got out very often. But you remember what the outside of the house looked like, so maybe that wasn't the only time you'd ever gone out."

"No, of course not."

"When we were at the house, you weren't that interested in what was upstairs. Why was that?"

Burton shrugged. "I don't know. It just wasn't very interesting. Just a normal house, I've seen a hundred like that. Nothing remarkable about it."

"You barely even looked at the bedrooms. Usually, kids remember which bedroom was theirs."

Burton raised his eyebrows, looking at Zachary blankly. "Why would it matter which one was mine?"

"People care about things like that. They want to belong somewhere. To have a room that was theirs."

It was one of the things that had bothered Zachary about foster care. He never felt like he had a place of his own. Even though he was assigned a bedroom in every house he went to, it was never just his, and changing homes so often meant that he never felt like he put down roots and had ownership of a place.

"I know where my room is in the house I grew up in," Burton said, "With my adoptive parents. That was my room."

"And the room you wanted to see in the old house was the basement."

"Yeah…" Burton trailed off, apparently unsure as to where Zachary was going.

Zachary nodded. He sipped the milkshake, taking his time. Letting Burton think about it and get used to the idea before concluding, "Because that was where you lived. That's where they kept you."

Burton's face became a thundercloud. "No."

Zachary cocked his head and let Burton think about it. He needed time to go through his memories and sort it out. Did he have memories of the upstairs? Did he have memories of the basement? Where had his jar and his name been?

Burton shook his head again, definite. "No. They didn't keep me in the basement like an animal. That's wrong."

Zachary nodded. "Okay. Tell me about it, then. What else can you remember about your house? You've had some time to think about it. Maybe some more memories have come to you since we talked last."

Burton's anger abated slightly. He ate a few French fries. His forehead was still creased with worry lines. "That would be cruel," he said. "No one would keep their kids locked up in a place like that."

"People do. I'm sure you've seen in the news from time to time. Not very often, but it does happen. Sometimes just one child in the family, sometimes all of the children. Maybe the basement, maybe a locked bedroom or closet. Kids go to the bathroom in a bucket or a corner. Get fed now and then, not regular meals. Maybe they don't have any way to keep themselves clean or have clean clothes. It's horrible, I agree."

"Why would anyone do that? How bad would a kid have to be to be treated that way?"

Zachary studied the expression on Burton's face. Guilt. Dread. They had undoubtedly conditioned him. Made him feel like it was his own fault that he'd been locked up like that.

"A kid wouldn't have to be bad at all. Parents don't do it because they have bad kids. They do it because they are bad parents. Evil people. Normal people would never treat their kids like that. You know how your adoptive parents were. They loved and protected you. They would never do something like that."

Burton shook his head. "No. Never."

"And that's how normal parents are. But the people that you were born to… they were not like that. There was something wrong with them, not with you. It isn't your fault that they locked you in the basement. It isn't anything that you did."

"No," Burton repeated. But he didn't look convinced. Deep down inside, he still thought he was that naughty child. The child who was so bad that his parents had to lock him in the basement. The cold, dark, damp basement with a dirt floor.

"I'm sorry they treated you that way. They were wrong."

Burton swallowed. He had a long sip of his drink. Cola and whatever had been in his flask. Zachary was sure he wished they had stayed in the lounge, where he could have ordered drink after drink to satisfy his craving. Instead, all he had was the weak mixed drink, and only one cup. His eyes started to rove to Zachary's cupboards and fridge. But he wouldn't find any alcohol in the apartment. That was one of the reasons Zachary had taken him there. He couldn't deal with hours of Burton drinking again.

"They wouldn't do that," Burton said softly.

"Some people would. When you got out and went on your walk down the street, people recognized that you had been badly neglected, and they called the police. The police connected you with your parents, and they were arrested and went to jail."

Burton's eyes were wide and disconcertingly childlike. He had been holding those memories inside for decades. He had always kept that part of himself separate. That child had remained locked up in the darkest corner of his mind, just as he had been locked in the basement.

"Who found me?" he asked.

"I talked to a woman named Elise Perry. She remembers when you were found. When you went out for a walk and saw the dog, and the neighbors called the police. They thought someone had dumped you there, but then the police traced you back to the Weavers. Or the people calling themselves the Weavers."

"How?"

"You knew where you lived. You probably showed them. The police watched to see what happened. When your birth parents discovered you were missing and went out looking for you, that confirmed to the police that they were the ones who had been holding you. They arrested them, went into the house, and would have found the evidence in the basement showing that you had been kept there, neglected."

"It was still my home," Burton offered.

Zachary nodded. "Yeah. The only place you knew. It must have been very strange to be taken away from there. Put into foster care and then to your adoptive parents. Lots of disruption, strange new experiences."

"How could anyone do that, though?"

Zachary sucked on his straw, trying to focus on the cold, sweet, thick milkshake. If he could keep his focus on his senses and physical surroundings, he didn't need to go back into the past. Isolation cells at Bonnie Best when he 'acted up.' Being locked in a closet for 'cognitive time' when he'd broken rules or done something to irritate his supervisors at one of his group homes. He hadn't been forced to live in an unfinished basement, but he'd had enough experiences with isolation to empathize with Burton just a little too much.

He didn't offer Burton another explanation for why his biological family had treated him like that. It was inconceivable to most people. But some adults needed power. They needed absolute power over those who were under their control.

A child who wet his pants or wouldn't eat his peas simply couldn't be tolerated. Such defiance was a slap in the face and had to be crushed in the strongest possible way. They had to show who was boss and make sure that the child had no way to fight back.

No way to express any more defiance or independence.

28

"What they did was unforgivable," Zachary said simply. "All that the state could do was to put them in prison. But that's not justice. That doesn't take away what happened to you or make you feel any better."

Burton shook his head in agreement.

"Do you remember Allen?" Zachary prompted after a period of silent contemplation.

Burton raised his eyes and looked at Zachary in confusion. "I lived down there with him? You're sure?"

"Someone wrote that name behind the furnace. Maybe you did. Maybe he did." Zachary didn't offer anything else, not wanting to plant any thoughts or false memories. Those things were indisputable facts.

"Maybe I wrote it," Burton said. "Maybe… Allen was an imaginary friend. Someone I made up to keep me company."

Zachary nodded. "Maybe you did."

Burton put his hand over his chest like it hurt. He shook his head. His eyes glistened with tears. Zachary waited. He hoped that Burton wasn't about to have a heart attack. That would put a definite crimp in the investigation. Burton was probably just feeling anxiety, like Zachary did when confronted with a truth he didn't want to face or a change that seemed insurmountable.

"Take deep breaths," he advised. "Nice and slow. Make sure you're breathing the air all the way out."

Burton's hand closed into a fist. The lines of his face hardened. Putting on a mask and trying not to let his emotion show.

"It's okay," Zachary assured him. "This is hard. Do you want to take a break?"

Burton looked around the kitchen and into the living room. "To do what?" he demanded. "There isn't exactly anything to do around here."

"You could stand up and walk around. Look out the window. Check your email. Just get grounded again."

Burton got up and left the table, left the rest of his food there and went to the big window in the living room. He looked down at the parking lot below. Zachary took out his phone and checked his mail, not wanting Burton to feel like he was under scrutiny. He clicked through a few of his emails. There wasn't a lot that he could respond to on his phone. The ones that weren't junk required some research or attachments. There was one from Lorne Peterson, his old foster father, and he made a mental note that he needed to call him. It had been too long since their last visit. Zachary needed to be more diligent about keeping up with him. He had little enough family; he needed to keep them close, let them know that they were appreciated. That Zachary didn't just reach out to them when he needed something.

"I didn't make him up," Burton said from the living room, not turning around, still staring out the window.

"Do you remember...?"

"Allen," Burton said, testing the name out. Rolling it around his mouth and considering the memories that saying it out loud brought back.

Zachary waited.

"He was... older," Burton said. "I think he was older than I was. He knew things I didn't. He was... my protector."

Zachary's own heart ached at the thought. The two little boys trapped down in the basement, Allen trying to protect five-year-old Burton. Allen probably wasn't much older than Burton, but he had put himself between his little brother and the adults who had all control over him. There was no way that he could protect himself or Burton against the abuse. But he'd been heroic. He had tried.

"He was my brother." It sounded more like a question than a statement.

Burton turned around to face Zachary, and Zachary saw the deep creases between his eyebrows smooth out. "My… big brother?"

Zachary did his best to look sympathetic, but not to nod or to feed Burton any more information. Burton needed to remember and work out what he could on his own.

"What can you remember about him?"

"It's so hard… it was so long ago."

"Yeah."

"He wrote the names. Do you think he wrote the names?"

"Is that what you think?"

"Yes. He must have written them. He was the one who could write. He knew… he knew things I didn't know."

"What things did he know?" Zachary wrote a few words in his notepad and waited for Burton to fill in the details.

"He was the one who knew about… dogs and cats. Other animals that he told me about."

"Because you hadn't ever seen them?"

Burton shook his head. "I don't know. I must have seen them before. What kid hasn't seen cats and dogs? I just… didn't know very much about them. We didn't have a dog."

"Most kids still see them on the street. Read about them in books. See them on TV."

"Must have," Burton mused. "I must have… I just remember the bugs. They were the creatures I knew best. What I could catch in my hands or my jar. We knew some of them… the spider that built its web in the corner. We would see it come out, watch it working on its web. Eating other bugs. The flies in the summer…" Burton's nose wrinkled. "There were so many flies in the summer, buzzing around us. Around…"

Zachary nodded. They would get a reprieve in the winter when the bugs were no longer flying outside the house and getting in through cracks in the windows or walls or through doors that stayed open too long. But during the summer, even in a cool basement, they would still be attracted by the smells of two little boys who were not properly cared for. Dirt, open sores, rotten food, excrement. Zachary could imagine how the flies would have plagued them.

"They get everywhere," he agreed.

Burton paced back and forth, rubbing his temples. He probably had a headache. All of the emotional work on top of being hung over and not having more to drink to numb it.

"What things do you remember about when you first went to your adoptive family?" Zachary asked. "Things that you were impressed with. Surprised by. Excited about."

Burton scowled. Maybe he was regretting that he had hired Zachary in the first place. It would be easier to just go home and not think about it anymore. Not to have to dig up and expose all of the old memories. "I don't remember a lot of specifics. I liked them. Mom and Dad. They were nice. I remember… they had lots of good things to eat. When I look at it now, they weren't anything special. But to me back then, it felt like… sort of like when you look at Christmas or Thanksgiving dinner. That there is just so much to choose from and everything looks, smells, and tastes so good. It felt like that. Like every day was another Christmas dinner. But when I think back to it now, it was just sandwiches. Oatmeal. Roast and potatoes. Not feasts. Not anything fancy. But it was all so good and made me feel… strong and healthy and like life was good because of it."

"You were very skinny when you got away. Malnourished."

"My mom says that's why my legs are a little bowed," Burton offered, looking embarrassed by the fact. "That it was from not having enough vitamins those first few years. But I thought… it just meant I didn't eat all of my vegetables. I didn't ever understand that I had… really been neglected."

"What else did you remember about living with your adoptive parents?"

"They had a nice house. Clean and sunny and everything neat and tidy. I had my own room. Nice soft bed with clean, white, fresh-smelling sheets. It wasn't even like I had special sheets with Batman or cars on them. I don't think they really had any idea about kids and what was popular. They were just clean, white sheets. And nice clothes. Whatever I wanted to eat."

Food again. It was probably hard for someone who had been so starved to think of anything else. That had been the most important priority in his life after his experience. Getting the calories that he needed. Filling his stomach. Food had been limited in Zachary's home, but he hadn't been as malnourished as Burton had been. Skinny and small, but he hadn't had rickets.

29

Zachary took a break from talking with Burton and called Aurelia Pace. He needed her input and confirmation before he could go back to the police department with any hopes of their getting a search warrant to look at the old house on Peach Tree Lane.

"Did you find him?" Pace asked immediately when she picked up the phone, and Zachary realized that she had been waiting for the call confirming that they had found the body of little Allen Weaver. He got a lump in his throat but tried to ignore it.

"No. We haven't gotten in yet. The police didn't have enough to go on. I've been interviewing Ben, and I have some more questions for you. I'm going to need your help if we're going to get them to look into it after all these years."

"I'll help however I can. What do you need?"

"I need some information on Ben after he was rescued and went into foster care."

"Yes?"

"Could he read and write?"

"What?"

"I want to know whether he already knew how to read and write when he went into foster care. Even a little bit."

"No... not that I remember. I would have to talk to his foster parents at the time, or maybe you could talk to his adoptive parents and find out whether he could read and write yet when he was placed with them. But I don't think so. He had been badly neglected. He didn't go to school. Would his parents have locked him down there and then taught him his lessons? Tutored him in his schoolwork? I can't see it."

"A lot of people choose to homeschool because they don't trust the state to do it. They may have felt like they had to teach him their beliefs and philosophies. That might have involved lessons in reading and writing."

"Maybe. Like I said, I would have to follow up to be sure, but I don't think so."

"Then he wasn't the one who wrote the names on the walls."

Pace was quiet for a minute as she thought about it.

"No. If he hadn't been taught to write his name, then he wasn't the one who wrote it."

That seemed obvious, and yet it had not occurred to her before.

"So someone else wrote it. That points to the possibility that another child did exist."

"Yes, I agree with that. I thought we had already established that there was another child at some point."

"You and I agreed… but the police say they need more. That maybe Allen is just a split personality or imaginary friend and never actually existed."

"Oh, I'm sure that's not the case."

"Still, we need a way to prove it."

"I suppose."

"It helps if we can say that Ben wasn't able to write his own name, and yet those names are written on the wall."

"I wish I had my file notes from back then, but I don't. If there were other things that he said or that we had concerns about, I would have written them down. But I can't remember now. Did he ever mention the name Allen? I wish I could say that he had. But he obviously never told me that he had a sibling, or I would have looked into it. It's very frustrating. It's horrible that this is only coming out now. If he'd only told us years ago, it could have been investigated at the time. We could have torn up the floor in that place."

"There's no guarantee it would have made a difference. Allen could be buried in the back yard. Or he could have been dumped in a dumpster or in the woods. There are a hundred different scenarios. There's no guarantee that we're going to find anything if we get a search warrant. And even if we find his remains… that is no guarantee that we'll be able to prove his cause of death or to charge his parents."

"I would like to be able to get justice for Ben. And for Allen."

"I don't know if either of us will ever be able to do that. There's nothing we can do to bring Allen back. Or to give Ben those first few years back. They were taken away from him forever."

Zachary dropped Burton off at the Best Western after another exhausting interview. While Burton's memories were getting closer to the surface, Zachary still wasn't sure they were going to find enough information to convince the police to issue a warrant to search the house and property for any sign of Allen's remains. All they had was Burton's memory and, as Mario had said, he could be trying to pull a scam. Trying to get attention.

But the emotions that Burton was going through, the reactions he'd had and the pain and grief in his eyes, those were all things that Zachary was sure were genuine.

He looked in the rearview and side mirrors as he pulled out to go to Kenzie's house for the evening. He was tired, but Kenzie would want to hear how things had gone, and he would sleep better if he spent time unwinding with her than he would if he went back to his own apartment and ping-ponged around it alone.

There was a motorcyclist stopped in the parking lot behind him but, as Zachary watched, he just sat there and didn't pull out. Maybe he had stopped to talk on his phone or to get something out of his packs, but he didn't seem to be going anywhere. Zachary pulled out and drove from the parking lot out to the main road. He turned the radio on to try to distract his busy brain from working on the problem of how to get a search warrant for the old Weaver home. He didn't want to go back to Kenzie with problems on his mind. He'd be distracted and she'd feel like he wasn't paying her any attention.

He resisted the urge to call anyone on the phone to discuss matters. Who would he talk to? He'd already talked to Pace and Burton. He didn't have anything new for Mario. He couldn't really discuss the case in any detail with anyone outside the case. There were confidentiality concerns, and he didn't have Burton's permission to share it with anyone else.

He glanced over his shoulder before changing lanes, then quickly corrected and slowed when he saw a motorcycle in his blind spot. The motorcycle shot past him, and he watched it weave through the traffic ahead of him. He checked the other lane, passed a stream of slower vehicles, and switched back again. The motorcycle was just ahead of him, holding its speed.

Zachary glanced at which exit he was at and noted the time. Ten minutes later, the motorcycle was still there, riding just behind him.

He was on a main thoroughfare. It was natural that other drivers would be going in the same direction as he was. But he had a bad feeling about the motorcycle.

He couldn't swear that it was the same one that he'd seen in the hotel parking lot. But if it was, it had been keeping just ahead of him way too long to be coincidental.

Zachary hit the brake, slowing a little. His distance from the bike should increase. Bikers liked to go above the speed limit.

But the space between him and the bike stayed the same. The bike had also slowed.

Zachary didn't like it. He sped up and blasted past the motorcycle and a few other vehicles, then settled behind a white van and watched the traffic behind him. Pretty soon, the motorcycle had also made its way past the cars that Zachary had. He didn't pull right in behind Zachary, but sat a lane over and just behind Zachary.

Who would be following him? His mind flashed immediately back to the members of the trafficking syndicate who had followed him and ended up shooting Luke. Zachary had neglected to spot that tail. They had used the cell phones that Luke and Madison had been using to track their positions. This time, they didn't have a cell signal to follow. Was it possible that one of them had spotted Zachary or had placed a tracker on his car sometime during the day and they were now moving in to deal with him?

He couldn't lead them back to Kenzie's house. Hopefully, they hadn't been following him for long and didn't already know about Kenzie and where she lived. He didn't think the motorcycle had been on his tail for that long, but there might be several other vehicles in the tail. Or motorcycle guy might have only been on Zachary's tail for one day, while someone else had been there previously. They wouldn't take that long to act, would they? They would strike fast, like they had before. They weren't patient enough to develop a longer-term plan.

Were they?

Zachary hit the Bluetooth button and called Kenzie. But what if they had put a tracker on his car and a bug inside where it could monitor his calls?

If they were that sophisticated, he was in trouble either way. They'd probably been on him for a while and listened to several other calls exchanged with Kenzie.

"Zachary. Running late?" Kenzie asked, upon picking up.

"Well, I wasn't, but I've run into some problems. I… might have a tail and I'm going to have to do something about it."

She didn't respond at first. "A tail?" she asked finally. "Who would be following you? I don't understand."

"I don't know. It could be related to an earlier case. I don't want to take any chances."

"You think it's the guys that shot Luke?" she discerned immediately. "Zachary, those guys are dangerous. I thought you said that they wouldn't be interested in you if they thought that both Madison and Luke were dead?"

"That was the plan."

"You don't think it's those guys, do you?"

"I can't think of who else would be following me now."

"You should be calling the police, not me."

"I don't think the police would do anything if I called them right now. They'd think it was a prank call or some crazy."

There was, again, a space of just too long before Kenzie responded again. Like she was considering whether he were paranoid, or whether what he said could really be true.

"Do you think they're tracking your phone?"

"No, I'm pretty careful about not opening any attachments or strange links. I don't see when they could have installed any kind of tracking on it. I'm sure it hasn't been hacked." Zachary thought some more about it, keeping an eye on the motorcycle, which so far was not taking any action, but was just sitting there, waiting for him to make the next move. "But why would they change tactics? Those guys know how to track people without being seen. They kept out of sight when they were tracking Madison and Luke. Why wouldn't they put a tracker on my car this time and stay out of sight?"

"Maybe they didn't have a chance. You surprised them."

"I'm not that hard to find. All they have to do is wait at my apartment building. Watch to see what vehicle I get out of, if they don't already know my license plate number."

"Your address isn't listed, is it?"

"No, but I know how easy it is to find someone."

"That's not exactly what I want to hear."

Zachary slowed his car, watching the motorcyclist for his reaction. He slowed and stayed behind Zachary.

"This guy is being pretty obvious," he said, relieved. "I don't think he's a professional."

"Then who is he?"

"I don't know."

Zachary watched him for a while longer. Where had he picked the motorcycle up? He had seen him at the hotel. Was it someone who knew Burton? Someone who was following him for some reason? It could just be something like a debt-collector. Zachary wouldn't be surprised if Burton had borrowed money from someone he shouldn't have or had gotten in deep with a bookie. He was the kind of guy who just dove into things that he knew he shouldn't be doing. Drinking, smoking, why not gambling? Maybe the guy on the motorcycle wanted to know who Zachary was and to see where he would go to find out if he had any money. If he could pay off Burton's debts, given the right incentive. It could be something like that.

"I'm going to see if I can lose him. I'll call you if I'm not going to be there within the hour."

Zachary hung up. He made sure that there was no one right behind him, then slowed abruptly and pulled up over the curb to sit in the grassy verge beside the road. The motorcyclist had to make a split-second decision as to whether to fall back and find out what Zachary was doing, or to keep going and hope to connect up with him again later. He could take the next exit, circle around, and come up on Zachary again from behind. See whether he was having car trouble or what was going on.

Either the motorcyclist didn't have fast enough reactions to pull over in time to stay with Zachary or he made the decision to go on so as not to look suspicious. Zachary watched him go on through the traffic, and kept an eye on him as far as possible. The motorcycle took the next exit ramp. Zachary pulled back onto the road and hit the gas, zipping down the thoroughfare as quickly as he dared. He wove in and out of traffic, took the exit after the one the motorcycle had taken, and took a few random turns that took him into a residential area. Once there, he pulled over to the side and watched for any sign of the motorcycle. If he showed up again, that meant that Zachary, his car, or something in the car was tagged with a tracking device.

He waited for half an hour without any sign of the motorcycle. He kept his ears pricked, and didn't hear any approaching.

He had lost the tail.

For now.

30

Hopefully, the fact that the motorcycle had been tailing him meant that the pursuer didn't know Zachary's name, where he lived, or anything about Kenzie. He would be safe going to her house.

Zachary waited for his heart to slow.

Eventually, he started the engine and worked his way through the quieter residential streets toward Kenzie's house. He didn't want to hit the main thoroughfare again, in case the motorcyclist was looking for him.

When he pulled to the curb in front of Kenzie's house, his phone rang. Zachary saw that it was Kenzie's number.

"Kenz?"

"I just wondered if maybe you wanted to pull into the garage. So your car is out of sight."

He considered for a moment, then shook his head. "No. I'm sure no one followed me here. And if they were following me, that means they didn't know I was coming here. You can keep your baby in the garage."

Kenzie's cherry-red convertible was her pride and joy, and he wouldn't want it on the street where it could be hit by a drunk driver. Or stolen. Kenzie might never forgive him if something happened to her baby.

"Are you sure? You could park in the alley."

"No. It's fine."

"Okay. See you inside."

She hung up the call. Zachary slid his phone away and removed his keys from the ignition. He locked the car once he was outside and checked the door. He looked at the house, looked up and down the street, and checked the handle again. He beeped it one final time to arm the alarm, and headed inside.

Zachary managed to get past the gatekeepers to reach Campbell about his case in the morning. Mario had clearly filled him in on the details that Zachary had previously provided.

"I understand your concern, Zachary, but I don't think there's enough for us to get a warrant."

"I've done a little more investigating, and I'm hoping we might be there."

"Okay." Campbell's chair squeaked as he tipped it back, and Zachary heard him take a noisy slurp of his morning coffee. "Tell me about it."

Zachary outlined what he knew, then waited for Campbell to think it through.

"I still don't know, Zachary. It's a stronger case, but I don't know if it is quite there."

"There was someone else in that basement with Burton," Zachary asserted.

"How can you be sure?"

"Because he couldn't write. So he is not the one who wrote those names on the wall. He was not able to read or write. Who do you think wrote them? The parents?"

"The social worker could be wrong. Maybe he could write his name. A lot of kids know that before they can read or write other things."

"I think she knew him pretty well. They would have had all kinds of examinations done to see what kind of shape he was in and what his IQ and educational levels were. They had to know all of that kind of thing to bring the parents to trial. They needed to know exactly how bad the damage was."

"Have you seen the tests that were done?"

"No. I would have to get in contact with the prosecutor and see if he still had all of the documentation on file and would let me look at it, and I haven't gotten the court documents yet to see who it was. You may have a lot of that information in the police file too, whatever investigations were done on your end. You could request them from storage and have a look."

"Yes, convenient for you, isn't it? Letting us do all of the work."

"I've put a lot of hours into it already. If you want me to look through the file, just let me know and I'll be at the police station the minute you want me."

"I know that," Campbell said, and Zachary could hear the smile in his voice. "I'm just teasing you." There was another sharp squeak from his chair. Zachary pictured him sitting up now, leaning over his desk, making some notes. "I'm going to have to think this through and see what we've got in the files. I wasn't around when this happened, obviously, so I don't have any background on the case. And I don't think we have anyone around who was here at that time."

"It was a long time ago, and the police department thought that they'd done everything that was required. They didn't know that there might have been another boy, or they would have looked into it then."

"Or maybe they did," Campbell pointed out. "I might open up that file and find that they already did a search at the time and didn't turn up any sign of the older boy."

"That's true." Zachary hadn't thought about that possibility. "You're right."

Maybe there wouldn't be any need for a search warrant at all. Maybe Campbell would call him back and say that the floor of the basement had already been dug up and there were no remains to be found.

"Have you looked for birth records for this other brother?" Campbell asked.

"Preliminary only, yes. I figured at the time that there was a possibility that the other boy had been adopted, so his name was changed, but the social worker said that they didn't have any idea there was another boy. He must have disappeared sometime before Burton was found."

"You don't think it means there wasn't another brother?"

"No. I think it means the births weren't recorded. The public records that I looked at never indicated that there were any children living with the Weavers. The census done during that time period states that there were only two adults living there. None of the neighbors knew that there were any children. I think the children were probably born at home and never attended to."

Campbell grunted. There were, of course, cases he was aware of where just that had happened. People didn't trust the government or wanted to stay off of the radar for some nefarious reason. Undocumented children. Ghosts who, as far as the government was concerned, never actually existed. They might be kept by the parents, as Ben and Allen had apparently been, or they might be trafficked or sold through black-market adoptions.

"I'll take a look from my end," Campbell promised. "It may take a few days to even get the files, so don't call me tomorrow looking for answers."

"Okay. You'll let me know what you find?"

"I'll let you know if I find anything actionable. No guarantee that I will. If we decide to investigate further or to get a warrant, I'll give you a heads-up. If not, I might not get back to you."

"I'll touch base next week, then," Zachary said. "Wednesday?"

Campbell grumbled. "I don't have time for this."

"That's why I'll call you. You have plenty else on your plate. You can give me an update then."

"Talk to you next week." Campbell hung up.

Zachary decided to spend the weekend with Lorne Peterson, his oldest friend and former foster father. He would have dinner with Lorne and Pat, his partner, and go see Joss and Luke, who lived closer to Lorne than Zachary did. Vermont was a small state, but it still took time to travel from one end to the other. However much Zachary enjoyed highway driving, he didn't have time to go back and forth twice over the weekend.

"Do you want to come?" he asked Kenzie. "Do you have the time, or are you busy over the weekend?"

"I've put in enough hours that I should be able to escape for the weekend. Unless someone calls in sick."

Zachary nodded. "I'll tell Pat that we'll both be there, then. If you end up not being able to go, he'll be disappointed, but it's not as inconvenient as showing up with another person who wasn't expected."

"I'm ninety percent sure I'll be able to go."

"Great." Zachary smiled at her. It was always nice to get away for a day or two, and they would enjoy a change of scene. As long as she didn't think he was planning a romantic getaway. He glanced back at her once just to be sure.

But they were still trying to work things out between them and Kenzie had promised not to push him into anything he wasn't ready for. As much as he wanted a close romantic relationship with her, his body and his PTSD brain set roadblocks in his way. He could push through them physically, but as he and Kenzie had discovered, that just resulted in his dissociating. Not being mentally present for the more intimate moments sort of defeated the purpose.

"It sounds nice," Kenzie said, catching his glance. He wasn't sure if she had picked up on his moment of anxiety or not. "It's always good to catch up with Lorne and Pat."

"Then, on Sunday, I'll be going over to see Joss and Luke. I'm sure it would be okay for you to go with me."

Kenzie drew in her breath and held it, thinking about the suggestion. She breathed out again. "I think I'll let you do that on your own for now. It's probably best for Luke if he doesn't have to worry about more people knowing where he is, and I'm not sure Joss would want me around."

"I don't know if she wants *me* around," Zachary pointed out. "I think she's prickly with everyone. It's certainly not just you."

"And then there's you."

Zachary opened his mouth, but didn't know what to say.

"I know it gets harder for you the more people who are there. It's pretty comfortable when it's just us and Lorne and Pat; they're laid back and you don't get too stressed out when it's just them. But with Joss… it's a lot more difficult to be around her. You're on edge, worried about doing or saying the wrong thing."

"Yes…"

"And then you add Luke in there. He's a whole different ball game. Lots of stress dealing with him too. Not personal, like with Joss, but worrying about all of the consequences of anything you say to him and what his future choices might be. And now knowing that Rhys is interested in him too…"

Zachary nodded more definitely. She understood him better than he gave her credit for. The combination of her experience with him and her intuition, and now the sessions with Dr. Boyle too… she really had a chance to get to know him more deeply than anyone in his life probably had before. Including Mr. Peterson. Including Bridget.

"So I think it's already stressful dealing with Joss and Luke, with all of the personal stuff and the potential repercussions. So maybe it's best if you don't have another person there to deal with as well."

"You don't stress me out."

"Not normally. But if you're trying to run interference between me and Joss or Luke… that's a different story. Or just having too many people in the room at once. I know it's not easy. You don't want to get overwhelmed."

Zachary nodded slowly. "Okay. Yeah. You're probably right. So you don't mind… staying at Lorne's while I go to Joss's?"

"Not at all. They always make me feel at home. And if they need some space, or I do, I can go over to the library or a coffee shop and get some personal time."

"Yeah. All right." Zachary considered the list of items that was starting to build up in his head. "I'll… I'll call Pat first, so I don't forget."

31

Spring came earlier in the southern portion of Vermont. It wasn't usually that noticeable, but things were definitely greener as they traveled south. When they arrived at the little white bungalow, Zachary saw Pat's tulips were coming up, splashing the yard with bright, welcoming color. He took a deep breath as he got out of the car, taking in the sweet smell of freshly-cut grass.

"It's so nice," Kenzie said. "I think we should stay here for a week or two until things catch up at home."

He looked at her quickly, then realized she was kidding. She might be able to get a couple of weeks of vacation since she had worked at the medical examiner's office for more than a year, but she would need to give them notice before just dropping off the map.

"It sure is nice," he agreed. "Sometimes, it seems like spring is never going to come."

They walked up the sidewalk together, Kenzie slightly ahead of Zachary, and Mr. Peterson had the door open by the time they got there.

"Kenzie, Zachary!" He pulled in each of them in turn for a hug, giving Kenzie a friendly kiss on the cheek. "Good to see you. Come in. Tell me how everything is."

Zachary always found himself examining Mr. Peterson for signs of aging and declining health. A fear that he could lose someone else in his life, one of the only people who had been there to support him over the years, almost since the fire. Lorne Peterson continued to age well. He was a little heavy around the belly, and his fringe of hair was completely white, but he still moved with vigor and always seemed happy and healthy. Zachary couldn't see any signs that he was declining.

They gathered in the living room to chat. Pat poked his head out of the kitchen, where he was cooking up something that made Zachary's mouth water, even with his suppressed appetite.

"Kenzie. Zach. How was the drive?"

"Great," Zachary answered, at the same time as Kenzie answered, "Pretty."

"Next time we'll be able to bring the convertible," Zachary said to Kenzie. Flying down the highway in a convertible with the top down was fun, but not pleasant if it were too cold. Kenzie was looking forward to when she could take it out again.

"Sounds good." Pat wiped his hands on the dishtowel he was holding, then flipped it over his shoulder. "Dinner will be on shortly."

Kenzie and Zachary each filled Lorne and Pat in a little on what they were working on. Kenzie was careful not to share too many details of her work, which was not generally acceptable for dinner conversation. When Zachary started to talk about Burton's case in general terms, Lorne laid down his fork and watched Zachary intently.

"I think I remember that case."

Zachary stared at him. "You do? But it happened upstate, and it wasn't even in the papers there."

"No. But we were still fostering then. That kind of thing goes through the fostering committee like lightning. Hearing that a child who has gone through that kind of thing is going into the system? Everyone follows it. Holds their breaths to see who gets him, wonders about what kind of problems he's going to have. Something like that… Well, to be honest, it's like what happened to you, Zachary. When the community hears about something so unusual or extreme, the whispers start. Even before the internet and texting, people would get on the phone and light up the lines."

Zachary nodded slowly. It made sense. It hadn't even occurred to him that Mr. Peterson would know anything about the case. He knew that foster parents weren't allowed to share confidential information about their charges with each other. But apparently, there was no such prohibition against sharing gossip and speculation about where such a child would go or what problems he might have. There would be no names or private information shared, but people who knew the circumstances might still spread it on a no-names basis.

And he hadn't thought about his own story being shared between foster parents before. He knew that the social worker would tell them what she thought they needed to know about the circumstances, but they also held things back, trying to make it so that a child sounded less damaged or needy than they were in order to get them into the right home.

He shifted uncomfortably. How much had the Petersons known about him before he was placed there? And later families and group homes?

"Did you hear anything about him after he was placed in foster care?" Kenzie asked.

It took Zachary a few moments to remember that she was talking about Burton, not him.

"Heard he was quiet, withdrawn. You never know, with a kid who's been through so much trauma, if he's going to be angry and destructive."

Like Zachary had been. He wasn't *actually* angry and destructive, but easily upset, impulsive, and making poor decisions. And foster parents and teachers had thought the worst of him. His social worker had been compassionate, but even she had dressed him down on more than one occasion, trying to get him to keep out of trouble. That had proved to be impossible.

"Do you know who got him? Did you know the family he went to?"

Lorne thought back, his forehead crinkling. "I think… oh, it was a long time ago… Marty and Kathy Anderson? I think… yes, I'm pretty sure they were the ones who got him. We had conferences that we attended in Burlington. Everyone in the state. So you got to know other foster parents, even if they weren't close by."

"You don't know what happened to them do you? If they stayed in the state? Still foster parents?"

"I didn't keep track of them. Maybe I could hire a private investigator to track them down." Mr. Peterson smiled and winked. "Sorry it's such a common name."

Zachary shrugged. "It makes it harder, but not impossible, if they stayed around. Helps if they stayed together too, but even if they didn't, I might still be able to find them."

"What would you ask them? They won't be able to share anything confidential."

"If I take Burton there, they can talk to him about his own case. Or he can sign a waiver allowing them to talk to me."

"Not sure of that. It's statute protected. They might need to get lawyers involved before they can say anything."

"If it's about a crime that was committed? Abuse and possible murder of another child? I think there's an exception."

Lorne nodded, conceding the point. "Probably. But they still might want to get a lawyer involved just to confirm the fact. People have to be careful these days. Such a litigious society."

"Yeah." Zachary nodded. He pulled out his notepad and wrote down the names before he could forget them, drilling Mr. Peterson to see what he remembered about where they lived, Marty Anderson's profession, and anything else he knew that might help Zachary identify and track them.

"Do you think they'll know anything that will help you with this case, though?" Kenzie asked. "They weren't involved until after Ben was taken out of the home. Social services probably didn't tell them all the details. And they couldn't share things they didn't know."

Zachary rolled his shoulders. "I don't know. They might know something. You never know what Burton might have said to them in the time he was there. Maybe he asked after his brother. Told them a few details. They wouldn't necessarily know that anything had happened to the brother. They might have thought that both boys were recovered and sent to different homes." Zachary looked at Mr. Peterson. "Did you know that it was just one boy? What would you have thought if one of your kids had started talking about a sibling you hadn't been told about?"

"I wouldn't have thought anything of it. Kids come from all kinds of diverse backgrounds. They might have step-siblings, half-siblings, foster siblings, kids that were raised in the same family, facility, compound, whatever. The native kids often refer to their cousins as brothers and sisters. I would have just assumed the other child was apprehended before him, or left and went to a different home with a different parent at some point."

Zachary looked back at Kenzie. "So he might have said something to them and they never even thought to report it."

"I guess so. Hopefully, you can find them and they'll remember something."

32

Dinner at Lorne and Pat's went well, as it almost always did. While it was sometimes awkward or overwhelming if there were too many people there, it was easy when it was just Kenzie, Pat, and Lorne. Zachary could relax around them and not feel like he was in the spotlight or had to put on a show all the time.

The next day was the visit with Joss and Luke, which wasn't nearly as comfortable. Zachary had to be careful of every word he said, worried that Joss would take it the wrong way and be angry or offended. He hoped that one day she would forgive him for his part in the family's breakup and the sequence of events that had happened to her, so he was always trying to make up for it and to play the part of the penitent, perfect brother. But it wasn't a role that he could fill.

He was more distracted this time by Luke and focused on him more than on Joss. Not just because he wanted to know how Luke was and how he was settling in, but how likely he was to reform and stay on the right side of the law, to recover completely from his addictions, and to possibly be someone who would be stable and a good example for Rhys.

It seemed like a long shot.

"Are you… making new friends here?" Zachary tried. He wasn't sure how to find out whether Luke was looking for a new partner and, if he were, whether he had found anyone who suited him. While Luke had been with Madison when Zachary met him, he knew that Luke had, in the past, had relationships with both boys and girls. He had no idea which Luke preferred, if he had a preference.

"Yeah, I'm meeting other people in AA and NA," Luke said casually. "I'm... pretty good at making people like me."

Zachary nodded uncomfortably. Luke's previous life had him luring young people of both sexes into the trafficking business. He was very charming and easy to talk to. He was handsome and had a way of appearing vulnerable and likable.

"Anyone in particular that you really click with?" Zachary still tried to keep the question casual, as if Luke's answer didn't mean anything to him. Just chit-chat. Small talk. Two people marginally connected with each other catching up with the other.

"No..." Luke stared off into space. "I don't know that I want to get involved with anyone at this point. I mean, a hookup, okay, hanging out together or calling when things get tough with the recovery. But someone special...? No. I don't really feel like I can trust anyone at this point. Maybe in the future... when people have had a chance to prove themselves. Right now. I don't really know anyone... *know* them. I don't want to get too close to anyone."

Zachary nodded. "You open yourself up... to being hurt, betrayed."

Luke clicked his tongue. "'Zactly. I'm not ready for anything... personal yet."

Joss cleared her throat. She rocked back in her easy chair, bringing her legs up to a crossed position in front of her. "So what are you doing in these parts? Checking up on us?"

"No... just came to see Lorne and Pat... thought it would be good to see everyone in one trip. Them. You guys. Catch up a bit."

"You didn't bring your girlfriend this time? Mackenzie?"

"Kenzie. I did, actually. She just stayed back at Petersons'. I thought... might be too much of a crowd here."

"How did she feel about that? I bet that went over well, you invite her along and then pawn her off on your friends."

"No, it was her idea, actually. I thought she would come all the way. But she knows me too well. Didn't want to make it more difficult by having to juggle..." Zachary motioned to Joss and Luke and made a third motion to where Kenzie would have been. "Dealing with everyone at once. She didn't want to be…" He couldn't think of the right word. Third wheel? Extra baggage? Nothing sounded respectful and appropriate. There wasn't anything negative about Kenzie being there with him. It might just have been too much for him to focus on, when he was trying so hard to heal his relationship with Jocelyn and evaluate how Luke was settling in and whether he was likely to maintain his new life or fall back into his old ways.

"She's smarter than she looks," Joss said coldly.

"Kenzie's very smart," Zachary told her, not sure how to take that. "She has a doctorate."

"Yeah, but that's book smarts. I'm talking about being people smart. I don't get the feeling she has a lot of experience in… dealing with people like us."

"Well… no. I guess you're right there. But she's trying. And she's been really good for me."

"You're lucky to have her."

"Yeah. I know. Trust me; I count my blessings every day she stays with me."

"Can't be easy for her. We're not exactly the easiest people to get along with."

"No." Zachary rolled his eyes. "She's had to put up with a lot of my crap. I try, but I don't always succeed in being… good relationship material."

Jocelyn blew out her breath. She made a noise in her throat and spoke to Luke. "You should have seen this guy when we were kids. He was always 'trying.' But man, did he like to screw up. There was always something. And it didn't matter what you did, how many times you told him not to do something, he'd always find another way to screw it up, or just plain disobey. Man, he gave me a lot of grief."

Zachary tried to swallow the lump in his throat. "I know, Joss."

"You were the most aggravating kid. You wouldn't believe that someone could want something so bad, and screw it up so royally."

Zachary nodded, unable to think of anything to say in his defense. She knew that he tried.

And he knew that he failed.

Every single time.

"You've been quiet since you got back," Kenzie observed.

They were on the highway again, back on their way home. Zachary was glad to be going home. And glad to be on the road, where he could zone out and not have to think about anything as he drove. It was one of the only times that he could reach what he thought of as a flow state. A time when his brain seemed to stay on track instead of running out of control, and he could stay focused and think things through more easily.

"Just thinking."

"About what? Joss and Luke or the case?"

"A bit of both. Burton's big brother. My big sister. The different ways our lives have taken us."

"Yeah. You lead very different lives. Imagine what yours would have been like if you had been adopted when you were five, and grew up in just one home."

Zachary thought of Burton's nonstop drinking and antisocial behaviors. Zachary had managed to avoid substance abuse. But he had gone off the rails in other areas where Burton seemed to be more secure. What would Zachary's life have been like if he'd been raised in a single stable home after age five, like Burton and Zachary's brother Tyrrell. Would it have helped him? Or would he have still had to deal with the same problems?

And what about if he had spent his first five years locked in a dark, lonely basement instead of growing up in the dysfunctional family he had? While he'd had to deal with violence and neglect in his own home, he'd had five siblings to play with. He'd had the great outdoors to stomp around in and run off his energy in. It had been a completely different start from Burton's.

"Different lives," he acknowledged Kenzie's comment. "I don't know if it would have been better to grow up in just one adoptive home, like he did."

Kenzie raised her eyebrows and looked at him. "Really?"

"I mean… I think that would have been better overall… but it would depend on what the parents were like… and the therapy and everything… I think Burton grew up in a pretty good home, but maybe that doesn't matter with the amount of damage that had already been done. To him. To me. Maybe once you reach a certain threshold… no amount of love and stability can fix you."

He stared at the road, thinking about it. He'd told Rhys that they were alike in that way, both broken inside. And so was Burton. Rhys had a good life with his grandmother, but she'd made her mistakes in the past, and what he'd had to live with the first fourteen years with his mother and his aunt and the loss of his grandfather... was her love and attention now enough to keep him on the right track? Zachary wanted to think that he would be okay. But he'd already seen warning signs. Rhys taking off on his own to go to Zachary's house in the evening, when he wouldn't be able to get back home before dark. Lying to Vera about where he was going and holding things back from Zachary. Now showing an interest in Luke, someone who was not just lost, but dangerous.

"Do you think it can make a difference? After the damage has been done, does anything make a difference?"

Kenzie sighed and looked out her window. "I don't know. I'd like to think so."

33

It wasn't as hard as Mr. Peterson had feared for Zachary to track down Marty and Kathy Anderson. Unfortunately, only Kathy Anderson was still alive. Her husband had died a few years earlier, and Zachary was still trying to figure out by her explanation that he'd been "taken suddenly" whether he had died of disease or accident. Not that it made any difference to his discussion with the widow.

They had introduced themselves at the door. Burton was quiet and more subdued than usual, not drinking openly or being difficult to get along with. All of the emotion he'd shown over Allen's name and what had happened to him was suppressed. He acted as if he remembered none of it. He introduced himself as Ben, one of Kathy's former foster children, and she hadn't shown any recognition at first. They'd fostered a lot of kids over the years. She had probably had others show up at her door in the past. She couldn't be expected to remember all of them.

They sat down in her tidy living room and made small talk for a while, Zachary saying more to Mrs. Anderson than Burton did. He asked about her home, how long they had fostered, and anything else he could think of that would make her comfortable and put her at ease before the more uncomfortable questions that would follow.

Eventually, there was no way to avoid it, and Zachary took the plunge.

"Ben's name when he was here as a foster child was Bobby Weaver. Do you remember that name?"

"We've had more than one Bobby," Kathy said thoughtfully, digging back deep into her memory. "Bobby Weaver…"

"He came to you after a very negligent home," Zachary went on. "He was quite thin and malnourished."

"He wouldn't be the only one." Kathy closed her eyes briefly. "Yes… Bobby. That was…" she looked at Burton for a moment, and then away, careful not to stare. "He'd—you'd—been kept in a basement."

Burton nodded.

"Oh, yes. I remember Bobby." Kathy Anderson's chin lifted as she thought back to it. What she had known at the time. Maybe other things she had learned since. It had been a big deal when he had been put into her home.

"I've heard that he was pretty quiet," Zachary said. "And he would only have been with you for a few months before he was placed with his adoptive parents."

"Yes. That's right. All of that is right."

"He wasn't disruptive?"

"Oh, no," Mrs. Anderson gave a short laugh and shook her head. "On the contrary. He had to be pushed into any new experience. Encouraged to try new things. To experiment. He was very quiet and would just sit there if you didn't get him doing something."

"And did he like… animals?" Zachary tried.

"Oh, yes. He was a bit scared. Especially with dogs that were loud or moved quickly. But gentler animals, yes, definitely. And his bugs!" Her eyes lit on Burton once more. "You probably don't remember how obsessed you were with bugs."

Burton gave an embarrassed grin. "Actually, yes. I do remember. They were… my whole world. Always trying to catch them, looking for something new."

She nodded agreement. "Yes. I never knew what I would find when I went into your room. You had jars, but sometimes there were escapees. Or sometimes, maybe, you didn't put them into jars in the first place."

Burton scratched the back of his neck, smiling. "Maybe." He admitted. "I didn't like them to be trapped."

They all sat and thought about that for a few moments. They all knew what Burton's experience with being trapped in on small room had been.

"Could Bobby read or write?" Zachary asked.

"No. He didn't have any reading readiness skills. We taught him the alphabet. Things like shapes and colors that he wasn't familiar with. Reading through books like *Richard Scarry's Cars and Trucks and Things that Go* to learn about things that were out there in the world that he had never experienced. And feeding therapy."

"Feeding therapy?"

Kathy looked at Burton, verifying with her gaze that it was okay for her to talk about it. Burton nodded.

"Normally, you start toddlers on soft, smooth foods, and then work your way up to different textures and learning to chew things properly. You expose them to a wide range of foods so that even picky kids have a lot of options to choose from and can stay healthy. Bobby had a lot of sensory defensiveness. He didn't like different textures or strong flavors. He had probably only been given pablum or oatmeal, or maybe some soups. So he would gag or spit food out a lot. We thought at first that he was sick, that there was something wrong with his stomach. But it was just that he wasn't used to eating what a normal child would."

Zachary made a couple of notes. Who could help but feel sorry for the little boy who had been so neglected he didn't even know how to eat properly?

"He was very quick to make up for lost time," Kathy said. "He was very curious about things and learned fast."

"So he couldn't write his own name?"

"No. Not when he came to us. It took a few days to teach him how, when he'd learned his alphabet and spent some time developing the fine motor skills for drawing and writing."

"Do you remember him ever talking about a brother?"

"A brother?" Kathy looked puzzled. "No. I don't think we knew about any brother."

"Allen," Burton said.

She looked at him, her brows drawn down. "Allen," she repeated.

They both waited for it to register, for her to access any memories she might have of the name. She shook her head slowly. Then, "Allen?" she said again.

Burton nodded.

"Let me think."

She got up from her seat and went over to a bookcase where there were volumes and volumes of large books. She ran a finger over them, looking at the spines. Then finally pulled one out. She sat back down next to Burton, and Zachary saw when she opened it that it was a book of photos.

"Do you want to see a picture of you when you came to us?"

Burton nodded wordlessly.

Kathy flipped pages until she found it, then pointed. Zachary didn't have a good vantage point, but he could see the small figure in the middle of the pictures. A little waif of a boy. All alone in the middle of the picture.

"This is the day you came."

Zachary looked at the pages of pictures, and the volumes of books on the shelf. "You took a picture of every child on the first day?"

"Once you've had a child run the day he's dropped off... yes. You don't ever again want to call the police and not have any pictures of the child you are trying to report missing."

Zachary nodded. Very practical. Kathy gazed down at the picture of little Ben. Except he'd been Bobby, then. Bobby Weaver, just rescued from where he'd been held in the cold, dark basement all of his life. Or at least, a good portion of it.

"Allen," she said again. "Allen was your brother?"

Burton cleared his throat. "I think... he was."

"But he wasn't with you when you... escaped that place. When the police went and arrested those... those horrible people."

"I don't know what happened to him. I'm trying to remember. To find out. And if I ever mentioned him to you... maybe the police will agree to look."

She gazed at him blankly. "Look? Look where?"

"In the basement."

"But they looked in the basement."

Burton looked at Zachary.

"We... would like them to see if there are any remains. If he was buried there."

"Buried in a basement?"

"There was a dirt floor."

"Oh." She shook her head sadly. "Oh, I hope not..."

Burton looked down at the picture of himself. So long ago. So small and forlorn.

"What do you remember about him?" Kathy asked.

"Not very much. He was there with me. He told me stories. Tried to protect me."

Burton touched the picture tentatively, as if doing so might help bring the memories back. Had they looked similar, as brothers often do? Maybe seeing his own face back then would help to trigger a memory, bring another fragment of it back.

"We know that he could write," Zachary said. "The boys' names were written on the wall. Bobby and Allen. If Bobby couldn't write them, then it must have been Allen."

"And he was older," Kathy discerned. "Because he had been taught how and Bobby hadn't. Maybe he even went to school at some point."

Zachary nodded. It was an avenue that he hadn't pursued, on the assumption that neither boy had ever seen the inside of a school. But who had taught Allen how to write? Their mother? A woman who didn't even seem to care about feeding her children properly? Why would she take the time to teach him his letters?

And if he had gone to school, what name would his records have been in?

"Do you know what their real name was?" he asked Kathy Anderson. "The name Ben went by was Bobby Weaver, but that wasn't their right name, was it? They were just trying to stay below the radar, taking on a pseudonym."

"Oh, yes. You're right. Bobby came into the system as Weaver, and we just left it at that. His birth hadn't been registered before then, and we didn't want there to be a connection between him and his parents. Particularly when he got into school. We didn't want any of the other children making that connection."

"Do you remember what their name was?"

"I might remember if you give me a few minutes." Kathy put her fingers to her temples and rubbed them, closing her eyes and concentrating. "Oh… O' something. It was so long ago, but of course we followed the story, because it impacted our family so directly."

Opening her eyes, she placed a tentative hand on Burton's shoulder. He swallowed and gave her a forced smile. Zachary wondered whether he remembered her at all. He had lived with her only a few months. Did he have good feelings about her, even if he didn't remember her clearly? Or had it been such a confusing, traumatic change that his feelings about that time had been negative?

There was no telling how the woman, despite her appearance of kindly compassion, had treated him in the time he had been there. She might have been gentle and encouraging, or she might have been a strict hard-liner. Or both. Sometimes the ones who flip-flopped were the most difficult of all.

"Dougherty," Kathy said suddenly. "That was it. Doughertys."

"Did you know their first names? Were they the same, or had they taken on different first names too?"

"I think they were the same. What were they?"

Zachary didn't answer immediately. "Do you want me to tell you? Or were you trying to remember?"

"Elizabeth. And Sam?"

"Then they kept the same names." That would, at least, mean that Zachary could look them up at the courthouse and see what had come out in the trials. And he could check to see if there were a birth certificate or any kind of announcement or social security claim for an Allen Dougherty. It was highly unlikely that he had survived and was still alive out there somewhere. It was always possible that he'd been pawned off on another family and ended up in the system, but the chances that Zachary would be able to find any records of him were slim to none. Chances were, Allen had never left that basement.

But Burton might have extended family out there who were decent people. Cousins, aunts and uncles, grandparents. Just because his parents had been pieces of crap, that didn't mean that everyone related to them was.

34

Zachary had worried that it would be hard to get Burton out of his old foster home. That he would be so happy to have some link to his old life that he wouldn't be able to leave Kathy Anderson behind.

But it had turned out not to be a problem. Even as Zachary was still asking Kathy more questions about what Burton had been like while he had been there and to ferret out any clues she might have that she didn't even know she had, Burton was making noises about wanting to go. He wanted a drink, Zachary knew. He wanted to wash everything away, to forget about his former life, foster mother included, and not to have to talk about it anymore. He was no longer the little boy in the picture.

Or maybe he was, and that was the problem.

He stood and motioned to the door, hurrying Zachary along.

Zachary rolled his eyes and followed him. "I'll call you if I need anything else," he told Kathy. Now that he had her information, he could circle back when he needed to. She had seen that Burton was fine with his information being shared with Zachary, and they could continue the conversation privately, without him shifting around and breathing noisily, like a six hundred pound gorilla in the middle of the room.

"Sure. Thank you for coming. It's always good to see one of our old kids again…"

Burton was hurrying out the door toward Zachary's car. He shrugged at Kathy. "Sorry. It's all been pretty difficult for him."

"Yes… I'm not surprised. We haven't had many that have come from such terrible situations."

Not many.

Just that phrase was shocking. It should have been 'he's the only one.'

But Zachary had heard of and read too many stories about children being the victims of such horrific neglect or abuse it was almost beyond belief. Some of them survived. Some did not. And of the ones who did survive, how many were too broken to ever fully recover?

Zachary followed Burton out to the car and clicked the key fob to unlock the door for him. Burton climbed in without a word and shut his door, isolating himself in a quiet bubble of space. Zachary took his time walking to the car and around to his door. Long enough for Burton to take a few breaths to steady himself.

Or, as Zachary saw when he opened the door and slid into his seat, a few belts from his flask. He didn't say anything.

"Don't act all judgy with me," Burton snapped. "You've got no idea what it's like."

Zachary knew how overwhelming his own issues were, how difficult it was for him to deal with flashbacks or to deal with reunions with his own family members. He didn't judge Burton for how he chose to handle it. That was his own business. Was spending most of his time drunk better or worse than having a complete meltdown? Or attempting suicide? There were just some things that were too harrowing for people with normal, unremarkable pasts to understand. There was no polite, conventional way to deal with the cruelties that Burton had survived.

Zachary was so deep into his investigations that he was barely aware that Kenzie was there. He should have put his computer aside and spent some quality time with her, but he'd felt like he couldn't leave what he was doing. He was startled when she sat down next to him and touched him on the arm. He looked at her, then looked at the system clock on his computer.

"Oh… sheesh, I'm sorry, Kenzie. I was… sort of focused on what I was doing."

"Sort of?" she teased.

"Uh... have I ignored you all night? Did we eat?"

"I ate." Kenzie looked to Zachary's side, and he saw a piece of pizza with a bite or two out of the tip congealing on a plate on the side table where he must have laid it down and promptly forgotten about it.

"Really. I'm sorry."

She slid her arm around him and snuggled in close. "When I was in school and we covered learning disabilities, I never really understood what they were talking about when they said that ADHD wasn't the inability to pay attention to something, but to regulate your attention in the usual way. It sounded like it was just semantics. They did say that people with ADHD sometimes hyperfocus. On things like video games or areas of particular interest. It sounded like an ADHD diagnosis was just an excuse for not doing your work, but playing games or doing what you liked instead."

Zachary nodded and rubbed his neck. He'd clearly been bent over his laptop in the wrong position for some time. He would probably have a stiff neck for days. "Hyperfocus," he agreed.

"You are the king of hyperfocus."

"I didn't mean to ignore you."

"It's a compliment. I know you're doing work, not just messing around on social networks. Your ability to dig in like that... that's what makes you such a good investigator. One of the things."

Zachary wasn't used to having his dysregulation complimented. If it had been Bridget he'd ignored all night... even for just ten minutes...

"So, have you made progress?" Kenzie asked. She reached around him to grab his plate and took a bite of his cold pizza. Then she handed it to him, and he knew he was supposed to finish it. He took a couple of bites. It was good; he just didn't feel like eating.

"I did find a birth certificate for Allen Dougherty. I think that, together with the fact that both the social worker and the foster mother agree that Burton could not have written the names Bobby and Allen on the wall, will be enough for the police to pursue a warrant."

"How much older was Allen?"

"Four years older than Bobby. Or Ben. He probably attended a year or two of school before... before whatever it was that happened that resulted in Bobby and Allen being imprisoned in the basement."

"You think there was a... trigger? An inciting event?"

"Maybe. Sometimes there's a specific incident that makes people start treating their children differently. They probably weren't great parents before that, but Allen knew how to read and write, and Bobby didn't. I think… maybe something happened in between."

"Maybe not. Maybe it was just a gradual descent into depression, abuse, addiction."

Zachary shrugged. "Maybe. I've ordered copies of the court transcripts, but I don't know how long it will take to get them. Maybe there will be something in there that will tell their story. They must have had something to say in their defense… some sob story. People like this don't take responsibility for their own behavior. They always blame it on someone else."

"Yeah, I've met people like that."

"I'm going to see if I can work out a family tree, too. If they have family in the area. Grandparents might speak up if they are asked now about Allen. Even if it's just to say that they don't know when he disappeared or what happened to him. They can at least verify that he existed. That they had seen him at some time."

"Are you going to be able to do that?"

"Dougherty is not a common name. Not uncommon, but if they have been in Vermont for a while, I might be able to find some obituaries or other information that will help me to build a family tree."

"How long did his parents serve?"

Zachary had been looking at his computer again, going through the information he had been able to collate on Allen and the parents. It wasn't much more than names and dates, but there were, at least, official records to back up the story that they had been trying to construct. He looked at Kenzie quickly.

"What?"

"How long did Ben's parents serve in prison? How much time?" When he didn't answer, she raised her brows. "What were their sentences?"

Zachary blinked. In his mind, anyone who did what Elizabeth and Sam Dougherty had done deserved to stay in prison for the rest of their lives. But he hadn't come across that detail yet. The news reports had been sparse to nonexistent, and neither the social worker nor Kathy had mentioned how long the Doughertys had been sentenced to serve, or even what they had been convicted of.

Murderers got out of prison. Not the worst ones, maybe, but plenty of people who had served time for murder got out after twenty years and continued their lives. Burton's parents had been convicted decades earlier. If they had killed Allen, no one had known it at the time, and at most they had been convicted of child abuse and negligence. Not likely to be life sentences.

He swore under his breath.

Kenzie sighed and nodded. "I doubt they're still in prison," she said gently.

"After all they did to that little boy? People knew what they had done and they wouldn't put them away for life? How could they be out when he is still suffering?"

"Yeah. It's not very fair, is it?"

"No." Zachary rubbed his fist against his forehead, fighting the impulse to beat it against his head. "No, no, no."

She put her arm around him and squeezed him to her. "I know."

Zachary leaned into her.

He knew that there was no justice for kids who were abused. While he blamed himself for the fire that had burned the family home down, and for all of the things he had done that had driven his mother to abandon them, he knew that his parents had been abusive. It took a lot of years in therapy to finally accept that the abuse had not been his fault. He had not brought that on himself. They had drunk too much, and they had hurt each other and their children.

The things that their mother had expected—for the older girls to look after the younger ones, for them to all stay out from underfoot, and for them to generally fend for themselves—had been unrealistic and unfair. Children didn't raise themselves. And yes, they made messes and got into mischief and had accidents. Even if Zachary had gotten into more than his fair share of trouble, that didn't justify beatings.

And not buying food or feeding the children much of the time hadn't just been a matter of poverty. There were programs available to help. But money had gone toward alcohol and other vices instead of food, food stamps had been bartered for other things, and if children were sent to bed hungry, they'd better not have the nerve to cry about it.

His parents had never gone to jail longer than overnight, usually for brawling so loudly that the neighbors had called the police. They'd never gone to prison for abuse or neglect. While Zachary and the others suffered through hardships in foster care, his parents had… done what? They hadn't stepped up to take responsibility.

Zachary had never investigated to see where they had gone after abandoning the children. Had they stayed together and eventually killed each other? Gone their separate ways and started two more families? He didn't imagine that they had reformed. That would not be consistent with the behavior he had observed as a child.

So he knew there was no justice for children like him and his siblings. The system had failed them. He only hoped that the youngest children had fared better. Tyrrell had gone through some tough times, but he said that he had been able to stay with the younger ones until he was a teenager, at least. He hadn't told Zachary much about Vince and Mindy, but he mentioned them now and then and Zachary knew they were still in touch through email. One day, maybe he'd meet them and find out their stories.

"They couldn't just let them out," he told Kenzie.

But he knew it wasn't true. He just wanted it to be true. He wanted to help Burton to recover, to be able to reconcile with his past, as horrific as it was. He wanted Allen to rest in peace, and maybe for Burton to be able to connect with extended family. The idea that the people who had forced him to live like an animal in a pen were walking around free was just too much.

"Maybe it's time to put all of this aside and relax for a while before bed," Kenzie suggested.

"Yeah. I'll clean up." But Zachary didn't move. He stayed leaning against Kenzie, taking comfort in her warm, soft body molded against his. He didn't want to move.

She rubbed his back in circles, not pushing him to tidy his things away or telling him he had to finish eating his pizza and put the plate in the dishwasher. He closed his eyes and just felt what it was like to be with her.

35

He didn't remember anything that happened after that. Probably not much actually happened. They just cuddled and talked quietly about things other than Burton and his abusive parents walking around free like they'd never done anything wrong. He must have cleaned up at some time and they had gone to bed, because that was where he found himself at two o'clock in the morning, wide awake after another nightmare.

"It's okay," Kenzie murmured sleepily, giving him a hug and a kiss on the cheek before falling back asleep with her head on his chest.

He stared into the darkness, trying to focus on the good things. On how nice it was to be there with her and have her comforting him. To lie there with her asleep on his chest, all warm and cozy. That he was in a better relationship now than he'd ever been in with Bridget, even in those early, honeymoon days.

He tried not to think about Bridget, when that was the subject that kept rising to the surface.

Kenzie had suggested before that when Zachary had dreamed about twins, it had been because of Bridget. Knowing that she was expecting multiples weighed heavily on his mind when he had wanted so desperately to have children with her himself. If he could change things around so that he was the one with Bridget and so that both Gordon and Kenzie had partners who made them happy and satisfied… and if the babies that Bridget was carrying were his and Bridget's, conceived in a loving, tender moment. Or in a lab after Bridget's fight with cancer, he didn't care.

He just couldn't let go of that dream.

He should have been thinking about his nightmare instead of the dreams he'd had with Bridget. Twin boys again, not four years apart like Allen and Bobby. Twin boys, both looking exactly like Bobby had in the picture that Kathy had taken. Except that they were dressed in clothes that hung off their bodies in rags. Like zombies in a B-movie. But they hadn't been zombies, they had been children. Children that Zachary had forgotten about, left alone and neglected when it was his responsibility to keep them fed.

He didn't know how anyone could do that. How had Elizabeth and Sam Dougherty consigned their children to the dungeon beneath their house while they walked around above, clothed and well-fed, free to come and go as they pleased, living out a perfectly normal life in a neighborhood that knew nothing about what was going on? How could they act like normal people when their children languished in the basement?

Had they ever felt that sickening guilt that Zachary had felt when he woke up, left over from the dream, still reaching out to help them before they dissolved from reality? Had they ever felt one twist of guilt and regret over what they had done? Or had they only felt like victims, sure that everybody else was out to get them, misjudging them, not understanding that it wasn't really their fault at all?

He shifted, trying to find a more comfortable position. Kenzie's head was grinding against his sternum, a bone that had been broken more than once before and was letting him know it with flares of pain. He loved having her against him; he just needed her to move a little bit to ease the pain radiating from his chest into his ribs.

"Are you okay?" Kenzie murmured. She hugged him, moving closer to his shoulder. Zachary breathed and rubbed his sternum tenderly.

"Yeah."

"Can't sleep?"

"No. But it's okay. Go back to sleep."

"I'm okay. I don't mind staying up with you for a bit."

"You need your sleep."

"So do you. You want to talk for a few minutes? Would it help?"

"No. I don't think so. I'm just… restless."

"You had a dream?"

"Yeah."

He wondered if he'd cried out in his sleep. He knew he could be pretty loud when he was fighting his demons.

"What about?"

"Nothing. The fire," he lied, not wanting to tell her it had been twins again, and to think that he was pining after Bridget. He was devoted to Kenzie. Bridget had her own life now. Another man in it. Another man's babies growing inside her.

He felt suddenly nauseated and lurched up to a sitting position.

"Zachary?"

Zachary knew it was too late to calm his body. After getting his feet free of the covers, he made a dash for the ensuite bathroom and reached the toilet just in time. He hit the floor on his knees. It was a long time before the vomiting and retching ceased and he was able to rest his head for a moment and try to catch his breath.

Kenzie waited until he had splashed water on his face and rinsed his mouth and blown his nose. Then she tapped on the door he had slammed behind him. "Are you okay? You got a bug?"

"I'm fine." Zachary wiped his mouth and nose with toilet paper, trying to eliminate all evidence of being sick. He rinsed his mouth with mouthwash. "Sorry, it's okay. Just go back to sleep."

"I'm worried about you. Is it something you ate?" She laughed at herself. "Of course it wasn't something you ate; you barely touched your dinner."

Zachary shut off the light before pushing the door open, so as not to blind her. Instead, he was nearly blind himself. Kenzie put a sympathetic hand on his arm.

"Probably just my meds."

"If they're making you sick, you should talk to the doctor about adjusting them. Lower the dosage or look at a different medication."

"Most of the time it's okay; I just get nauseated. Just this time…"

She stroked his arm and guided him back toward the bed.

And then the car alarm sounded.

36

Zachary froze for an instant. And then he was to the bedroom window, sure that it was his alarm sounding. Even as he took the few strides to the window, he knew he would get there and there would be no reason for his anxiety. It would be someone else's car, a proximity sensor that was too sensitive and had been set off by a tree blowing in the wind or an animal. Nothing to panic about.

But when he peered between the slats of the blinds, he saw that it was his car. The lights had come on as well as the siren blaring. And his alarm was not a proximity sensor. It was a break-in alarm that would only be set off by someone lifting the handle, putting a key in the lock without disarming it first, or breaking the glass.

There was a man standing beside the car. Zachary didn't recognize him. He was too far away to be sure of the details, but he seemed to be an older man. In his sixties or seventies, but the type who still looked vigorous and strong. A tough guy Zachary would not want to tangle with or come face to face with in a dark alley.

"Zachary?"

"Can you hand me my phone?"

He could hear Kenzie moving around behind him. She picked up his phone and handed it to him. "Is there someone there?"

The man was already moving away and, by the time Zachary got his phone turned on and switched into camera mode, there was not much to see but the man's retreating form. There was no point in calling 9-1-1; he would be long gone by the time the police managed to get there.

He lowered his phone and watched the man disappear from sight.

"Who was it, did you see?" Kenzie asked when he turned around. "What happened?"

"No one I recognized. A man. Trying to get into my car or messing with it. I need to go out and take a look."

"It could be dangerous."

"He's gone. It's fine."

"He could come back. He could have a partner."

Zachary turned and watched out the window for another minute. But he couldn't see any other sign of life. "I'll be careful."

"It's times like this that I wish you carried."

"A gun doesn't help in a situation like this. Like you said, he could have a partner, and they could be armed. Me walking out there with a gun would just escalate things. If I'm not armed, I'm less likely to be shot. Besides… well *you* know…" He couldn't vouch for his own safety with a gun in the house.

Kenzie sighed and didn't argue it any further. "You could at least take a baseball bat. A kitchen knife."

Zachary looked out the window one last time. "There's no one out there."

Before she could argue any further, he headed for the front door. Kenzie disarmed the burglar alarm. He slipped his shoes on without untying them and they flopped under his heels as he walked up to his car. He looked around him carefully, then examined the car. No glass was broken. So the man must have tried to open the doors or messed with it in some other way. Zachary clicked his fob to disarm the security system and unlock the doors, and had a quick look inside. Nothing appeared to have been touched.

It was too dark to see anything underneath the car; he'd have to take it to Jergens his mechanic for a quick look before he did any driving around. He brought up his bug sweeping app on his phone, but it didn't detect any radio transmissions or magnetic distortion. Other than the vehicle recovery module he'd installed himself. If the man had put a tracker on the car, it wasn't transmitting yet.

Zachary locked the car and rearmed the security system. He returned to the house. Kenzie had pulled on her robe and was waiting for him, arms crossed and looking anxious. Her phone was in her hand. Ready to place an emergency call if something went wrong.

"Everything is fine," he assured her. "I'm okay." He looked down at himself as he kicked off his shoes. It might have made sense to pull something on before going outside in his boxers. He cleared his throat, face warm.

"You think it was just a random thing? Someone checking for unlocked cars or something valuable left on a seat?"

"Probably." But Zachary's mind went back to the motorcyclist who had followed him. First a tail, and now someone trying to break into his car? It was probably just a coincidence, but he didn't like coincidences.

"It's not like you're hunting some serial killer." Kenzie gave a weak laugh. "Not this time."

"No. Burton is probably my biggest case right now, and that's something that happened decades ago. I can't see how I could have stirred anything up with my inquiries."

"And it isn't the guys who had Madison? It could be, couldn't it?"

"It's possible, but I can't see why they'd have any interest in me since Madison and Noah are both supposed to be dead. Or why they would come here and then not do anything. If it was those guys... there probably would have been bullets through the door."

Kenzie seemed reassured by this. "Yeah."

Zachary approached Kenzie and offered a hug. She cuddled into his arms, and he gave her a reassuring hug. She had tried to calm him earlier, and now it was his turn to make her feel better. "Let's get you back to bed."

"You too."

Zachary shook his head. "I'm going to... keep an eye on things."

"You said he won't come back."

"And he won't. But I won't be able to get back to sleep. I'll just keep you up. Better if I keep myself busy."

"I don't know if I'll be able to either."

"You will." He gave her a nudge in the direction of the bedroom, and they walked down the hall together.

Kenzie climbed into bed, and Zachary sat on the edge.

"Are you going to read me a bedtime story?" Kenzie teased.

"Shh. No more questions. It's time for sleep. Be a good girl."

Kenzie closed her eyes, holding his hand. "Reminds me of putting Amanda to bed," she murmured.

Zachary didn't say anything, waiting for sleep to take her.

37

Zachary made the decision to reach out to Elizabeth Dougherty's parents to see if they could be of any help. He figured that between the two parents, Elizabeth was the more sympathetic figure and her family would be more likely to help him if he showed some compassion toward her and claimed to want to hear her side of the story.

What he really wanted, of course, was information about Allen. Had they known about him? Had they seen him? Did they know what had happened to him? Hopefully, whatever they could provide, together with the little bit of information that Zachary had with Allen's birth certificate and the few details they knew would be enough to convince the police to try for a warrant to search the house, including breaking up the basement floor. They had x-rays or radar they could use to look through concrete, so they might be able to see whether there was anything down there before beginning.

Elizabeth Dougherty had been born Elizabeth Johnson. Her parents, Sylvester and Edith, were still alive, as far as Zachary could tell. He didn't call ahead, but went to their door and rang the doorbell. It was a pleasant little house. Not the best neighborhood, but not the worst, either. Better than the one Elizabeth had lived in with Sam, Allen, and Bobby. She had, presumably, grown up there or in a similar house.

A woman came to the door after a couple of doorbell rings, opening it slowly and peering out at Zachary. She was bent and white-haired, but her eyes seemed clear and alert. "Yes? Who are you?"

"Mrs. Johnson, my name is Zachary Goldman. I'm here to ask some questions about Elizabeth and her children."

Her face was immediately shuttered. She started to push the door closed. "No comment."

"I'm not a reporter." Zachary put his hand against the door. She could still shut it, but it did stall her for a split-second. "I know Bobby."

She stared at him. Eventually, she opened the door again and motioned for him to enter. Zachary was directed to the living room and sat down. He looked around. Books. Displays of china. Pretty furniture. A feminine, grandmotherly room. Little male influence, if any. Edith didn't say that her husband would be joining them or that he was lying down. The doors to the closet at the front door were closed, so he couldn't see if there were any men's clothing or shoes.

Edith sat down in an upholstered chair. "You know Bobby?"

"His name now is Ben. He came looking for the house he grew up in. He's been… unraveling his story, trying to remember what happened and to put it all together. I'm helping him with that, and I thought you might be able to answer some of his questions."

"I didn't have anything to do with any of that business. I don't know anything."

"What do you think it would be like, not to know the things that had happened to you when you were younger, in a different life? You would still react to things, but not have any idea why. You would have vague, shadowy memories, visceral reactions, but not know any of your origins. Your heritage."

"I can't help any of that."

"You can, because you can provide some of the pieces he is missing. Not everything, maybe, but you can still help him. He wants to know more about what happened. About the family he came from."

"Why would he want to know about anything that happened back then? It was horrible business. Nothing that anyone should have to hear, let alone go through. That poor boy. To have something like that in your family…" She shook her head, looking angry. "It's a black spot on our name."

"I know it is. Maybe we can start this from another direction, and that would make it easier. You haven't had any contact with Bobby, of course, with all that happened. Social Services never offered kinship care?"

"No. They never tried to contact us. Never tried to place him with family."

"I guess in a case like this… they wanted to make a clean break. Make sure that Elizabeth and Sam would never have any more contact with him."

Edith shrugged.

"What about Allen? Had you met him?"

Edith's eyes widened. "Allen?"

"Bobby's older brother. That was his name, wasn't it?"

She nodded automatically.

"Mrs. Johnson," Zachary leaned toward her slightly. "What happened to Allen? Do you know?"

She looked around the room, not meeting his eyes. Zachary waited. It was awful for him to expect her to answer questions like this about her own child and grandchild. To admit to what had happened and the fact that they had not been able to stop it.

"We kept expecting someone to talk about him. To say what had happened… but no one ever mentioned him. It was like he had disappeared off the face of the earth."

Zachary had been afraid she was going to relate some fiction about Allen being adopted by another family, maybe informally. She would claim he was still alive out there somewhere; they just weren't sure where he had ended up.

The clean break was better. They had known about him, and then he had disappeared and no one had ever mentioned him again.

"Did you ask Social Services about him? You must have been confused."

"We asked… once… but they looked at me like they didn't have any idea what I was talking about. I didn't mention it again. I hoped… I didn't want to know… I wanted it to be a happy ending. And if I asked them… then it wouldn't be."

"So you never asked the authorities again."

"No."

"What about Elizabeth?"

Edith's lips pressed together.

"Did you ask Elizabeth what had happened to Allen?"

She swallowed and looked down at the carpet, staring at it as if mesmerized. "No. I never did."

He didn't need to ask why. She wanted to believe to herself that her other little grandson was still out there, somewhere, healthy and strong, living a happy life.

Like Bobby.

Except that Burton's life wasn't happy either. It should have been. He'd had good parents after that initial five years. They had given him everything he had needed. They had been loving and kind and pleasant. They had, by all accounts, done everything right. But Burton needed more. He needed to know his past to become an integral person. He had to know the past to move into the present and to see past the bottle in his hand into the future.

"Did you meet Allen?"

She smiled, the sun bursting through the clouds. "Oh, yes. He was a lovely baby and little boy. Such a sweet little fellow."

"And… when did things change? When did you notice that something was wrong?"

"We had a falling-out… a series of fallings-out, really. Sam was… not well. He was making strange choices. Always paranoid. Like he really did think that people were after him, talking about him. He was sometimes violent. Elizabeth and Allen would have bruises. They never admitted that he hit them, but what other explanation is there? They came over less and less, and it didn't matter what we said to Elizabeth, we couldn't convince her to leave him, to go somewhere safe."

"It had to be her own choice."

"Yes. And she wasn't going to listen to her mother. She always was the rebellious sort, didn't like to be told what to do. She knew better than her mother. She was an adult and could live her own life."

Zachary nodded. Independent. Dysfunctional. Butting heads with her parents who didn't think she was safe staying with her boyfriend or husband. She knew him, they didn't. So she had let herself stay in a bad situation, thinking she could change Sam, help him or fix him, or that if she just made all of the right choices, he wouldn't blow up at her. If she could just get things right.

"So they disappeared from your life when Allen was…"

Edith shook her head. "It must have been around the time she got pregnant with Bobby. She wouldn't return calls. They moved and didn't let us know their new address. We couldn't contact her at all. She just disappeared."

"And you didn't hear anything about her until five or six years later?"

"I don't know." Edith avoided his eyes and shook her head. "Then we were hearing about this boy they had found, this boy in terrible condition, horribly neglected, held in a basement. They didn't have the names right. Sam had talked her into taking a different name. But as soon as we saw their pictures on TV, I knew it was her." Edith put her hands over her eyes, reliving the horror of it. "Oh, that poor, poor boy. I couldn't believe that she could do anything so cruel. I've never seen anything like that before."

She had undoubtedly seen pictures of starving children before, but always in other countries, other contexts, not where she'd been so personally connected with what had happened.

"Did you see Elizabeth after that? Or did you stay away?"

"It was a while before I saw her. She was in jail, then in prison."

"And did you talk to her about what she had done?"

"She said it wasn't so bad." Edith's voice grew lighter, apparently imitating Elizabeth's answers. "She said it had all been exaggerated. She hadn't done anything to hurt Bobby. He had food and shelter. All of his needs were taken care of. What business was it of anyone else what room he had slept in? What difference did that make?"

"He just… slept in the basement? That was her answer?"

"More or less. She said it was all just an exaggeration. People trying to make her bad so that the jury would send her to prison. I couldn't stomach it." Edith shook her head. "It made me physically sick. I couldn't bear her excuses."

Zachary remembered being sick the night before at the thought of Bridget's twins. They hadn't even been born yet and he was worried about them. Bridget didn't have a great track record for being a kind, loving person. She might be a wonderful mother toward them. But he was familiar with the sharp edge of her tongue. He'd been faced with it too many times.

"It must be pretty upsetting, knowing that your daughter could do something like that."

"Yes. I thought we would go to the trial to begin with. Show our support. Be there every day. But I couldn't listen to it. I couldn't keep going, knowing what she had done. And that she wasn't…" She bit her lip. "She wasn't innocent. She was not locked down there with him. Them. She never called for help or to take him away to somewhere safe. She was… a participant. Not just a woman who was abused and trying to avoid getting hurt again."

Zachary nodded. He could understand how hard it must be, even though he'd never been in that situation. He knew how hard it could be to believe that someone close to you was not what you thought they were. To have those buried layers revealed and exposed to the light of day.

"So if you didn't attend the trial, you don't know if they ever mentioned Allen?"

"They didn't. If they had, it would have been in the news. There would have been more charges, more police investigation. No one knew about little Allen."

And she hadn't stepped forward to tell about him. She had been willing to ignore what had happened to him to spare her daughter the additional charges and prison time. While Zachary knew it couldn't have been an easy decision, he had a hard time understanding how she could have made the one she did.

Because she loved her daughter.

Despite everything she had done.

"Now that Bobby knows about Allen… it may come out. You'll need to be prepared for that."

Edith stared at Zachary. "Why would you do that? You can't… it was so long ago. What would be the point of making it public now? Let Allen rest… wherever he is. What good would it do to say anything?"

"No one has had to pay for what happened to Allen."

"But no one knows what happened."

"Someone does. Several people do. And they think they got away with it."

She shook her head in disbelief. "You can't do that… just out of revenge. It has nothing to do with you."

"How long did Elizabeth end up serving? Do you know where she is now?"

Edith turned her head toward the hallway at the sound of running water. Her husband was apparently up from his nap or whatever he'd been doing when she answered the door. Zachary glanced at the time on his phone, trying to plan the next few things he would have to do to get the ball rolling with the police department.

There were footsteps in the hallway. Quiet, for a man.

"Mom? Is there someone here?"

38

A woman walked into the living room and looked at Zachary, her brows drawing down. Zachary got to his feet, shocked into action. He didn't know if Edith had more than one daughter, but she had looked toward the hallway when Zachary had asked where Elizabeth was. It had to be her.

"I was just on my way out," he told her. "Mrs. Johnson, it was nice to meet you. Thank you for your help."

Elizabeth was staring at him. She looked out the living room window at his car parked out on the street, then back to him again.

She was in her fifties. Younger than her husband. He was more the age of the man who Zachary had seen trying to break into his car the night before. Zachary took a few steps toward the door, feeling like his feet were on some kind of time delay. He always felt awkward when he had to change his pace or walk backward, ever since a spinal injury shortly after he had met Kenzie. After their first date, actually.

He was tripping over his feet to get to the door before Elizabeth could get through the thought process clearly taking place. He had no idea what her reaction to his presence there would be.

Nothing in his research had pointed to Elizabeth living at the same address as her parents. There had been a few possible addresses, all of them probably places she'd rented in the previous couple of years, moving from one place to another.

And now she was back to living with her mother.

And Sam? Where was he?

Zachary reached the door and twisted the doorknob.

"Hey!"

He ignored Elizabeth's shout and kept going.

"Who are you? What do you think you're doing here?"

He moved as quickly as he could, his toes hitting cracks in the sidewalk two strides in a row so that he was sure he was going to trip and fall flat on his face. But he managed to recover and keep his balance. He didn't know whether to watch the sidewalk in front of him to avoid any further cracks, or to focus on his car, his goal, all the way down the sidewalk and a few vehicles down the street.

Elizabeth didn't follow him, but stayed behind to talk to her mother. Until, apparently, Edith told her what Zachary had been there for, and then she let out a shriek.

Zachary couldn't run, but he did his best, bounding toward his car at his top pace.

He really needed to spend some time with a physiotherapist learning how to run again. He felt like an ungainly giraffe.

Elizabeth came out of the house. Zachary hit the buttons on his key fob to unlock the door, unable to look down at it to press the right one. He knew the layout of the fob, but he couldn't remember it or instinctively hit the right button in the heat of the moment. The lights of the car blinked. The horn beeped. The trunk clicked open.

Not quite the results he had been hoping for.

He got close enough to grab the handle of the driver's door and just about sprained his fingers lifting it up when the door didn't unlatch for him. Still locked. He pushed buttons on the key fob again, trying to do it more slowly now. Elizabeth was still coming after him.

The lights blinked and he saw the locks pop up. He wrenched the handle again and the door opened. He fell into his seat and pulled the door shut so quickly that he nearly shut his leg in the door. He hit the armrest button to lock the door, but nothing happened. He was trying to fit his key into the ignition at the same time.

He looked at the armrest to find the right button to lock the doors and managed to hit it just before Elizabeth reached the car. She banged into the side of the car and grabbed the door handle, but the door didn't open. She howled again and bashed her fist on the window.

He turned the key in the ignition and the car roared to life.

Thank you.

He stepped on the brake and shifted the car into drive. He didn't hit the gas right away, but took his foot off of the brake and let the car start to roll forward. He didn't want to run over Elizabeth, no matter what she had done to Ben and his brother or what she had intended to do to Zachary. He didn't need that on his conscience. She stepped back from the car slightly, still banging on the window and screaming at him that he'd better not ever come back again and that if she ever saw him again…

Needless to say, she didn't welcome his return. She didn't have any trouble thinking of creative ways she could hurt him if he happened to show his face again.

As the car pulled away from her, he put his foot gently on the gas and sped up. She ran after the car, but of course, she was no bionic woman and she couldn't keep up with it. He drove away, leaving her behind.

He drove directly to the police station. He hoped he hadn't royally screwed things up by going to Edith Johnson's house. He had not intended to confront either of Ben's parents. He had just meant to talk to his grandparents, to find out what he could about Allen. But now Elizabeth was in the know, and if she contacted Sam, he would be too. If he didn't already strongly suspect that Zachary was going to cause trouble for them.

Judging by the motorcycle that had tailed him and the man who had tried to break into his car the night before, Zachary suspected that Sam was already fully aware that Zachary was on the case and was determined to get him off of it as quickly as possible.

His heart was still hammering hard when he got to the police station. He sat in his car for a minute, breathing slowly, trying to bring his body back under control, but he didn't have much success.

At least he wasn't having an anxiety attack. Those always seemed to be caused by emotional issues rather than imminent physical danger. He might not make the best decisions when he was facing a challenge, but he at least didn't fold.

He'd kept it together. He was fine, and he had a job to do.

He got out of the car, testing out legs that were quivering like Jell-O. But they held his weight. He carefully locked the car, armed the security alarm, and walked from the parking lot into the police station.

"I don't know if he'll be free," he told the officer of the day, "but I'm looking for Joshua Campbell. It's Zachary Goldman, and it's… somewhat urgent. If you could tell him that there have been developments…"

The officer of the day took down the information and nodded. "If you'll have a seat, please, Mr. Goldman. You'll be called up when we have an answer for you."

"Thanks."

He wobbled over to the seating area and selected a seat that wasn't too close to anyone else. He was glad to get off of his feet so he could be sure that he wasn't going to topple over anytime soon. For the first few minutes, he just sat there, breathing, trying to calm himself down, and pretending that he wasn't watching the OD for any sign of whether he had been able to reach Campbell and whether Campbell was going to have anything to do with him.

He would probably end up getting shunted to someone junior. They would take his statement, roll their eyes, and tell Zachary that someone would get back to him.

Which they wouldn't.

Ever.

Probably.

He checked his email and answered a few quickie questions. He didn't want to deal with anything more complicated, so he switched over to his social networks to see what was happening. But all the time he was browsing through the mixture of friends' posts, memes, and fake news, his brain was working away on what Edith Johnson had said.

She had provided him with what he needed to get started. And Zachary knew where Elizabeth was. Or where she had been. There was no guarantee she would stay at her mother's house for any longer than it would take to pack a bag and get out the door.

But maybe she would have to wait for Sam, if they were still together. They had obviously been in communication, or she wouldn't have looked at

Zachary's car when she saw him, ascertaining whether he was the person that Sam had told her was investigating the old child neglect case, and who might be digging into something that could send them to prison once again.

Whether or not they were together, they were still communicating.

Somehow, their relationship had survived their prison terms. Elizabeth had probably been out for longer than Sam. Unless there had been clear evidence given that Elizabeth was the worse offender. People didn't like to give long sentences to young women, and she had been a young woman at the time. A young woman who, she could claim, had been abused and coerced into something that she hadn't wanted to do.

It wasn't her fault, of course. It was his.

"Mr. Goldman? Mr. Goldman!"

He looked up from his notepad. A young officer stood in front of him. Zachary straightened up. "Sorry. Far away thoughts."

The young officer looked at him, evaluating whether he was high or crazy.

"Just distracted," Zachary said. "Thinking through a case. Is Campbell available?"

The officer considered for a long moment, then nodded. "Yeah. This way."

Zachary pushed himself back to his feet. His legs were steadier, the chase fading from his mind and the adrenaline spike gone. He couldn't quite keep up with the pace that the officer set, but the man slowed down, realizing he was outstripping Zachary, and settled into an easier speed for him.

39

Campbell was sitting at his desk, chewing on a pen. He pointed to the visitor chair facing the desk. Zachary sat down. The young officer stood close by, not leaving as Zachary had expected him to.

"Well?" Campbell demanded. "What's happened?"

"I have more details for you, hopefully enough that you can get a warrant. But I also… ran into one of the suspects. Unintentionally."

"And he knew who you were?"

"She. Yes. Afraid I spooked her and she may be on the run already."

Campbell grunted and shook his head. "Nothing we can do about that. We can't go after her until we have the evidence that she committed a crime. Which we won't have until we get a warrant. Which we don't get until you give me the rest of the details you were able to find."

Zachary nodded. He settled back into his seat. Campbell was right, of course, there was nothing they could do to make sure that Elizabeth didn't run. They had to go through the proper channels and hope that they'd be able to catch up with her later.

"I have evidence from several sources that there was an older son named Allen," he told Campbell. He detailed the birth certificate and what Edith had said about Allen's existence—and subsequent disappearance.

"She didn't think it was important to tell someone at the time that there had been another child?" Campbell demanded, shaking his head.

"She knew that if she did, it would mean a longer sentence for Elizabeth and more notoriety for the family. She decided to avoid that."

"How the public expects the police force to do their job when they won't do their duty and report what they know, I'll never understand."

Zachary had to agree. "I guess… she loves her daughter and didn't want her to have to suffer the consequences of whatever she did."

"And she's letting the woman live with her now? Knowing what she did to her own children?"

"I don't know if she's living there or I just happened to catch her there, but yes, I think she is… it would appear that all is forgiven and Edith would prefer to forget about it."

"Do you think the father is living there too?"

"Probably. They must be in contact with each other." Zachary told him about the tail, the attempted car break-in, and Elizabeth immediately looking at the car and realizing who Zachary was.

"So they might both be on the run now."

"Possibly."

Campbell pulled a form out of one of the stacks of paper on his desk and filled in a few details. He reached toward the young officer who was still standing by. "Get that to Judge Wilkes ASAP. He's expecting it."

Zachary raised his brows. Campbell smiled.

"I knew you would eventually get the information we needed. We'll get the warrant and then see what we can find. How confident are you that the boy's remains are buried in that house?"

"Not one hundred percent. They could be buried somewhere else on the property, or taken out to the woods or dropped off a cliff or into a lake somewhere. But it feels to me like… the basement is the most likely place. That's where the boys were kept. No one in the neighborhood knew they even existed. It feels to me like… they would have kept him very close."

"You think that even with Bobby there, they buried Allen in the basement."

Zachary turned this over in his mind. Had it happened right in front of Burton? Had he watched his brother being buried? Wasn't that taking an unnecessary risk?

"I can't be sure, of course. But… I think so. They didn't expect Bobby to get out. They didn't expect to be discovered. They buried one boy there, and probably assumed they would bury the other there too. Maybe even used it as a deterrent for Bobby. 'If you don't do what we tell you to, the same thing will happen to you.'"

Campbell grimaced. He didn't argue with Zachary's assessment. "I've got the equipment lined up so we can visualize what's under the concrete floor without having to tear it all up. No guarantees, of course. Depends on how thick the cement is and how deep the bones are buried under that. We could be looking for something twelve feet deep. But I doubt it. These are not criminal masterminds. They didn't think anyone would be looking for him. And they were right, in the beginning."

Zachary imagined that the grave would be very shallow. Just deep enough to cover the boy's body. Elizabeth and Sam didn't strike him as the industrious sort.

Zachary had discouraged Burton from going back to the house for the search, telling him that it would probably take quite a long time and would be too upsetting for him. He'd already seen how Burton reacted to the empty basement and to talking about any of his memories or his family. It wouldn't be good for him.

He thought that Burton would agree and be happier staying at his hotel room drinking until Zachary got back to him with the results. Then he could be assured of getting the news at the earliest possible opportunity, but wouldn't have to see the remains or deal with the emotion of being at the house again. It was the best possible solution.

But Burton did not agree. As soon as he heard that they were heading over to the house and would begin the search the second they got word that they had the warrant, he wanted to be there. Nothing Zachary said dissuaded him, and eventually he agreed to pick Burton up so that he could stand outside the house until they got some word from the police. By the time they got to the house, the police were stringing yellow tape around the perimeter, even though they were still waiting on the warrant. They were staying off the property, stringing the tape on the outside of the fence.

Zachary found Campbell, but stayed back, knowing that he would be busy and wouldn't want Zachary getting in the way. Campbell noticed him after a couple of minutes and nodded to him as he continued to talk with his men and get things organized. There was a truck stopped in the street with equipment on it that Zachary assumed was the x-ray or radar or whatever the technology was to look through the concrete for the remains.

Campbell eventually approached Zachary, looking at his watch. "We should be able to start any time now. Is this...?" He looked at Burton questioningly.

"Yes, Sergeant Campbell, this is Ben Burton. Formerly Bobby Weaver. Ben, Sergeant Campbell."

Burton nodded. He held out a tentative hand. "Thank you for looking after this."

"I hope we can find something. Hate to drag everyone out and have it go belly-up. And it must be very stressful for you."

"Yeah." Burton ran one hand through his hair. "I just feel like... I left Allen behind here. Everybody left him behind. And we need... we need to find him. Lay him to rest."

"I hope we can do that. And that we can bring your parents to justice."

Burton frowned slightly at this. He looked at Campbell, then at Zachary. "But... they're already in prison, right?"

Zachary took a deep breath, looking at Campbell. Campbell did not jump in to give Burton the bad news.

"No," Zachary said gently. "They're out. I don't know what their original sentence was; I don't have the court documents yet." He looked at Campbell. "Unless you know?"

Campbell cleared his throat. "Father for two years. Mother for one."

Burton looked at him, wide-eyed. "One year? They only put her away for one year after what she did to us?"

"After what she did to you. Not for what she did to Allen. That will have to be considered once we know whether we have a body or not. And yes... I realize it's completely unfair. There's no way that they should have been able to get out so quickly. Unfortunately, that is the law." He shook his head. "I'm sorry. I'm just glad that she couldn't find you. If she had come after you, tried to get you back..."

"So that means... she's out?" Burton looked around him at the strangers gathering on the sidewalk and in the street. "She could be here. She could be anywhere. She's just out, walking free, as if nothing ever happened?"

"Yes."

"And Allen." Burton motioned to the house. "He's still in there. And me. I'm still trapped in there."

Zachary touched Burton tentatively on the back. "I'm sorry. If he's in there, the police will find him and get him out. And you… part of you will always be in this place, but the rest of you, you're walking around free too. More free than her, because you don't have the guilt for what happened."

"Oh, don't I?"

"Well… you may feel guilty," Zachary knew that he still carried around a lot of his childhood guilt. He blamed himself for a lot of the things that had happened to him and his siblings. Even though, as an adult, his logical brain told him that they were not his fault. It wasn't his choice as a ten-year-old to send himself and his siblings into foster care, where they would suffer more abuse and other terrible situations. "But you're not at fault in any way. It doesn't matter what you said or did as a kid; you did not deserve for this to happen to you. That was the choice of cruel, evil adults who had the responsibility to make better choices."

There was a shout from one of the officers gathered around a couple of squad cars. He straightened up and waved to Campbell. "We got it!"

"We got the warrant?" Campbell demanded, double-checking. There could be no ambiguity. Not *it*, but *the warrant*.

"We got the warrant," the officer confirmed.

Campbell nodded to the teams gathered around him. "Let's go, then. Time to get started."

He and a cadre of experts walked into the yard and up to the door. The householders had been watching everything from inside and opened the inside door to talk to them. Campbell explained that a warrant to search the house had been issued, and that they could let him in, or they could wait until the paper warrant got there so they could examine it.

"We don't own the house," the woman told him, her voice screechy. "We just rent. I don't know what you're looking for. We haven't done anything wrong. We haven't broken any law."

"We aren't looking for something that you did. We're looking for something that has been here for many years, long before you moved here. Do you have the owners' phone number?"

She read it to him through the door, and Campbell called the owner and had a discussion with him. There was a lot of back and forth, and, by the time he was granted access, another officer had arrived with the freshly-inked warrant. They displayed it to the residents as they entered but, by that time, no one was asking to see it. They had been told to let the police in and didn't have any argument to make.

"Why don't you go out for a while?" Campbell suggested. "Go out for dinner or a drink. We're going to be here a few hours, at least."

"What are you going to do? You can't go through all of my personal property!"

"We won't be pawing through your drawers, ma'am. We will be looking under the basement floor, in the backyard, maybe in closets or the attic. We will not be looking through your personal items."

She clearly did not believe him but, in the end, decided that she did not want to be on hand during the search. Zachary remembered what it was like to be trying to sell a house and having to vacate for people to look at it. He didn't like the feeling of someone invading his territory, but it was just something a person had to put up with. As a child, it hadn't been up to him to make that choice. Nor as a married man when Bridget wanted to upgrade to something nicer.

She'd upgraded now. Zachary had seen her home with Gordon, and it was like a showcase.

40

Then there was nothing to do but wait. They couldn't see what was going on in the house, though Zachary imagined it in vivid detail. The cops and experts going down the stairs to the basement. Turning on the dim lights and looking around the dismal little space. Getting out the equipment to be rolled across the rooms in narrow lines, back and forth and back and forth until they found something.

Burton paced. He drank. He spoke to Zachary in fits and starts. Phrases and sentences that seemed to come out of nowhere, without a cogent connection. Blurting bits of what came to his mind as he stewed in his fragmented memories.

Zachary saw the man who had stopped and talked to them the first day. The biker man. He was standing around in the crowd, curious like everyone else, wanting to know what they were looking for. People speculated on what the equipment that had come off of the truck was for, some of their guesses bizarre and some uncannily accurate.

Zachary watched the biker, thinking about the motorcycle that had followed him. Had that been the neighbor? Was he Sam Dougherty, or did he know Sam? Was he the one who had decided to tail Zachary to see where he took Burton and where he lived afterward?

Campbell was inside, and Zachary didn't know which of the officers outside would listen to him and take his claims seriously if he suggested that the biker might know something about what was going on or where to find Sam Dougherty. He kept an eye on the man, trying to decide what to do.

An hour later, his phone buzzed. Zachary took it out of his pocket. A text notification. He didn't have them display on his lock screen, just in case it were something confidential that he didn't want a client or interviewee to see. He unlocked it and touched the messaging app to see who the message was from. He tapped the bolded number and the message popped up. A photo. It was monochrome, lights and shadows. Like an x-ray or ultrasound.

He remembered being dragged along to one of his mother's ultrasound appointments. He had been on school suspension at the time and his mother had not wanted to leave him home alone in case he got into something.

The ultrasound screen had seemed mysterious and magical. He could actually see the baby that was inside his mother's belly. The ultrasound technician had pointed to a curved line of dots.

"They call it a string of pearls," she explained. "That's the baby's vertebrae. His spine."

Zachary had stared at it in amazement. He twisted his arm behind him, feeling the knobby bumps along his own back. He had a spine. And the baby, growing inside his mother, had a spine. And translucent little arms and legs that the technician traced on the screen. And a heartbeat, fluttering like a little bird.

But the string of pearls that Zachary saw on his phone screen did not come with a heartbeat. There were limbs angled off this way and that, and a small, round, skull, but no heartbeat.

Burton looked over Zachary's shoulder. He grabbed at Zachary's phone. "Is that it? What did they find? Did they find him?"

Zachary couldn't very well stop Burton. There was no point in telling him that they hadn't found anything. There was no way to spare Burton's feelings.

"It looks like he is," he said gently, holding on to the phone, but angling it so that Burton could see it better. "This here, what looks like a pearl necklace, that's his spine. And…" he pointed to the chicken wings. "His arms.

And his legs." Drawn up to his chest, as if he had curled up into the smallest ball possible, knowing that he was going into the womb of the earth. Back to the dust.

Burton sat down on the sidewalk. "Allen! Allen, oh Allen!" He drew his own knees up, rocking and sobbing. "They found you." He cursed softly. "They found you, Allen."

He broke down and wept openly. Zachary circled an arm around his shoulders and squeezed, trying to comfort him. How could he make Burton feel any better when he had just had it confirmed that his brother was dead? After three decades of repressing all that had happened to them there in the basement of the cursed house, he finally had his answer.

That was where he had lived, had been tortured, and where his brother had died. That was where he had been buried without ceremony or sanction. Buried where they hoped he would never come to light again.

41

Zachary tried to get Burton to move from the place he had collapsed to the sidewalk, but Burton wouldn't budge. Zachary wanted to get him into his car, away from prying eyes and ears. Somewhere he could have a little privacy and gather his thoughts.

But Burton didn't care what anyone saw or heard or thought of him. He wasn't moving from the spot. He was going to stay there forever, glued to that one place, the place he'd been when he found out that Allen had been murdered and buried just feet from him.

Eventually, Burton's tears and loud sobs and groans slowed. He leaned against the chain-link fence, hands over his eyes, body gradually relaxing. Zachary had ignored the men going past him with more equipment. Jackhammers and shovels and other heavy tools. He didn't want to draw Burton's attention to them. He was already going through enough without picturing them digging up his brother's bones.

Zachary rubbed Burton's back and brushed back his hair a couple of times. "How are you doing? This is terrible for you. Is there anything I can do? Anything I can get you? Do you want to talk to someone on the phone? Your mom and dad?"

He shook his head. "No, no one." He felt his pockets for his flask and eventually brought it out, but it was empty. He threw it away from himself, sending it clanking into the street.

Good riddance. Zachary hoped that Burton never went to get it back and that it got driven over by a truck, crushed flat in the street. He hoped that this one moment would sober Burton up enough to see that he was wasting his life crawling into a bottle, that it was time to start living. One of the Dougherty boys had survived, but his spirit was still stunted, like his body had been when they got him out of the basement. It had never been allowed to grow up. It was time for him to start living.

"He was my brother and I let him die." Burton's words were anguished.

"You were four or five. There was nothing you could have done to save him. You are not responsible for anything that happened."

"I should have been able to stop them. I should have helped him. He helped me. He protected me. And I didn't do anything. I just… stood there!" There was horror in Burton's voice as if he couldn't believe it. How helpless and paralyzed he had been. He didn't believe what Zachary had said. He saw himself as the cause of Allen's death.

"There was nothing else you could have done. You were too small. No matter how hard you'd tried to fight them, you couldn't have saved him. And they might have killed you too."

"They should have! They should have killed me too, and I wouldn't have to go through this. Why couldn't I be the one who died?"

Zachary continued to rub his back, trying to find some way to soothe him. "He wanted you to live. He was your big brother. He was trying to look after you."

Burton leaned forward and buried his face in Zachary's shoulder. "Allen, Allen…"

"He loved you. And your adoptive parents love you. You're not alone. You should call them."

"No." He choked the word out. Zachary wondered what his relationship with his adoptive parents was like. They had, by his account, done everything they could for him, and he had done everything self-destructive he could. He didn't share with them that he was looking for his house, didn't want to share the news about his brother. There was clearly a rift between them. He had, perhaps, been too old and too traumatized to bond with them properly. Those early years were vital for relationship development. Zachary wondered about his own ability to form normal relationships. He didn't have a lot to show for his efforts. An ex-wife, a struggling relationship with Kenzie, one foster father.

He did love his brothers and sisters. He'd developed those relationships early, like Burton. Before he was broken.

He couldn't think of anything else to say. He was quiet, staying close to Burton and trying to give him the moral support he needed, watching the curious watchers. The biker dude was still there. Pretending he was watching the house more than he was watching Zachary and Burton. Zachary saw him take out his phone to make a call. He quickly slid his own phone out and tapped a message back to Campbell, inside the house.

There is a man out here who confronted us when we were here before. I think maybe the one who followed me.

He didn't know whether Campbell would take out his phone and look at the message, or whether he would be too busy with what was going on inside. It would be loud and close and he might not even notice that he'd received a text.

Is it Sam Dougherty? Campbell fired back.

Don't know. Could be. Or a friend.

What's he doing?

Been watching us. Making a call now. Maybe to Sam?

There was no answering text from Campbell for a few seconds. No dots to tell Zachary that he was composing his message. Then his phone rang. He held it up to his ear. "Hello?"

"Officer Blau is going to come talk to you. I want you to point this guy out to him. Discreetly."

"Okay. Sure."

A heavyset officer approached. Belly straining over his duty belt. He rocked side to side as he lumbered toward them, looking like a bear or a Sasquatch. He looked at Burton, then Zachary. He leaned closer, talking to them with a voice that was raised instead of confidential.

"Everything okay here, sir?"

Zachary glared at him and spoke quietly. "You need to check on the guy behind you. By the red truck. Doo-rag on his head and tats down his arms."

"You should go home," Blau said loudly. "There's nothing to see here. Nothing is going to be happening here tonight. You're making a scene."

"The black and white doo-rag," Zachary insisted.

Blau straightened up, hitching up his belt. "See to it. You'd better be moving on your way soon, or I'll do what I have to to see you off the property. We don't want drunks and meth-heads hanging around here."

He wheeled around one hundred and eighty degrees and walked away again. Zachary tried to reconcile what had just happened with what Campbell had said on the phone. He knew what he was supposed to do, but Blau had appeared to be totally off-script. Like he thought he was there to protect the scene and see Burton and Zachary off rather than looking into the biker dude.

He watched Blau walk around the edges of the onlookers, eventually working himself into a position behind the biker, who had finished his phone call and was chatting to another neighbor while he kept his eyes glued on Zachary and Burton. Blau tapped him on the shoulder and he turned slowly, unconcerned, then froze when he realized that he had been flanked. He said something and looked like he was going to make a run for it. Blau grabbed his arm and stopped him cold. There was no struggle, but the biker dude suddenly had his arm twisted up behind his back and couldn't seem to move out of the hold.

Zachary turned to face Burton to prevent anyone seeing his grin. He had thought that Blau was stupid, but he'd been anything but.

Burton was wiping his face, looking at Zachary with his brows drawn down. He didn't understand what had just happened or why Zachary was smiling.

"I have a right to be here. No one is chasing me away."

"No. You're fine. It was just a distraction. He didn't mean it."

"He didn't mean it?"

"He just needed to know who I wanted him to talk to." Zachary glanced at Blau and the biker out the corner of his eye, not making it obvious he was looking at them again. "Him." He nodded sideways. "They need to talk to him."

"Why?"

"He knows something. He might know Sam."

"Who is Sam?"

"Sam is your birth father."

Burton's eyes went over to the biker. "That's not him, though. That's the guy that talked to us before. Last time."

"Yes. That's right. But… I think he followed me the other day after I dropped you at the hotel. And he's here again, watching us, calling someone on his phone."

"You think he's calling… my birth father?"

"He could be. Or I could be totally wrong. It's not like I haven't made mistakes before." Zachary rolled his eyes. "Plenty of times. But the way he was acting… I think he knows something, even if he says he doesn't."

"You don't think he was here back then? That he knew Sam when we lived here. In this house."

"He might have. People don't usually stay in this neighborhood that long, but he could be an exception. Or he might just know Sam and moved here coincidentally. You know 'Hey, Sam, would you believe that I just moved onto your old street?' That kind of thing does happen. But I don't like coincidences."

"When did he follow you? You didn't tell me anything about this."

"You have enough to worry about. I didn't want to bring it up. Nothing happened, and I thought… that it might have been connected with an old case, something that I'd already wound up. I didn't realize until later that it might be related to this case."

"Or not at all."

Zachary conceded. "Right."

Burton rubbed his eyes, which were red and swollen. He sniffled loudly and looked around. He seemed to have cried himself out. At least for the moment.

"What are they doing in there now? They found him, so… now what?"

"They'll declare it a crime scene. Take what evidence they need."

"How?"

Zachary didn't want to give too much to Burton. He didn't want Burton to see it in his head. "I don't know all of the details. They're going to need to remove… the remains. And they'll have lab work that needs to be done. There may be other pieces of evidence to examine. Maybe clothing or jewelry that survived."

"Allen didn't have any jewelry."

"No, of course not. But there could be things that would last longer than cloth. A belt buckle. A zipper. Pocket rivets or buttons. I don't know what else."

Burton nodded, sniffling and snorting some more. He rubbed at his eyes, which Zachary imagined didn't make them feel any better, just rubbing whatever grit was on his face and hands into his eyes.

"I can't… I can't believe they would do that to Allen. Just… bury him there. Leave him there. No one knew? No one knew anything?"

"Just them. I don't imagine they would have told anyone. Criminals can be stupid, but they had to know that if they told anyone, it would mean more charges against them. They had to keep it a secret."

"How could anyone not know?" Burton shook his head. "How could everyone just forget him?"

Zachary had the same questions. Elizabeth's mother had known about Allen, but she had kept quiet to spare her daughter. How many other people had known and not said anything? Sam's parents were still living too; wouldn't they have known Allen before Sam started 'acting funny' and being paranoid, eventually locking the boys up? What about neighbors? No one missed him? School teachers and friends? Had no one asked whatever had happened to the Dougherty's boy?

"I don't know. But now we found him. Now they'll have to pay."

"I can't believe that they weren't sent to prison for the rest of their lives. Wouldn't you? You wouldn't let someone like that just get out and go free in a year, would you? You know… that they can't be let out to just… do it all over again." He swallowed and looked at Zachary, thinking the same thing as Zachary had. "What if… they had other children? Does anyone know? Was anyone watching to make sure that they couldn't ever do it again?"

"Probably not. They might have had parole rules when they got out initially… but that was years ago now. They can't watch people forever. Eventually, they have to let people just go free and stop monitoring them."

"They monitor sex offenders."

"Yeah."

"Why wouldn't they monitor murderers? Do they seriously think that just because someone has done their time that they're not going to do it again? Sex offenders re-offend, but murderers don't? What kind of logic is that? Why don't we have monitoring for killers?"

42

The biker had been discreetly removed from the scene, maybe taken to the police station for questioning. Zachary and Burton waited for some word from inside. It was starting to get cooler, the sun beginning to sink toward the horizon. Most of the curious neighbors dispersed, deciding there was nothing to see.

There were still a few onlookers on the street and in nearby homes but, for the most part, Zachary and Burton and the officers who were watching the perimeter had it to themselves.

There was a buzz from Zachary's phone. He pulled it out. Another message from Campbell.

Prepare Burton. We're going to be coming out.

Zachary slid the phone away again. When he looked at Burton, his eyes were already on Zachary.

"They're getting ready to come out."

"Does that mean... they're finished?"

Zachary nodded. He didn't know whether the police would need more time at the scene, but the part that Burton was concerned with was done. They had recovered Allen's remains.

"What are they... what will happen?"

"They'll be bringing the remains out. They'll take them to the police lab.

They'll examine them, try to make an identification and determine cause of death."

"We already know his identification." Burton's voice was angry. "It isn't like there were any other children in the basement."

"I know. But they still need to confirm it scientifically, if they can. We all know who it is."

"I told you. I told you he was in there."

"And we managed to get them to look. They were able to recover him. You were right, and because of you, Allen will be laid to rest somewhere… more appropriate. Somewhere you can put a headstone and visit if you want."

"When?"

"I don't know how long it will take. A few days to a few weeks." Kenzie would know. She would be involved in checking the remains in, cataloging everything, maybe involved in the post-mortem with Dr. Wiltshire. "They'll get it done as soon as they can."

Burton looked toward the house, waiting. Zachary was cramped and cold sitting on the ground with Burton. He rose to his feet, and in a moment Burton followed suit, looking like a newborn horse or deer testing out its legs.

"You okay?" He touched Burton's arm to steady him.

"I'm fine."

Zachary withdrew his hand and let him be. "It won't be long, now."

The front door opened as if on cue. The officers started coming out. A couple of them with the x-ray and digging equipment first. Then behind them, several in a line, men carrying boxes. They were closed and sealed and marked as evidence. They didn't joke around and talk among themselves like police officers often did, but walked in a solemn procession. The officers who were standing around outside removed their caps and stood watching. The equipment was loaded onto the truck, and the evidence into a white van. Campbell joined Zachary and Burton.

"How are you holding up?" he asked Burton in a low, respectful tone.

Burton wiped at his eyes, leaking at the corners again as he watched them put the bones of his brother into the van. He shook his head. "I can't believe this is happening. It feels like I stepped into a nightmare. I keep waiting to wake up, but… I can't. I just keep getting deeper and deeper."

Campbell nodded. He slapped Burton on the shoulder. "I'm sorry about all of this. You shouldn't have to go through it."

"Why didn't they find him back then? How could they just leave him there? Pour concrete over top of him?"

"They didn't know. If they had known, they wouldn't have left him there. At least you remembered, when you came back here, what had happened."

Burton's eyes slid to the side. He looked at Zachary, and then back at Campbell.

"We'll set up a time to meet tomorrow," Campbell suggested. "I'll need to document everything you can remember."

"But… I don't know if I can do that."

"It was a long time ago, and your memories will be hazy. We'll take that into account. But we need your statement. You are the only witness, other than your parents. At least, I assume that is the case."

Burton tried to nod and shake his head at the same time. "I don't remember…"

"We'll have some experts available. They'll be able to help you to retrieve some of those memories. We have psychologists, hypnotists, other kinds of experts. You may not remember a lot, but every little thing will help."

Burton's arms wound around his stomach and he held himself like a child with a stomachache. He looked at Zachary again.

"You've done fine so far," Zachary told him. "You did remember things. Even though you thought you couldn't. You remembered the house, what it looked like, and where you had been. You found your bug jar and the names on the wall. You remembered Allen's name and you knew that we would find him here. That's a lot."

"But it's not enough." Burton's eyes were wide and worried. "That's not enough to put them back behind bars."

"You let us worry about building the case," Campbell said. "We'll get the evidence we need and pass it all on to the prosecutor. We'll have enough. We're not going to drop this."

"He was only a little boy." Burton wiped his face with one hand and went back to holding his stomach. "We were just little."

"Yeah. That's one of the horrible things about it. He was so young. He never had a chance. But we're going to do something about it." He squeezed

Burton's upper arm. "We don't forget innocents. We're not going to let them get away with it."

"How will you stop them? How will you even find them?"

Campbell glanced at Zachary. "We already have some leads on that. Don't worry about the police work. We know what we're doing. All you need to worry about is getting a good night's sleep tonight so that you'll be ready to give your statement tomorrow." He paused, weighing his words. "We'll expect you to be clear and sober."

Burton scowled. "Would *you* be?"

"This isn't a question of how I would be. I'm sure I would be an absolute wreck. This is about you and what you can do for your brother. You need to hold it together for his sake. You need to be alert and coherent. You don't want alcohol blurring things. You need to be able to give a legal statement, which you can't do if you're under the influence."

"I *can* stay sober," Burton growled. "I don't know what nonsense Zachary's told you. I'm perfectly capable. I can speak for myself. I don't walk around here letting everybody else speak for me. No matter how much I drink, I can still function just fine."

"I'm sure you can," Campbell said without any hint of sarcasm or criticism. "And tomorrow, you will need to be that person. Sober and ready to make your statement."

"I will be."

"Good man." Campbell gave a nod. "I'll see you tomorrow, then. First thing?"

Burton looked suddenly trapped. He looked at Zachary for rescue. "I might…"

"I don't think I can be there in the morning," Zachary said. "And I'd like to be there for moral support. Could you do early afternoon instead?"

Campbell gave him a disapproving look. "Suddenly this isn't the most important thing on your calendar?"

"I have a doctor's appointment in the morning. You know I can't miss those. Besides, it's been thirty years. A few more hours isn't going to make that much difference. Maybe in the afternoon, you'll have a preliminary report from the medical examiner. What they've found on gross examination of the remains."

"Fine. Afternoon, then," Campbell agreed. "I'll make time for you on my calendar. And I'll have the experts in, so if you don't show up, you're going to be wasting a lot of people's time."

"We'll be there." Zachary looked at Burton and raised his brows. "Right?"

Burton nodded. "We'll be there. Early afternoon. No problem."

"It better not be."

43

Campbell walked away from them once more to talk to his men as they took the last of the evidence out of the house and moved it safely to the van. The police started to take the yellow tape back down and, after a few minutes, Burton turned away, finally ready to go.

"That's it. That's all they're going to do."

"They'll still be doing more behind the scenes. There's lots to do in the lab, and they need to track down Elizabeth and Sam, which will be more difficult if they have bolted. They're done here, but there is still more to do."

Burton looked at the house one more time. Committing it to his long-term memory, Zachary thought. Making sure it was something that he would never forget again. Saying goodbye. Reconciling himself to the fact that he would need to go on with his life. He had found Allen, and now it was time to go on.

"Come on," Zachary invited. "Let's go."

He didn't grab Burton by the arm, but waited patiently for that last goodbye to be finished. Then Burton turned and followed him to the car.

"Thanks for…" Burton cleared his throat uncomfortably. "For talking to the cop, telling him it would have to be tomorrow afternoon."

"No problem. I actually do have a doctor's appointment tomorrow morning."

"Oh. What for?"

While he would normally have considered it an invasive question, a client stepping over the line and trying to become too involved with his life, Zachary felt like it was only right that after Burton had lain bare his soul that there should be some kind of reciprocation. Zachary knew everything personal and private about Burton's life, and Burton knew nothing about Zachary's.

"She's a therapist. I have a lot of… mental health issues to be resolved. She helps me work through them."

Burton buckled his seatbelt, thinking this through. "So, like, depression?" he asked. "What kinds of things?"

"It can be depression. I get very depressed before Christmas, but it can actually hit at any time of the year, and then it hits me all the harder because it is unexpected. I have anxiety issues, compulsions, PTSD. My girlfriend and I have started couples sessions so that she can help me to get better at relationships, at… overcoming some of the traumatic stuff I've had to deal with."

Burton motioned to his window, back toward the house as Zachary put the car into gear and started to pull out. "Traumatic stuff like this?"

Was it a competition to him? Pull out their respective traumas and compare them, see who had suffered the most? Who had bragging rights?

"That's private. But… yes, some pretty nasty stuff. I didn't see my brother killed in front of me… though sometimes I was afraid I would."

Burton closed his mouth and thought about that as they drove into the rapidly-falling darkness.

Zachary was glad that his appointment with Dr. Boyle was by himself, and not a couples session, as had originally been planned. Kenzie had a coworker call in sick, and she had been asked to help with the post-mortem of Allen's remains. Something that Zachary had encouraged her to do, both for his own sake and for Burton's. Though he had initiated the couples sessions, he found them much more difficult than individual sessions. After all of the emotion that he'd dealt with in helping Burton get through the previous day, he didn't think he could have managed a couples session.

"How are you doing today?" Dr. Boyle asked, smiling at him and giving him a chance to think about what had happened in the last few days since their last session. Zachary thought of the nightmares, about visiting with Joss and Luke, and about the events with Burton.

"It's been… a busy few days."

"Professionally? Personally? What's been going on?"

"A little of both. And I haven't been sleeping very well."

"Do we need to talk about a prescription sleep aid?"

"I've already got those… but I don't like to use them."

"It's important for your mental health for you to get enough sleep."

"Yeah. But… I had that episode before when I had a reaction to mixing them with a painkiller, and… I just don't think it's a good idea for me to take them."

"Well, ultimately, that's your choice, of course. But I think that having a blanket policy that you'll never take them, even if you need them, isn't the best idea."

"I still have them. And if I was going to go all night without sleep for a few days, I would take them. But just for the odd night having a hard time… I don't want to do that."

"So you only occasionally have restless nights? It isn't anything serious and it doesn't last?"

"Well… no. You know me, most nights are difficult. But things were going better. I was having better sleep. I think this is just temporary."

"Do you know why you're having a hard time? Can you tell me what kind of sleep trouble you're having? Do you have trouble getting to sleep, problems with waking up in the night? Nighttime restlessness? Waking up too early?"

"Well, any of those. But lately… nightmares. Ones where I wake up and I still *feel* the feelings that I had in the dream. Where I don't know when I wake up that it was a dream and that it's gone. I'm still looking for something or feeling panicked. Still almost in the dream."

Dr. Boyle nodded and made a notation on her notepad. A few words to remind her of this later. "Yes, I know what you mean. I've had dreams like that."

"Sure." Zachary nodded, feeling relieved. "I'm sure I'm not the only one."

"Is there anything similar between the dreams you've been having lately? Any one dream, or a recurring image or theme? Is it always the same feeling when you wake up?"

"Kenzie thinks it's because of Bridget. Her being pregnant."

"Oh? Why?"

Zachary realized that he'd skipped a step. "I've been… dreaming about twins. It's kind of been related to a case that I'm working, because there are two boys, brothers, and I've been helping him to find out what happened to his brother."

"But they were not twins."

"No. Four or five years apart."

"But in your dream, they're twins."

Zachary nodded.

"Sometimes dreams are like that," Dr. Boyle said. "Our minds flip a switch, change something up. It could be, like Kenzie suggested, because you're thinking about Bridget and her expecting twins. Or it could just be that you didn't have a good mental image of this brother, so you made him identical, to give him a concrete form that you recognized."

"Yeah, maybe that was it," Zachary agreed, nodding eagerly. He didn't want it to be about Bridget.

"Have you been thinking about Bridget a lot when you have been awake?"

Zachary looked at the questions from several different angles. He didn't want to answer it. Which in itself was an answer. Dr. Boyle wrote something else down. Zachary couldn't see, from where he sat, if it was 'thinks excessively about ex-wife' or something else. Maybe a note to herself not to forget to pick up milk at the grocery store.

She waited for him to answer.

44

Zachary shifted, trying to find a more comfortable position, and cleared his throat.

"I guess."

"You guess what?"

"That I've been thinking about Bridget a lot. Or about her babies a lot."

"Is it a package deal, or do you think about them separately?"

"It just feels so unfair. That she would refuse to have children with me, insist that she never wanted to have children of her own, and then to get pregnant with Gordon. And have two babies, or even more. It's just... so unfair. I wanted to have children with her. I always wanted to have children, even though she had said she didn't want them."

"It is unfair," Dr. Boyle agreed. "I can see that it would be tough to deal with that."

Zachary warmed to the topic. "Was it because of something that Gordon has that I don't? Or did she just change her mind? Suddenly became aware of her biological clock?"

"Hard to say without talking to her." Dr. Boyle held up a finger. "And I am not suggesting that you talk to her. In fact, I'm telling you not to."

Zachary nodded. He knew that if he tried to make contact with Bridget, followed her in his car, or just happened to be in the neighborhood, she would take out a restraining order. And he could go to jail because he'd been warned before.

"Instead, let's just unpack this a little further. Why do *you* think she agreed to have children with Gordon? It isn't possible that it was just an accident? And they decided to go with it?"

"No. She had her eggs frozen before she had radiation. She couldn't have had children without them planning it."

"Okay. So we can assume that it was planned. And that's the reason she's having multiples as well, because they fertilized more than one egg to give her a better chance of conceiving."

Zachary nodded.

"So why do you think she chose to have children now, if she was against it before?"

"Her new husband… he's a very persuasive guy. One of those guys who's really… dynamic. I guess, he just talked her into it."

"That's a possibility. So how does that make you feel?"

"Like… I should have tried harder, instead of just accepting it when she said she didn't want to have any children. Maybe I just needed to push harder, to come up with a better argument. Maybe she was waiting for me to say something that would convince her. To step up and insist… say that I wasn't going to stay with her unless she agreed to have kids."

"Do you think that's how Gordon convinced her to have children?"

"No." Zachary looked down at his pants and scratched at something that had spilled and hardened there. "I doubt he needed to make any threats."

"You don't think so?"

"He's… like I said, he's really persuasive. He would just talk to her, and she would agree. And maybe he didn't need to say very much. Because he's a better man than I ever was."

"In what way?"

"He's very wealthy. He owns an investment banking company. I mean… he could buy and sell any business in the city. And he's not arrogant and stuck up. He's a very nice guy. Always very respectful, not the kind who would call me names or make comments about me, even though Bridget gives him permission. He's always been really nice to me."

"Well, that sucks," Dr. Boyle said.

Zachary laughed and nodded. "Yeah, it really does. I wish he would at least be a villain! I wish I could hate the guy and pick away at all of his shortcomings, but I can't. He is a good guy. He's good to Bridget; patient, but he doesn't put up with a bunch of nonsense. He's firm, stands up for me if she starts to run me down."

Dr. Boyle called Gordon a name and Zachary snorted. Dr. Boyle was right. It really did gall him that Gordon was such a perfect guy for Bridget. The kind of guy that Zachary could never have been, even if he'd tried his whole life.

There was a tickle in the back of his brain. While he believed that what he said was true, he did have the tiniest of doubts about Gordon. He had worried that Gordon had been involved in the death of one of his employees, but had been proven wrong in that regard. And he didn't believe the claim that the victim's sister made that Gordon was a manipulative egomaniac.

At least, he didn't think so.

Bridget would not have gotten together with someone like that. She liked to be the one in control. She had married Zachary thinking that she would be able to control him, to fix him and make him behave the way she believed he should. She hadn't understood what a huge undertaking that would be, and that Zachary's behavior wasn't always a matter of choice. And being broken definitely wasn't. He would have changed. He would have been what she wanted him to be, but he couldn't.

"Zachary."

He blinked and focused back on Dr. Boyle again. She did not comment on his momentary mental vacation. "So do you think you are focusing too much of your time and energy on Bridget and her unborn twins?"

He sighed. "Yes. Of course. I shouldn't be thinking about it at all. It isn't anything to do with me. I've moved on. She's moved on. We're in different relationships, and what she chooses to do or not to do is her own business. It doesn't affect me at all."

"So what are strategies you can use to focus less on her and more on the things that are important in your life?"

"Spending time with Kenzie… telling myself to stop and having something else to distract me. Visualization." He shrugged. "I know what I *should* do."

"But it isn't always that easy, is it?" Dr. Boyle sounded sympathetic. "Have you examined the reasons that you should be focusing your attention on Kenzie and other things instead of Bridget? Look at your motivations and think about what you are getting out of obsessing over Bridget and what things you want in your life? I think it's important to be motivated, or you're not going to follow through on any of the things you know you *should* do."

Zachary shook his head slowly. "I don't have any reason to think about Bridget and the babies. I don't know why I do it. I don't get anything out of it, and if I was focusing on Kenzie or a case, or even just meeting my own needs, that would make a lot more sense than thinking about her."

"Why do you think you do, then? What benefit are you getting out of thinking about Bridget?"

He rubbed the center of his forehead and thought. He had never considered that he might be getting some kind of reward from thinking of her. It was just where his mind went. His mind wandered and he thought about her, about his regrets, worried about the babies, wished that he could get back together with her and try again. To make it work this time.

"Um... wow. I guess... part of it is fantasizing about the great life we could have if she would just take me back."

"Because you had such a great life when you were together?"

He knew that wasn't true.

"Well, in the beginning, it was really good. She complimented me, made me feel good. And she was so pretty and so popular, it was like... I was suddenly *that* guy. I was lucky. I had everything. All the good things that I'd never had before."

"But that didn't last long."

"No. Because... she started making little digs... trying to 'motivate' me. She was impatient that I wasn't the perfect date. That I wasn't making enough progress toward the mold she was trying to press me into."

"And those little digs escalated."

"Yeah. By the time we got married, she would go into full-blown banshee mode... screaming at me for what I thought was a little thing, or for something that I couldn't help."

"And why didn't you confront her about that? Why did you stay—and get married—when you saw this happening?"

"Because when she wasn't screaming at me, it was good. I felt good. She would be kind and empathetic. She wanted to hear about me, about my life, my worries and concerns..."

"And that made you feel good. Did you recognize it as the cycle of abuse?"

Zachary hesitated. "No."

"Do you recognize it now?"

"Maybe… but I have a hard time seeing it like that. I think… most of the time, things were good. She was kind and loving. But then I would screw something up, and she would lose it. And that wasn't her fault; she was doing the best she could dealing with my crap. It was my fault, because I couldn't toe the line. Couldn't do the things that she asked me to, even though they were perfectly reasonable."

"Were they? Give me an example."

Zachary tried to pull one thing out of the mess that had been his life with Bridget. "Uh… letting her know where I was going to be. When I was going to be late for dinner or a planned event."

"So she expected you to let her know ahead of time?"

"Yeah. And that's just being considerate, you know. People expect that. Especially if it's an event with other people and she's going to end up being there alone. People talk. They think that I'm just blowing it off, that I don't think she's important enough to make sure that I'm there."

"And did you try to let her know when you were going to be late for something?"

"Yes, of course. But… with my work, I don't always know if I am going to be out on a case a particular night. If a subject under surveillance was on the move, things were going down… sometimes I didn't know much ahead of time, but I just couldn't get away."

"Uh-huh."

"Or else…" He ducked his head, embarrassed even though she already knew all about his failings and foibles. "You know, with my ADHD, I'd forget I was supposed to be somewhere, or not give myself long enough to get there in time. That really drove her nuts." He thought about the other night, when he'd completely blocked out Kenzie, not even able to change his focus for long enough to eat dinner. If that had been Bridget, he would still be smarting from her verbal lances.

"Is that something you can control?" Dr. Boyle asked.

"Well… I try. But I get distracted by a case, or I hyperfocus on something… and everything else just falls by the wayside. It isn't intentional."

"Did Bridget know that?"

"I tried to explain it to her."

"And how did she take that?"

Zachary shook his head. "She didn't. She wouldn't accept… my ADHD as an excuse."

"So… going back to the question about the cycle of abuse. If she was verbally abusive because of something that you could not control, then is that your fault or her fault?"

Zachary shrugged. They both knew the answer, but he didn't want to voice it aloud. He didn't want to think or say that Bridget was an abuser. He had dealt with enough abusers in his life, and he liked to think that he had gotten himself out of that cycle.

Even though he hadn't.

Not with Bridget.

Kenzie was different. While he always expected her to go off like Bridget would have, she didn't. She'd been there for him. She'd been supportive. Exasperated sometimes, yes. Pulling out of the relationship when he wasn't able to handle it. But she hadn't yelled and screamed. She hadn't belittled him or hit him. She was different.

"Do you think that maybe with Bridget, you were seeking a familiar experience? The same kind of relationship as you had been in before. The way your mother treated you. The way that you were judged by school teachers and professionals as being obstinate instead of having challenges?"

"Yes." They had discussed this before. But he didn't like it, and it didn't stop him from thinking about Bridget when he should be thinking of other things.

"So one of the things that you got out of your relationship with Bridget was familiarity. Being in an environment that felt the same as your home environment."

"Yes, I guess."

"And you got her kind words and strokes when she was in a good mood."

"Yeah."

"And if you could go back to her and start over, what would you get?"

Zachary shrugged. "Nothing, I know that's just a fantasy."

"But when you think about her, you think of those good times. Your brain gets those same good feelings as when you were together and she was showing you love and attention."

"I guess, yeah. So you think that's why I think about her and worry about the babies so much?"

Dr. Boyle cocked her head.

Zachary replayed the question in his head, but didn't know what it was that had caught her interest. "What?"

"*Think* about Bridget, but *worry* about the babies."

Zachary furrowed his brows, thinking about that for a minute. The dreams he'd had hadn't been nice, soothing, happy dreams about newborn babies. They hadn't been happy, cuddly dreams. They were full of menace and danger, of the specter of death.

"Do you think… I'm worried about the babies because of what happened to Burton?"

She raised her brows. "I don't know what you're talking about. You'll need to give me context."

"Um—my client. I've been helping him to connect with his past. He was badly abused and neglected. Yesterday… we found the remains of his brother. He was killed thirty years ago, by one or both of his parents. And buried in the basement."

Dr. Boyle winced. "Yes, that could certainly cause nightmares. And concerns about how Bridget and Gordon are going to treat their children."

Zachary closed his eyes, letting the feelings wash over him. He'd been trying to suppress the emotions and to compartmentalize. Keep Burton and his brother in one box, and Bridget and the babies in another, and his own history in yet another. Now he let go and let them mix.

45

The image that bubbled up and rose into his mind was not Elizabeth Dougherty and Allen and Bobby, or Bridget and the babies.

It was his mother.

He again saw her after the births of the younger children. Too tired to get out of bed or show any interest in them. Easily angered if one—or more —of the children got in her way. Zachary and the older girls had done what they could to take care of the younger ones. He remembered carrying them with him, rocking, feeding, and changing them.

They were, in his mind, the best part of his day. He dragged himself off to school and dealt with schoolwork and teachers and bullies and distractions, but when he got home at the end of the school day, he didn't see taking one of the babies as a penalty, but as a reward.

What could be better than holding and playing with a baby? They sometimes cried, but they didn't hit him or scream and criticize him. They didn't steal his lunch, make fun of his stained clothes, or tell him to do his homework. They just loved him back.

He knew that his mother didn't see them that way. She complained about their demands. She didn't nurse and preferred to let one of the other children bottle feed them. She would, eventually, get out of bed and once again take up her responsibilities of making dinner and trying to keep the house in some kind of order. An impossible task with the number of children in the house.

She and their father drank and fought frequently. Joss and Heather and Zachary tried to keep the little ones out of their way and shelter them from the violence. Sometimes they were successful, and sometimes they were not. Like Burton, he was too small to stop an adult who was intent on violence. He could run and hide, but he did not have the strength to stop them.

"Do you want to share?" Dr. Boyle asked.

Zachary opened his eyes and just sat there for a moment, pondering. "Maybe I am worried about how Bridget will be able to care for them," he said cautiously. He certainly didn't want Dr. Boyle calling Social Services to say that Bridget needed to be investigated. The babies hadn't even been born yet. He was sure that she was getting all of the prenatal care she needed. That would not have been a problem for Bridget.

But when they were born? What then? He assumed that there would be a nanny. Bridget would not be responsible for all of their care. She had a maid and other employees to help around the house and grounds. She was bound to have someone to help with child care as well, especially with twins.

"If I married Bridget because she reminds me of my mother..."

"And you know how your mother treated you as a child."

"And the littler ones. I didn't care so much about how she treated me. I mean, I did, but I could try to be better and not to irritate her. But the babies couldn't do that. We had to... look after them."

"You personally?"

"Yes. Me and Heather and Jocelyn. We tried to take care of the little ones and make sure... nothing happened to them."

"You were not very old yourself."

"I was eight when Vince was born. And six when Mindy was born. That's old enough to help."

"To help... yes. But it sounds like you're talking about a little more than that."

Zachary nodded.

"I'm interested in hearing that you had that much responsibility. Usually, when you talk about your childhood, you're talking about the trouble you got into. And I don't think that the whole of your existence consisted of getting into trouble."

"Well..." Zachary cleared his throat. "Mostly. That's what I remember. Always being on edge, trying to avoid screwing anything else up."

"That's what I mean. You were trying to be responsible. You weren't just ignoring everything your parents or teachers told you and willfully getting into things. Seeing you as an adult... I don't think you spent very much time intentionally breaking the rules."

"No. But I got in plenty of trouble anyway. Ask my sisters. Joss says I was always getting into trouble, and," he swallowed, "getting her into trouble too, because she was supposed to be watching me and keeping me out of mischief. I don't remember that, but I do remember my mom saying that I was incorrigible and could never behave. And my dad... didn't talk so much as he took action."

"He punished you for your behavior, a lot of which wasn't your fault, but was the result of your ADHD and learning disabilities."

"But I still did stuff that I knew I shouldn't."

"So do all kids. How do you think you would treat a child who broke a rule? Or who got into some other mischief? How do you think Bridget will react?"

"I don't know." Zachary scratched the back of his neck. "She'll have help. And Gordon isn't like my father. He'll make sure she has someone to help with the babies."

"That's good. Does that make you feel better?"

"On the outside," Zachary said slowly. "I get it logically. But on the inside... I guess I'm still worried."

46

At the police station, Burton and Zachary didn't have to sit in the hard chairs of the lobby waiting area. The officer of the day had been told that they were coming and had another officer escort them to an interview room. It was a comfortable room, with soft boardroom chairs rather than the hard plastic tubular chairs that Zachary knew were in the interrogation rooms intended for criminals. It was more the type of room that a family would be invited to when they had bad news. Or where a couple of chiefs might meet to discuss their teams.

Burton looked around and fidgeted a lot. He wasn't looking good. He had probably not obeyed Campbell's advice and abstained from alcohol the night before, but he'd been up for long enough to have time to think about what he was being asked to do.

A woman joined them after a few minutes and introduced herself as a therapist who was experienced in meeting with victims and helping them to provide statements that would help the police to investigate crimes and could later be used for the prosecution. She didn't introduce herself as 'doctor,' but as Harriet Sonbaum, and invited Burton to call her by her first name.

"I don't really remember anything clearly," Burton said uncomfortably. "I don't have a picture in my head of what happened. Just… feelings and impressions."

"That's fine," Harriet assured him. "Let's start with that." She settled herself into a chair and pushed a strand of dark hair back behind her ear. It was obvious that it was not long enough to stay there and would swing free again as soon as she shifted. "You came here, if I understand correctly, looking for the house that you had lived in when you were young."

"Yes."

"What feelings did you have about that? You wanted to come home?"

Burton considered that.

"Well. No, I don't think that was it, no. I didn't want to move here, or to have some kind of reunion. I wanted… to see it again. To know where I came from."

"What did you know about the life you had before you were adopted?"

"Nothing, really. My parents only talked about my life after I was adopted. Before that… everything was kind of a blank. I don't know if they thought I remembered, or if they thought that if they didn't talk about it, I would forget, and that was better."

"Did you ask them about it as an adult?"

"No. I don't want to hurt them. I don't want to challenge them about it. I just… needed to have some kind of connection to… the *before*."

"And after Mr. Goldman helped you to find the house, how did you feel? When you first saw it and knew that it was the right place."

"I was… I don't know. Stunned. I didn't know how to feel. But I wanted to see inside. To walk through it. Looking at it from the outside-in was not what I was looking for."

"You probably hadn't seen it much from the outside as a child, from what I understand."

"I guess. I just… needed to be inside. Where I had been."

"Because it was familiar."

"Maybe. I don't know why. I just wanted to be there."

"Okay."

Burton looked at Zachary. He looked back at the therapist. "I don't know what else you want."

"Tell me about going into the basement. How did you feel? What were you thinking?"

"I wasn't thinking that my brother was buried there, if that's what you're asking," Burton growled.

"No. So what were you thinking?"

"I was thinking… that it wasn't the same. Too much had changed. It wasn't the same place as it had been before."

"What had changed?"

"I don't know. I guess the floor had been poured. That was the biggest thing that didn't seem right. When I was there before, it had been a dirt floor."

"Anything else?"

Burton shook his head. "Everything. It had been open before, no smaller rooms. No closet around the furnace. All just one open area."

Harriett nodded. "Yes?"

"And… you know, there were finished walls and floor and the carpet. And the lights weren't there before. Not like that."

"What kind of lights were there before?"

"I don't know. It was dark. All of the corners were dark. Black. So I guess they weren't very good lights. Low wattage. Maybe just… a couple of bare bulbs."

"What do you feel when you think back to the way it was before? When you lived there?"

"Nothing." He shook his head slightly. "I just lived there. That's all. It was… like my room. My house."

"You felt like you belonged there? Like it was your possession?"

"I don't know. If I was so little when they started to keep me down there… then I would never have known anything else, would I? So how would I judge it? I wouldn't know if it was a good or bad place; it was the only place I knew."

"That's true." Harriett let some silence pass. "How about the people? Do you remember your biological mother and father?"

"No, I don't think so. I don't… have a picture in my mind. It's just… nothingness."

Though he had been pretty sure that the motorcycle dude wasn't his father.

"How about Allen?"

Burton rubbed his chin. He looked around the room. He looked down at the table and his hands clenched into fists and then released again. "I don't remember him," he said finally. "It was just… too long ago. I can't help the police with anything that they're looking for."

"Don't worry about the police. Don't worry about helping anyone. Just relax and explore the basement in your mind. You knew that your bug jar was behind the furnace."

"I didn't know it was there."

Harriett didn't ask any questions, just waited for him to clarify.

"I knew... something was there. I knew the furnace was there, somewhere. I knew that. But that's not really anything special. Any house in the neighborhood has a furnace."

"Of course. But not everyone would be concerned about it and want to look at it. Unless they were, say, a furnace repairman."

"So I wanted to look at it for a reason."

"Your jar was there."

"Yeah. And the names."

"What did you think when you saw the names?"

"I don't know. I didn't think anything. Until Zachary said that was my name. Bobby Allen. I thought it really was." He pushed his chair back from the table slightly. "You see? I didn't know about Allen. If I knew about Allen, I would have known that wasn't my last name. That it was his name."

"Maybe." Harriett said. "And maybe you did."

"No," he shook his head with certainty, "I didn't."

Harriett let it go. She looked at the clipboard she had brought with her.

"When did you start to remember that Allen wasn't your last name, but was a separate person?"

"I didn't. Zachary did."

Zachary shook his head. "No... I told you it wasn't your last name. But that maybe it was your first and middle name. Or a double-barreled first name. You were the one who kept asking 'who is Allen?'"

Burton patted his pockets, then went still again. He scratched his head anxiously. "Allen was my brother," he said, answering his own question back across time. "My... big brother."

"Yes."

"He was the one who wrote the names on the wall. Not me. I didn't know how to write. Or to read the names. But he'd gone to school, so he knew."

Zachary listened, fascinated. They hadn't had any confirmation before that Allen had gone to school before being shut in the basement.

"He went to school?" Harriet asked.

"Yes. He must have."

"Did he got to school while you were at home in the basement?"

"No. No, I don't think so. It was... a long time ago. He told me stories, but he didn't go to school anymore..."

Harriett nodded. "What other stories did he tell you?"

Zachary remembered Burton saying that Allen had told him about animals. Nice, furry animals rather than the many-legged denizens of the basement. Dogs and cats and animals in other parts of the world. What had Burton thought when Allen told him about those things? Could he picture them? Did he think they were fantastical, like unicorns and dragons? Did he think that Allen had just made them up for entertainment?

"I don't know." Burton closed off immediately. Every advance was followed by a retreat. Fear kept him from moving forward.

"What did he tell you about school?"

"I don't know. It was where you went to learn. There were lots of other kids there. Teachers to tell you what to do. There were... slides and swings."

Burton said 'slides and swings' like they were something mystical. And to him, they must have been. He was attached to the ground. He didn't know about sliding from a high ladder. He didn't know about swinging way up above the ground, until the horizon seemed like it was at his feet.

"Yes," Harriett agreed with an appreciative laugh. "That must have been very puzzling for you. Like a rollercoaster or jet plane is to someone who has never even seen a picture of one. Did you want to go to school?"

"Of course. He did, so I did. He made it sound wonderful."

"Were you disappointed when you eventually went to school?"

Burton considered this for a few moments. "I was and I wasn't. It was not as grand as what I had imagined... and it was more. I just didn't have anything to base it on."

"Your experience was very limited."

"Yes."

"Do you remember," Harriett said slowly, "anyone coming down the stairs to see you?"

This time she hadn't suggested specific people like his mother and father. And she had added in a new trigger, something that had to be part of Burton's experience. People coming down the stairs.

They could not have fed him or taken care of any other physical needs without coming down the stairs. They could not have killed and buried Allen without coming down the stairs.

Burton shook his head at first, but no one said anything and he had some time to think about it. He must have also known that people had to have come down the stairs at some point. So he made himself remember. But was it really a memory, or was it something his brain created because it should logically have been there?

"I… didn't like it when people came down the stairs," he said slowly. "That scared me."

"Did it? But there must have been good things about someone coming down the stairs too. Food to eat or other new supplies."

Burton nodded. Zachary thought about the foods they had talked about before. How Burton hated mac and cheese and fish sticks. How when he had gone to the foster home, he had not been able to eat textured foods without gagging, and had to be taught to eat. He ate pablum and mush. A few soft things. His diet had been very restricted.

Had his mother fed him by hand like she must have done when he was a baby? Spooning food directly into his mouth? Playing 'airplane' to try to get him to eat it all up?

"There was food," Burton agreed. "I don't remember it being very good… about being hungry for it. I had to eat it when they brought it. That's all."

"How about Allen?"

Burton pushed back immediately. "I don't remember Allen!"

"Okay."

There was a period of silence. Burton rubbed his face and jaw and the back of his neck. He was holding it back. He didn't want to remember.

He didn't want to have to compare notes. He didn't want to say what his parents had or had not done. Logically, they must have come down the stairs at some point. But he didn't have to remember more than that.

"Let's skip ahead to when you were rescued," Harriett suggested after letting some minutes pass in silence. "What do you remember about that?"

"I don't exactly remember being rescued… but I told Zachary… I can remember walking down the sidewalk and seeing someone walking a dog. I wanted to pet the dog."

"That must have been a very big step for you. For someone who had never seen an animal before, a dog could be a big scary thing."

"I guess Allen never told me they could be scary. So I wasn't scared. I thought… that all dogs were friendly and nice."

"Ah. That makes sense. Still. Approaching a stranger and a strange beast that you'd never seen before seems like a really big step in your life."

Burton gazed off into the distance. He nodded.

"Did the man walking the dog call the police? Did other people come to help?"

"I guess. I just remember petting the dog."

Zachary could picture it. The thin little boy he had seen in the picture, stroking the big dog's silky fur. Just enamored with the dog and ignoring the rest of what was going on around him.

4 7

There was a knock at the door, and Campbell entered. He must have been watching the interview on a monitor somewhere, and he had decided it was time for him to take over. Zachary still thought that there was more that Burton could remember, but he clearly wasn't ready or willing to share it yet. Campbell hadn't wanted to unwittingly color any of Burton's memories prior to his working with Harriett, but probably felt that they had hit an impasse and it was time for him to move things forward with the information he had.

Burton eyed Campbell and the thick folder in his hands warily. Campbell reintroduced himself and sat down.

The file folder looked old. Like it had been in storage for many years. When Campbell opened it, it was filled not with perfect computer printouts and photocopies, but lots of handwritten notes, carbon copies, and copies made on machines that were precursors to the modern laser and inkjet technology. Lots of different shades of gray and purple.

Burton stared at the file, mesmerized.

"This was the initial police investigation after you were discovered," Campbell explained the obvious. "From the time that you appeared on that street, it was clear that something was wrong. You were alone, you were ragged and unkempt, and malnourished. The police were called and began their investigation."

Burton nodded.

"You were several houses down the street from the house we searched yesterday. You were able to point it out to the officers who talked to you, letting them know that was where you had come from. You were only five and your speech wasn't entirely clear—" Probably the result of the fact that he had been kept away from all human contact, "—but you were able to make yourself understood."

Campbell flipped through the dusty pages and lifted the edges of the top pages to show Burton fading photos of the house as it had been thirty years previously. Zachary looked at it curiously. It had not changed very much at all. The fence and the exterior of the home looked newer, but the shapes were still the same. There was not much vegetation. It was a summer picture, but there was no green grass, only brown, dusty, dead grass dotted with green weeds that had been able to force themselves up through the sod.

There were no tricycles in the yard. There were no outdoor toys at all like a family with children would normally have. There was nothing to show that the children lived there.

"The police investigated the owners—actually, the renters—of the home without making direct contact with them. They decided that there was enough to get a warrant to search the house. They had it under surveillance and, before they could get the warrant, the male subject was observed making his way down the street looking for something."

"Something?" Burton echoed.

"Or someone. He was calling quietly, looking into neighboring yards, checking under cars that were up on blocks, into side yards, various places that a small boy might have been able to crawl. He was detained."

Burton's eyes were wide. He again patted his pocket, but apparently he'd had the presence of mind to leave his flask back at the hotel room so that he wouldn't be tempted to drink while he was at the police station. An action that he probably regretted now. He was used to anesthetizing his emotions, and now he couldn't. Confronted with the reality of what would happen, he had no buffer to keep it at a comfortable distance.

Campbell flipped through a few more pages, then displayed a photo to Burton of a man in his forties or fifties, in classic mugshot poses. Zachary studied the lines of the man's face and hair. The same man who, thirty years later, had tried to break into Zachary's car, but then made a run for it when the alarm had sounded? He hadn't been close enough to see his features clearly.

Burton's mouth opened and closed. His face turned gray. He stared at the monster who had kept him in the basement all of those years ago. Sam. His biological father. Zachary touched him on the back, trying to steady him.

"That's him!" Burton said in a choked voice.

Campbell nodded. It wasn't obvious whether Burton remembered him, or whether he was just shocked at seeing the man for the first time after so many years.

Campbell waited to see whether Burton would say anything further and, when he did not, Campbell continued. "As I said, the police were already in the process of getting a search warrant. They amended the application to add the new facts on the fly, and waited for it to be granted. It was not granted until the next morning when judges were back at their desks and in their courtrooms, but they had kept surveillance on the house to ensure that no one could escape before they had a chance to enter the premises."

Campbell showed a copy of the warrant that had been granted, but it didn't have any effect on Burton.

"At ten o'clock the next morning, police entered the house. Elizabeth Weaver, who was actually Elizabeth Dougherty, was still in the home. She had made an attempt to clean up any incriminating evidence but, as she had not had the opportunity to leave the house, everything was still on the property. Soiled rags, a bucket that had clearly been used for some time as a toilet, worn and ripped clothing. It was all logged into evidence."

Burton nodded mechanically. Zachary was expecting to see pictures of these items, but Campbell apparently thought that too cruel.

"And the basement?" Zachary inquired.

"The basement was a hole in the ground. Undeveloped. No floor. But a child had clearly been playing there. There were broken bits of plastic bottles or Corelle dishes that had been used as digging tools. Buttons and coins and other small objects that were toys."

And a bug jar behind the furnace that they hadn't identified as something of value to little Bobby Weaver.

And two names written on the wall out of sight, not just one.

"The female subject was Mirandized, questioned, and gave a preliminary statement. She was arrested and remanded."

Campbell looked at Burton's face, searching it. Burton gave a tiny nod, his eyes on the papers. Campbell released several pages so that the photo of Elizabeth Weaver fell into place.

Zachary probably wouldn't have recognized her. She bore little resemblance to the woman he had seen at Edith Johnson's house. Her face and body looked wasted, her long blond hair oily and bedraggled. She had obviously not been at her best, waiting for the police to arrive. She had to have known that they would be arriving sooner or later. She had a distant look. An addict, Zachary suspected. Addicted to what? Heroin? She was better now. Maybe she had gotten cleaned up in prison. Bobby's escape might have saved her life.

Burton covered his face with both hands. He choked back sob after sob, trying to stop them, releasing one choked gasp after another.

"It's okay," Zachary told him. "Do you need some time? Maybe a break…?" He looked at Campbell.

Campbell shifted to get up, but Burton shook his head. "No," he managed to gurgle out. "Get it done."

Campbell settled again. He looked at Zachary, then at the thick file before him. He waited for Burton to calm himself down.

Burton wiped his nose. Zachary looked around the room and found a tissue box and handed it to him. Burton blew and wiped and used several tissues to dab at his eyes, trying to slow the waterworks. He shook his head.

"Why would I cry? I don't care about her."

"No," Zachary said softly. "You care about Allen. About what happened to him."

"They buried him in the floor!" This brought a fresh stream of tears. Burton looked at Campbell for confirmation. "*He* did it. He dug a hole and put Allen in it!"

Campbell nodded wordlessly. Saying nothing that would change Burton's recollection of the events, if he did, in fact, remember what had happened so long ago. It had been so traumatic, Zachary wondered if he would ever remember it in any detail. And it was best for him, perhaps, if he didn't.

"I dug holes. I buried things." Burton wiped his eyes again and sucked back the mucus running down his nose and throat. "I wanted my Allen."

His entire body shuddered. "If I dug too close, he beat me. Told me he'd cut off my fingers. And he would have."

Burton put down his head, sobbing wildly. Zachary rubbed his back, murmuring soothing words that meant absolutely nothing to Burton.

"So I just… sat down there. Sat and looked at where he was buried. Forever."

Zachary looked at Campbell, wondering if they had the medical examiner's report yet. Had the bones shown a clear cause of death?

Campbell correctly interpreted Zachary's look. He closed the file and watched Burton, waiting to see if he would calm down. If he should or shouldn't discuss what they had discovered about Allen in the previous twenty-four hours.

Burton grabbed another handful of tissues and tried to stanch the flow of tears and snot.

"Do you know how Allen died?" Campbell asked quietly.

48

Burton's eyes and nose were red and raw. He held cupped palms over his eyes, waiting, willing his body to stop. His Adam's apple worked up and down.

"We were sick. He gave me his food. He…" Burton's mouth opened and closed, unconsciously simulating what he remembered. "I was getting better. But he couldn't… he couldn't feed me anymore. I tried to feed him." Burton wiped his eyes. "He just laid there."

Zachary licked his dry lips, unable to take his eyes off of Burton. He opened his mouth to prompt Burton for more, but he couldn't.

"He buried him," Burton said in a loud protest, skipping ahead in his story. "He dug a hole and…"

Campbell opened a slim file. He laid it flat on the table before him, looking at Burton. "Allen got sick and died?" he asked, looking down at the white sheaf of papers.

Burton shook his head. "Noooo…"

"What happened?"

Burton sniffled. "*She* did it." He gulped. "Allen wouldn't get up. She wanted him to…" Another sob and gulp. "…to carry the bucket up the stairs. But he wouldn't get up. So she…"

A child too weak to eat, and she had expected him to get up and carry the bucket of filth up the stairs for her. Zachary closed his eyes and shook his head. He thought of his own mother, how she would react to a child she deemed to be oppositional.

It had not only been his father who had beaten him.

Zachary put his arm around Burton's shoulders and hugged him close. "Okay."

Burton leaned into him, sobbing.

Campbell closed the file again, nodding.

"Will you be able to find them?" Zachary asked. He wiped at the corners of his own eyes, which seemed to be leaking.

"We already have. Mr. O'Sullivan, your biker, knew how to reach them. They are in custody now. We wanted to know what Mr. Burton could remember before going any further."

Zachary let out a long breath.

49

Zachary rang the doorbell. He thought about his parting from Burton, driving him to the bus depot to go back home to his adoptive family. Burton was, as usual, on the edge of being drunk. He thanked Zachary for the work he had done and for helping him through the voyage of self-discovery. He slapped him heartily on the back and swore that he was going to go home and go to an AA group. He'd get on the wagon, and he'd get back on track with his life.

Zachary doubted it would be that easy. But he smiled and encouraged Burton and shook his hand warmly one last time before he left.

And then he got into the car and drove south again. He hadn't made arrangements, but figured she would be home by the time he got there.

But it was taking her a long time to answer the door, and he wondered if he should have called ahead. He hadn't wanted to have to explain.

Eventually, he could hear footsteps, and the door opened.

Zachary looked up at Joss, a few inches above him. He stepped up over the threshold so that he would be at her level. Joss stepped back slightly, her forehead wrinkling.

"Zachary? What are you doing here? What's up?" There was an edge to her voice. She had told him before to set up a time, and not just show up on her doorstep. And, once more, he had disobeyed her instructions.

Zachary put his arms around Jocelyn and squeezed.

Her body went rigid and she tried to pull away. Zachary held on. Not so tightly that she couldn't break his grip, but tightly enough to let her know that he wasn't willing to relinquish his hold so quickly. She was still for a moment and then put her arms uncertainly around him.

"Thank you," Zachary murmured.

"For what?" Joss demanded. "What's wrong?"

"For being my big sister and looking after me. No matter what the consequences."

She didn't move for a minute. Then she squeezed him to her. "Of course, Zachy. You're my brother."

Did you enjoy this book? Reviews and recommendations are vital to making a book successful.

Please leave a review at your favorite book store or review site and share it with your friends.

Don't miss the following bonus material:
Sign up for mailing list to get a free ebook
Read a sneak preview chapter
Other books by P.D. Workman
Learn more about the author

Sign up for my mailing list at pdworkman.com and get Gluten-Free Murder for free!

JOIN MY MAILING LIST AND
Download a sweet mystery for free

PREVIEW OF SHE WAS AT RISK

CHAPTER 1

Zachary gazed out Kenzie's living room window at the pleasant, suburban view. He hadn't realized how much he was missing by living in apartment buildings instead of a nice little house like Kenzie had. When he stared out the window at his apartment, he saw nothing but sky, or looked down at the dirty parking lot, complete with homeless people going through the trash for bottles. He didn't know his neighbors within the apartment building well. They were familiar enough to nod to in the elevator, but that was about it.

What he was missing was the green lawns, the children walking to school, the flower borders and gardens. People smiling pleasantly each other when they passed on the street or even stopping to talk to each other. It was a postcard picture day, and unlike the way he felt when he looked at the typically Vermont trees and hills covered with snow as Christmas approached, it was a scene he could enjoy.

Maybe he should have moved into a house like Kenzie's. Maybe sometime in the future, he would. Maybe with the way that his relationship was progressing with Kenzie…

He pulled his thoughts away from the possibility. He didn't want to presume on anyone's kindness. He had lived with Mario after his previous apartment had burned down, and it was better to be on his own two feet. He got lazy relying on someone else to do the work and keep him on track.

The thought stirred Zachary, and he got up and went into the kitchen. He put in a pod and made himself a cup of coffee and poked his head out of the kitchen for a moment to listen and try to decide whether Kenzie was up yet. He couldn't hear her stirring. No point in making her coffee before she was up, it would just be cold by the time she got to it.

But while he was in the kitchen, he rinsed the dishes that were sitting in the sink, put them into the dishwasher, and wiped the counter, eliminating the rings from his previous cups of coffee. He put the washcloth back in its place and gave himself a mental pat on the back for at least doing something to help keep Kenzie's place tidy.

Fresh coffee in hand, Zachary returned to his place in Kenzie's living room. Since he was there most weeknights now, he had asked Kenzie whether she minded him getting a mobile laptop table that he could use while he was sitting on the couch or in the easy chair, if he kept his space tidy and it didn't detract from the decor of the room.

Kenzie shook her head, bemused. "Sure, of course. You should have some kind of desk instead of sitting hunched over that thing all the time. It's not good for your body."

He was often sore after a couple of hours sitting with it, so he knew she was right. "I just… didn't want to presume."

Kenzie shrugged. "Of course. You're here. I like having you around, having… a few touches that remind me of you when you're out. I don't mind at all."

So he had browsed online until he found one that he liked, and it had been a good purchase. He could sit and type, read documents, or browse databases with better posture, which helped to keep him going for as long as he needed to.

Zachary's phone vibrated in his pocket. He slid it out to look at it, and felt frown lines crease his forehead.

Gordon Drake.

Gordon didn't have any reason to be calling Zachary. Zachary had stayed away from Bridget, his ex-wife. He hadn't been following her or spying on her. They hadn't accidentally run into each other anywhere.

Not lately.

Zachary had cleared everything up at Drake, Chase, Gould after Ashley's death. There was no reason for Gordon to call Zachary back. With the killer behind bars, there shouldn't have been anything else for Gordon to call Zachary about.

Unless there had been another death.

Unless something else untoward had happened.

But even if it had, Zachary would have expected Gordon to go somewhere else to get help. Bridget had not been happy with Zachary looking into Ashley's death, and Zachary didn't think that Gordon would do anything he knew would antagonize her.

Especially not since she was pregnant.

Zachary picked slid his finger across the phone screen to answer the call.

"Gordon? Is everything okay?"

"Zachary, it's been a while since I saw you last. How are things with you?"

Zachary chewed the inside of his cheek. "I'm fine," he said cautiously. "What's going on with you? Everything okay at Chase Gold?"

Gordon chuckled. The nickname for the investment banking firm left out his name, which was a bit of a slap in the face considering he was the principal partner and owner. But he appreciated the appropriateness of the name.

"Yes, everything is fine at Chase Gold," he agreed. "Better than ever. And I have... put some extra controls in place as far as the interns are concerned. We don't want any more... hospitalizations."

"Yeah, that's good." Zachary waited for Gordon to explain why he had called. It wasn't just for a casual chat and to catch up on each other's lives. They didn't have that kind of relationship. Although Gordon had always been very cordial toward Zachary, he knew how much animosity Bridget had toward him. He usually respected her desire to have nothing to do with him anymore.

Unless he needed something.

"I guess you're wondering why I called. I was hoping that the two of us could get together."

"I suppose," Zachary said slowly, feeling his way along. "What did you want to meet about?"

"I would... prefer to leave that for our meeting. It's a rather delicate matter. I prefer to discuss it face to face, somewhere quiet and discreet."

"Okay. If you're sure. Where would you like to meet? Your office?"

"Heavens, no." Gordon was silent for a moment as if considering, though surely he must have known before he called Zachary that they would need an appropriate place to meet. "I can book a private meeting room at my club. Do you know the Ostrich?"

Zachary knew of it. He wasn't a member and had never been there. He wasn't aware of anyone in his circles who was a member. Other than Gordon, clearly.

"I know where it is. What's the dress code?"

"They are fairly relaxed now. No blue jeans or track pants. Clean, neat, and pressed. Collared shirt. No tie required."

Zachary didn't think he even owned a tie. When was the last time he had attended an event where he had needed one? Probably not since he and Bridget had broken up. He had gone to fancy dress parties with her. Lots of places that had required a tie or even a tux with a bow tie. Not the clip-on ones. They had to be proper tie-up bow ties, Bridget had informed him. No shortcuts. People could tell when they looked at you whether you had taken the time or not. They could see right through you.

If that was the case, then he didn't know what point there was in wearing a bow tie of any kind. If people could see through his clothing to what kind of a person he really was, then why try to masquerade as a society man by wearing clothes that didn't suit him?

But he didn't say that to Bridget. He had shaved and dressed up and stood still while Bridget tied his bow tie and made sure that it was straight and everything else was in its proper place.

But he could manage business pants and a polo shirt. He didn't have to go out and rent or buy anything for that. Gordon would be in a three-piece suit if he was coming from work, but he had not told Zachary that he had to be formally dressed. He would probably just stand out more if he tried to look like an upper-class businessman anyway. People paid no attention if he looked like he was working-class or a bum.

"Okay. What time do you want to get together?"

"I have a rather full schedule," Gordon said, a note of apology in his voice. "But I would like to see you as soon as possible. Could you do lunch today? I just had someone cancel on me."

Lunch at Gordon's fancy club.

"Sure. Lunch at the Ostrich Club. Do I… check in with the maitre d' when I get there? I haven't been anywhere like that before."

"There is a reception desk. You can tell Danielle that you are meeting me. She will direct you to which room I have booked or someone will escort you up."

Zachary nodded to himself. He looked at the system clock on his computer. He'd better start getting cleaned up if he was going to look presentable by lunch.

CHAPTER 2

The Ostrich was pretty much as Zachary expected it to be. Dark woods, plush carpets, polished waitstaff right there whenever you looked for them. He was escorted to the Roosevelt room by a pleasant young man who didn't try to make conversation or ask him what he was doing there.

Gordon was already seated at the table, his laptop out, working on some document or project. His expression was serious and focused. He didn't look up for a few seconds, but then he closed the lid of the computer and looked into Zachary's eyes, giving him a warm smile of welcome.

"Good to see you, Zachary. Have a seat. What do you want to drink?"

Zachary looked at the young man who stood attentively. "Uh… just a Coke, please."

The man nodded, acting as if that was a perfectly normal drink order. Apparently not everyone at the club was ordering hi-balls or tea. Or if they were, the waiter would never give it away. Gordon ordered some kind of French wine and the waiter nodded and wrote it down, expression not changing. Zachary couldn't tell if it was an expensive vintage or something out of a box. Given the setting, he assumed the former.

"And what would you like to eat?" Gordon asked.

"Uh…" Zachary looked around for a menu. "I don't know…"

"They're equipped to make any popular dish. What do you feel like?"

Zachary cast around for a suitable dish. "I'm not that hungry yet. Maybe just… a sandwich?"

Gordon nodded. "Sure. What do you like? Roast beef? Chicken?"

"Maybe cheese? Grilled cheese?" He felt a little silly ordering something juvenile at such a fancy place. But he didn't have much of an appetite. His meds made him nauseated for a few hours after taking them.

"How about a Monte Cristo?" Gordon suggested. "Grilled cheese and ham?"

"Sure," Zachary agreed. "That sounds good."

"Would you like salad or fries on the side?" the waiter asked.

Zachary shook his head. "Just the sandwich."

He nodded. Gordon ordered some kind of skillet. After the waiter was gone, he turned his attention to Zachary.

"So, things are going well for you?" he asked. "How is business?"

"Going pretty well." A few big cases had padded out his bank account and gotten his name out in the media, so he was doing all right.

"Anything interesting? Haven't captured any serial killers recently?"

"No. I think I'm going to put in all of my listings that I don't do serial killers. Too much time and effort," Zachary deadpanned.

Gordon looked at him uncertainly, then smiled. "Well, you might as well advertise the kind of cases that you actually want to get," he agreed. "I haven't seen much in the news lately. Has there been anything big?"

"I just finished with a man who was looking for his childhood home. Which ended up being where his brother was buried. So that was pretty intense. And the main one before that was a missing girl. Human trafficking. Prostitution."

Gordon shook his head slowly. "You do get around, don't you? Nasty business."

Zachary shrugged. "Yeah. Most people don't come to me because they won the lottery."

"I imagine not. People are coming to you at the worst, most vulnerable times of their lives."

"Yeah. Exactly."

Gordon stared off into space. He looked like a man with something heavy on his mind. Zachary waited for him to spit it out. Since he wanted to meet, Zachary had to assume that there was something he wanted to be investigated. He wouldn't be going to Zachary with personal problems.

Some people were much better qualified than Zachary to sort out relationship problems.

Gordon looked at his watch. A big, highly-polished gold number. "This is rude, but do you mind…" Gordon gestured to his laptop. "There are a couple of things I'd like to put through while I still have the time."

Zachary shrugged. "Sure," he agreed. Gordon wasn't yet ready to present what it was that he wanted. Maybe he was waiting for the food to arrive so they wouldn't be interrupted partway through. Or maybe he would wait until after they were finished eating to turn to the business he'd asked Zachary there for. He hoped it would take that long for Gordon to get to the point.

While Gordon opened his laptop again, Zachary pulled out his phone. He checked his email, even though there wasn't likely to be anything important that had come in since he'd left Kenzie's house. And he browsed through his social networks. He wasn't big on social networks, but sometimes he did find interesting news stories or something that impacted his work. It was a good way to connect with family or friends, but Zachary wasn't quite ready to put that much of himself on public display. As a private investigator, he didn't want people to be able to track him down too easily. And he knew from experience that people shared way too much on social media. He'd been on the investigating end of a lot of those.

He and Gordon worked independently until the waiter arrived with their dishes. Then they both put the electronics aside and thanked the waiter. Zachary took his first bite of the Monte Cristo sandwich. It was crisp but not greasy, with just the right amount of cheese and ham pocketed inside.

"Mmm. This is very good."

Gordon nodded. "Good kitchen staff. We have world-class chefs. They don't disappoint."

Zachary nodded to Gordon's meal of grilled vegetables and seafood. "That looks good too."

"Yes." Gordon took a few bites, then he pushed the dish a few inches away from him as though he was full. "Zachary, I know I can rely on your discretion. You've proven yourself imminently capable in the past."

Zachary nodded. "Yes. I won't share any company secrets."

"This one isn't for the firm." Gordon was staring off into middle space again, considering. Making his final decision as to whether to proceed or to jettison the whole thing. He swallowed and put his hands palms-down on the table to physically brace himself. "It's Bridget."

Zachary had been half-expecting this. He had tried to convince himself that it was about Gordon's firm, but Gordon was perfectly capable of handling his business without bringing Zachary in. He was the one who knew about investments and financial stuff and all of the ins and outs, not Zachary. Zachary would be hard-pressed to help Gordon with a case of fraud or some other business-related area. Maybe if he wanted to find out if one of his partners was out fooling around where he shouldn't be, but nothing about the business itself.

Zachary swallowed. He was going to have to tell Gordon no. He couldn't work on a case that had anything to do with Bridget. He was trying to put Bridget out of his life, out of his thoughts. He didn't want to be thinking about her when he was with Kenzie. He didn't want her creeping into his dreams or keeping him up at night. He just wanted to be able to leave that part of his life behind and to move forward.

"What about Bridget?"

Gordon traced a circle on the polished tabletop. He had a quick sip from his glass and poked around at the seafood on his platter. But he wasn't interested in the food. They weren't there to eat lunch. He was a man with something far more pressing on his hands than his next meal.

"You know that she's pregnant."

Zachary nodded.

"Of course you do," Gordon said quickly. "Of course. I told you that when she was in the hospital. She's been quite sick with this pregnancy. It hasn't been easy on her."

"Right." Zachary had, in fact, thought that her cancer had returned. He was relieved that wasn't the case, but he wished he didn't have to think about Bridget pregnant either. He had wanted children when they had been married. She had not. She'd had a pregnancy scare before her cancer was diagnosed, and she had no interest in carrying it to term. But she had not been pregnant, so that disaster had been averted.

"What I don't think I told you is that she is expecting twins," Gordon said slowly, enunciating his words as carefully as if he was being graded on his diction. "Two girls."

Zachary nodded again. He swallowed. His mouth and throat were very dry. He irrigated them with a good amount of Coke. "I guessed as much," he agreed.

Gordon looked at him for a moment, then nodded. He didn't ask how Zachary had guessed. That was not the point.

"In the beginning, Bridget agreed to try to get pregnant." Gordon couldn't have any idea the kind of pain that this disclosure caused Zachary. He had failed on so many levels with Bridget. "She was a little reluctant at first, but she agreed to give it a try, see how things worked out. Neither of us knew whether she would even be able to get pregnant and be able to carry the baby to term."

The doctors hadn't expected her to have viable eggs after the cancer treatment. Instead, she had banked them before she started treatment. She had been very sick, and it had taken a lot of coaxing on the part of the doctors. They didn't like leaving a woman with no options. She might change her mind in the future. She might decide, after the crisis was past, that she did want to expand her family or at least to have those choices open to her.

And apparently, she had done just that. They had fertilized a couple of frozen eggs and she had become pregnant with twins.

Gordon fiddled some more, not able to come to the point yet.

"The further along she has gone with the pregnancy; the more difficult things have become. She has had a lot of second thoughts."

But what was she going to do? Terminate the pregnancy? That was what she had threatened Zachary with after she had a positive pregnancy test. She didn't want her body ruined by pregnancy. Didn't want to be burdened by children who depended on her. She didn't think that Zachary would be able to man up and be a good father to them. He could barely take care of himself; how was he going to help with children?

"Has she decided… that she doesn't want to continue?" he prompted.

"She is getting older and we don't know how many chances she will have to get pregnant. How hard it will be to terminate and try again."

"Try again? If she wants to terminate, why would she try again?"

"It changes from day to day," Gordon sighed. "Maybe she's not ready. She could try again in a year or two when she feels more ready, though that will be pushing against her biological clock. Or sometimes she decides that twins will be too much and she should only carry one to term. They can do selective reduction... And other days, she is convinced that there is something wrong with the babies."

It wasn't that surprising that Bridget would be worried about her pregnancy. Many women had anxiety over such a significant change in their lives. It was something so utterly different than anything they had done before. For Bridget, it would mean a big change in the way she lived her life. Being a mother, tied down to two children, instead of being able to go wherever she wanted whenever she wanted to. Things were different for parents, even if she did get a nanny to help.

"What does she think is wrong?"

"Well, up until now, it has just been 'something'—*What if* there is something wrong with the babies? Something doesn't feel right. I think something is wrong.—But I'm not willing to operate on 'somethings.' I need answers. Concrete evidence."

And he had found something. But what? Why did Gordon need a private investigator?

"And... you found something?" Zachary ventured.

Gordon tapped his computer. He took a couple more bites of his grill.

"She decided to have prenatal DNA testing done. Just to make sure that everything was okay. It's not just Down Syndrome anymore. They are very sophisticated now. They can do all sorts of testing for genetic problems and predict a lot of developmental issues."

Zachary nodded.

"I went along with it," Gordon said. "I thought this would help her to move on. She would know that everything was okay, so she would feel better about continuing the pregnancy. I thought it was a good solution. Rule out all of those things that she was afraid of."

"But, something came up on the test." Zachary still didn't have a clue why Gordon would want him involved. He couldn't fix genetic issues with his magnifying glass.

Gordon sighed. "Both babies are at high risk for developing Huntington's Disease."

She Was At Risk, Book 10 in the *Zachary Goldman Mysteries* series by P.D. Workman can be purchased at pdworkman.com

ABOUT THE AUTHOR

Award-winning and USA Today bestselling author P.D. (Pamela) Workman writes riveting mystery/suspense and young adult books dealing with mental illness, addiction, abuse, and other real-life issues. For as long as she can remember, the blank page has held an incredible allure and from a very young age she was trying to write her own books.

Workman wrote her first complete novel at the age of twelve and continued to write as a hobby for many years. She started publishing in 2013. She has won several literary awards from Library Services for Youth in Custody for her young adult fiction. She currently has over 60 published titles and can be found at pdworkman.com.

Born and raised in Alberta, Workman has been married for over 25 years and has one son.

Please visit P.D. Workman at pdworkman.com to see what else she is working on, to join her mailing list, and to link to her social networks.

If you enjoyed this book, please take the time to recommend it to other purchasers with a review or star rating and share it with your friends!

facebook.com/pdworkmanauthor
twitter.com/pdworkmanauthor
instagram.com/pdworkmanauthor
amazon.com/author/pdworkman
bookbub.com/authors/p-d-workman
goodreads.com/pdworkman
linkedin.com/in/pdworkman
pinterest.com/pdworkmanauthor
youtube.com/pdworkman

CPSIA information can be obtained
at www.ICGtesting.com
Printed in the USA
LVHW050737080121
676040LV00010B/249